# Finding Gwen

DELAINE WALSH

A DARK ROMANCE

# Finding Gwen

## DELAINE WALSH

For the readers who are trying to find themselves.
It's okay to start over, to find a different path,
to take that jump into something new.

# Content Information

*Finding Gwen* is a single dad x nanny romance with hints of darkness. This book contains mature themes and content intended for readers 18+ but may not be suitable for everyone.
Your mental health matters.


Topics covered include:

 Physical/verbal abuse (not between MCs)

 Sexual assault by drugging (not between MCs)

 Knife violence (not between MCs)

 Panic attacks

 Self harm

 Kidnapping of FMC and child

 Mentions of drug and alcohol addictions

 Death of parents (off page, in the past)


There are also multiple explicit sex scenes between fully consenting partners, featuring:

 Restraints

 Forced orgasms

 Begging

 Lots of praise

# Chapter One

## Gwen

"Honestly, what was the point of even hiring a nanny?" my boss screamed.

She had been going on and on for the last thirty minutes about how I could never do my job correctly. Her voice became background noise as I debated whether or not this would be the last straw.

Mrs. Watson hired me two weeks ago, and we have butted heads every step of the way. She micromanaged me at every opportunity. Add to that the inability to leave the house for anything besides a quick walk around the block, and I was slowly losing my mind.

I loved being a nanny, and handling parents came with the territory. They were the bosses after all. At the end of the day, their word was law.

"Mrs. Watson, I'm going to have to ask you to stop raising your voice at me," I said, finally able to get a word in. I did my best to keep a professional tone. "I would be happy to have a conversation about your expectations if you are willing to do so calmly." *Maybe she would be willing to talk like adults.*

"Stop raising my voice?" Her question was laced with sarcasm and hatred. "How hard is it to do your fucking job? Are you stupid?"

*Nope, nevermind.* I had no idea what had put her in a bad mood today, but it no longer mattered. It was time for me to take my leave.

"I believe this arrangement is not a good fit for either of us." Her eyes grew big, and she opened her mouth as if to say something, but I continued. "Consider this my formal resignation. I quit, effective immediately." Gathering my stuff, I made my way toward the front door.

"Gwen, do not walk away from me! Gwen!" Mrs. Watson's shrill screams echoed through the house. She would undoubtedly wake up her daughter with all the noise.

I closed the door behind me, not daring to give that woman the satisfaction of looking back.

*Not my circus, not my monkeys.*

I parked on the street outside my house, my head falling to the steering wheel as I fought back the angry tears that burned the back of my eyes.

*What a fucking day...*

Not giving myself time to sit in self-pity, I got out of my car, and walked up the empty driveway. My fiancé, Matt, insisted he needed it all to himself. He was a car enthusiast, and his red Jeep was priceless to him. I left him to it whenever possible. It was never worth the headache to try convincing him the driveway was more than big enough for both of our cars.

As I made my way inside, a shiver ran up my spine. All the lights were on, the couch pillows were tossed onto the floor, and one of the kitchen stools was knocked over. A loud thump came from the back of the house. Panic washed over me.

*Had someone broken in?*

The front door had been locked, but there was still the back door. Setting my bag by the front door, I crept to the closet and grabbed the old baseball bat my dad gave me when I got my first apartment. I had laughed when he gave it to me, but now, I silently thanked him. The smarter move would have been to call the police instead of going after whoever had broken into my house, but I was still high on rage. I was ready to start swinging.

Creeping down the hallway, the steady thumping coming from the bedroom gradually grew in volume. As I got closer to the door, grunting joined the commotion. Gripping the bat a little tighter, I reached for the doorknob to the bedroom and began turning it, when a high-pitched moan froze me in my tracks.

"Oh, fuck! Yes, Matt! Yes!"

*No, he couldn't be...* I wanted to be wrong, but the sight that awaited me when I opened the door had my stomach flipping. My fiancé was at the end of the bed with his pants around his ankles and his dick buried in some random brunette, doggy style.

"What the actual fuck?" My voice sounded muffled through the ringing in my ears. Matt froze, his head whipping sideways to face me.

"Gwen! This isn't–We're not—" He pulled out, and tripped on his pants as he tried to take a step. I turned away and stomped back down the hall.

A loud thud sounded from the bedroom, followed by an even louder, *"Fuck!"* I could only assume Matt fell, and I hoped that he flattened his dick in the process.

"Wait, Gwen!"

I heard him trying to get his pants up, his belt clanking as he struggled. Standing at the edge of the living room, I closed my eyes and took a minute to breathe. Overwhelmed didn't even begin to describe how I felt at that moment. Rage surged like electricity through my veins, biting at my skin.

His hand on my shoulder had my eyes flying open. Repulsed by his touch, I pulled away, turning to face him. The bat in my hand raised, I pointed it at Matt, who flinched slightly as it brushed past his legs. "Do not touch me," I snapped.

Matt didn't move, anger flashing across his features. "Gwen—"

"I don't want to hear your fucking excuses, Matt!" I yelled, twisting to walk away. Before I could take a step, the air left my lungs as I was slammed harshly against the wall, Matt's forearm pinned against my chest.

The bat fell from my hand as I clawed at him. Screams to get off of me were cut off by a harsh slap to my cheek. Tears instantly swelled in my eyes. My vision blurred as the last two years of abuse rushed to the surface.

*"Lazy bitch... Fucking useless..."*

The words stung, but I kept telling myself it could be worse, so I defended him.

Then it did. Bruises constantly covered my upper arm from being grabbed too hard, and the first time he slapped me...

But Matt had apologized, bringing home a bouquet of roses like he always did after we fought. He convinced me I was the problem, and I believed him.

*Maybe this was my fault, too...*

*No.*

I don't know when he had stepped away from me, but when I blinked away the tears pooling in the corners of my eyes, he was standing against the opposite wall.

"Gwen, I'm–" I put up my hands, his voice trailing off. Bending down, I picked up the discarded bat while glancing at Matt.

"Don't follow me." My voice was shaky and barely above a whisper, but I refused to cry in front of him. Flinging open the front door, I grabbed my bag and let the door slam shut behind me. My feet sunk into the grass as I ran across the lawn to my car, quickly throwing my bag and the bat into my passenger seat as I climbed inside and started it up. Driving away, my destination was unknown, but when I came to the end of the street, a familiar car caught my eye.

I pulled up behind the red Jeep and the stupid stickers on the back window confirmed what I thought—it was Matt's.

Not thinking, I stepped out of the front seat, bat in hand. Without hesitation, I swung the bat and made contact with one of his taillights. As I stood there, staring at the red plastic scattered at my feet, all the adrenaline left my body and the severity of my situation finally hit me. I was unemployed and homeless.

*Fuck.*

"That fucking asshole." Ivy handed me a glass of wine and a bag of peas. Sitting cross-legged on my best friend's couch, I stared at the glass in my hand as I put the peas against my warm cheek.

While driving to her apartment, the floodgates opened, and I showed up to her front door with puffy eyes and a dripping nose.

She immediately wrapped me up in her arms, giving me the biggest hug, then lead me to her couch. There was anger in her eyes There she glanced at my cheek.

There was no doubt in my mind—my best friend was ready to commit homicide.

Ivy and I met in college. To be honest, I couldn't tell you details of the "when" or "where." It felt as if we had known each other our entire lives. All I knew was that after graduation, when I moved in with Matt, she insisted on staying close by, so I would always have a friend. *"You never know,"* was what she always said.

Right now, words alone could never express how grateful I was for my friend's crazy intuition.

Ivy laid a blanket on my lap before sitting on the edge of the couch with her own glass of wine. This was one of the biggest reasons I loved Ivy: she never pressured me to say or do anything. When I was upset, she simply let me sit in my feelings and held space with me.

But she also knew when to ask the right questions.

"You ready to talk about what happened, sweet pea?" she finally asked.

"I quit my job," I blurted. "The mom came home and started tearing into me yet again. I walked out. When I got home, I found Matt balls deep in another woman in our bed." I took a drink of my wine, hoping it would help.

"Did he do that?" Ivy gestured to my cheek with her wine glass.

"Yeah, he did," I muttered. "When he chased after me, begging me to listen to his stupid excuses, I lost it. He pinned me against the wall, and when I screamed at him to let me go..." I didn't stop the tears from falling. Dropping the peas into my lap, I chugged the rest of the wine.

When Matt hit me the first time, I called Ivy. She wanted me to leave him right then and there, but I couldn't. "I'm trying to convince myself this isn't my fault, but what if it is?"

"Gwendalyn Brookes..." Ivy meant business when she used my full name. I clutched the empty glass in my hand, trying to hide the tremors. Ivy took it from me, and placed both our glasses on her coffee table, then sat cross-legged directly in front of me.

"I don't know what I'm going to do, Ivy." I buried my face in my hands, avoiding her gaze.

When Matt proposed after only a few months of us living together, he did it in front of his family. My parents had passed unexpectedly in a car accident when I was in college, so the promise of a new family, even Matt's, pushed me to say yes. Our relationship wasn't perfect, but the scariness of the unknown made me want to stay where I was comfortable. The endless cycle of calm before the storm even stopped once we started planning our wedding.

Well, until today, when I came home to a cheating fiancé and everything started making sense.

Ivy's hand on my knee pulled me back to the present as she cleared her throat before speaking.

"Gwen, listen. First of all, none of this is your fault. Matt is an asshole. He never deserved you." I wiped my face with my hands before looking up at her. "Second of all, I know what you're going to do. You're going to take some time to clear your head and figure out what you want. We'll make a game plan tomorrow. You're not alone in this. It should go without saying, but you can crash on my couch as long as you need."

"But Ivy—" I started, but was quickly cut off.

"Nope, not gonna hear it. Plus, now that we found out he's a cheater, we get to go Carrie Underwood on his stupid Jeep. Should we start with keying the sides or slashing tires?"

I chuckled at Ivy's suggestion. She would help me hide a body if I asked.

"I may have already taken my baseball bat to a taillight."

Ivy bursted out laughing, and after a beat, I joined in.

"That's my girl." Standing up, Ivy walked to the kitchen and came back with the opened bottle of wine. After pouring a hefty amount into both of our glasses, she sat the now nearly empty bottle on the table before handing me a glass. Plopping down beside me on the couch again, she pulled some of the blanket off my lap. Palming the TV remote, she gave me a knowing look. "So, *Dexter*?"

"Absolutely."

"To morally gray men!" Ivy held up her cup, and I clinked mine against it, chuckling in the process.

"To morally gray men," I replied.

# Chapter Two

## *Gwen*

Several loud knocks on the front door woke me up the next morning. A wine induced headache had a vice-like grip around my head. I rolled over on the couch and pulled the blanket up under my chin in an attempt to block out the world. Sinking back into the couch, I ignored whoever was at the door in the hopes they would leave.

Just as I could feel sleep tugging me back under, another succession of knocks had me sitting up and outwardly groaning.

As I was about to stand, Ivy's bedroom door opened, and she walked out. Tying her robe around her waist, she pointed at me. "You better lay back down, sweet pea. I got this."

Chuckling, I wrapped my blanket back around my shoulders and curled up on the couch. Ivy's slippers padded on the kitchen tile as the stranger at the front door started knocking again. The back of the couch faced the front door, so I wasn't able to see who it was when she opened it.

"What do you want?" Ivy was not using her customer service voice, so it was someone she knew. Curiosity was about to get the better of me when a voice I recognized spoke.

"Ivy, I know she's here. She doesn't have anywhere else to go. Let me talk to her."

*Matt.*

"You have some nerve showing up here, demanding to talk to my best friend after everything you did." Ivy was the kind of person who was calm and collected, even when she was mad. Her emotions didn't always show, but right now, I could hear the fight in her next words. "I suggest you wait until Gwen is ready to listen to your bullshit."

"This is ridiculous! Let me talk to my fiancé."

*Fuck, the ring...* Looking down at my hand, annoyance washed over me at the sight of my engagement ring still prominently sitting on my finger.

The sounds of struggle grabbed my attention, and I slid off the couch to face the door. Matt was trying to push it open while keeping a foot between it and the frame so Ivy couldn't close it. She may look tiny, but Ivy was strong. I had seen her take down men twice her size in her self-defense classes.

"God damn it, just let me in!" Matt yelled, and I flinched, even though I was across the room with a door and my best friend between us.

Hesitantly, I rounded the couch and headed toward the kitchen. Ivy would take a bullet for me but I knew what Matt was capable of and I didn't want her getting hurt.

"It's okay," I say, trying to inflict confidence into my words. Ivy looked at me over her shoulder, her brows raised as if asking me if I was sure. I nodded my head.

Ivy took a step back and the door swung open, hitting the back of a dining chair. Matt stumbled forward.

I hugged myself in an attempt to hide the tremors in my hands.

Ivy stood next to me, her own arms crossed in front of her chest. She stared down Matt as he righted himself and looked between the two of us. He held a bouquet of flowers in his hand that appeared to have seen better days. It was a mix of different colored roses and I could feel a new headache forming behind my eyes.

Clearing my throat, Matt's attention stayed on me. There was a softness in his eyes that I wished was genuine, but I knew this man too well. He didn't have a sympathetic bone in his body.

"Matt, what are you doing here?" My voice somehow came out more confident than I felt. I silently thanked my best friend for having my back.

Matt extended the roses toward me, as if expecting me to take them. I started to politely decline them when Ivy beat me to the punch.

"Gwen's allergic to roses, asshole," she scoffed before walking forward, ripping the bouquet out of his hand and throwing them over his shoulder through the open door. They landed with a soft thud in the hallway. I stared at them, not surprised Matt didn't bother to remember my allergy.

He never did.

"Gwen, I'm trying here. Just come home. We'll figure this out, we always do." I heard the frustration in his voice, and there was a part of me that wanted to go with him so all of this could just be over. Another piece of me, though, wanted to call him out for the way he had treated me. Ultimately, tears won. Warm trails of moisture coated my cheeks as I looked at Matt once again.

"I don't want to go home with you, Matt," I whispered. "I need some time." The confidence from moments before was now gone as I wiped away the tears with the back of my hand.

"Come on, Gwen. I already said I was sorry. What else do you want from me?" His brows pitched together as if he didn't understand.

I shook my head, trying to clear it enough to form words. Matt took a step toward me and panic surged through my body. Before I could truly react, Ivy planted herself between us.

"She said she didn't want to go with you. That means you need to leave. Now."

Matt looked between the two of us, presumably shocked by the rejection. The confusion on his face quickly warped into rage. It was the only warning I had before he lunged forward, stepping around Ivy and attempting to grab my arm.

Ivy latched onto his forearm right as his fingers brushed my wrist, and she forced herself in front of him once more. I backed further into the kitchen, stopping when my back pressed into the counter. Using his own momentum, Ivy flipped Matt over her shoulder and slammed him onto his back.

Matt groaned in pain as Ivy squatted down next to him, getting close enough so that she didn't have to speak above a whisper. "You have exactly five seconds to leave with your tiny ass dick still attached to your body. Otherwise, the only way you'll ever get fucked again is by another dude." *Damn, it was scary when she did that.* "I'm a strong believer in fuck around and find out, Matt. What's it gonna be?"

I watched from a distance as Matt stood and limped his way to the open door, mumbling under his breath, "This isn't over yet."

Ivy followed behind and yelled after him, "Yes it is!"

I sank to my knees on the kitchen floor as fresh tears free-fell down my face. Ivy sat with me, gathering me up in a hug and letting me work through every emotion that flowed out of me.

Anger.

Fear.

Sadness.

All of them.

After what felt like an eternity of us sitting on the floor, I laid down on my back with my eyes closed to let the coldness of the floor help center me. Ivy laid down beside me, and grabbed my hand in hers.

"I'm sorry, Ivy." My voice was a whisper; I didn't trust myself not to get choked up and start crying again.

"Sweet pea, you gotta stop apologizing for things outside of your control."

I forced air into my lungs, and tried to let her words sink in. After several more moments of silence, the gravity of everything that just happened sank in.

If I had been alone... The thought sent a chill up my spine, and my body shuddered. Ivy squeezed my hand in silent support.

"You're not going back to him," Ivy whispered next to me. I felt her eyes on me, but I couldn't bring myself to look at her. "I'm not letting you this time. You're staying here. I'll lock you in my closet if I have to. "

"Ivy, I can't ask you to do that..." I muttered. She sat up with my hand still in hers, and urged me up, too. Meeting her gaze, I noticed the concerned expression and worry in her eyes.

"You're not asking, I'm offering," she said, effectively shutting me down. "I'll help you find a new job, a new apartment, whatever I gotta do. I don't want to lose my best friend. Not when I know I could have done something to prevent it." Sadness coated her eyes, her bottom lip quivering slightly as she spoke.

Sighing, I nodded my head.

She was right, after all. If I went back to Matt, the cycle would start all over again. This was my chance to be free, to find out who I wanted to be.

"Sweet pea, are you sure you're okay? I can reschedule this meeting," Ivy asked while she finished gathering her work things. We had spent most of the day after Matt's departure being potatoes on the couch until Ivy's boss had called asking if she could come in.

"I'll be fine, I promise. I'm gonna make myself some coffee, then update my resume so I can start applying for new jobs."

I held up the pod of coffee, being playful by giving it a little shake, so Ivy knew I was okay. She chuckled at my move before throwing her bag over her shoulder.

"Alright, then. I'll be back in a few hours. If I were you, I'd throw a shower on your to-do list, too. You're looking like a hot mess, babe!" she yelled over her shoulder, heading out the front door.

I started a cup of coffee, then headed to the bathroom, freezing in front of the mirror as I took in the sight before me. Since last night, I've had my hair up in a messy bun on top of my head. It was no longer the cute, messy kind, but the kind that screams, *"I can't remember the last time I washed my hair."*

Taking down my bun, I ran a brush through my hair before putting it back up. I loved my wavy, dirty blonde hair, something I got from my grandma, because it paired with my blue eyes perfectly. Groaning, I made my way out of the bathroom, deciding it was time for that cup of coffee. I followed the smell of my freshly brewed cup to the kitchen.

Pulling out the creamer that Ivy buys especially for me, I turned my black coffee into a beautiful light brown color before I took a large sip. I let the warmth flow through me and did a mental happy dance when the flavor was perfect.

Matt had always criticized my love of creamer. *You shouldn't be drinking coffee if you have to add creamer.* I shook his words from my mind, not wanting to dwell on him. Feeling way more energized, I decided it was time to start taking on the world.

Grabbing my bag, I dug out my dead phone and plugged it in on the kitchen island before turning on my laptop. I carried it and my coffee to the kitchen table, diving into updating my resume and looking for potential jobs.

Sometime later, I realized my mug was empty, and I had been staring at my computer for over an hour. As I made my way back toward the coffeemaker, I turned my phone on and let it go through the startup sequence while I started brewing a second cup of coffee. After it finished turning on, the vibrating was constant.

I wanted to completely ignore it, but caved and picked it up. I started slowly going through the overwhelming number of notifications. There were several missed calls from Mrs. Watson, as well as several texts telling me I needed to return her calls. *Not going to happen.*

Then I got to the texts from Matt. I sat my mug down on the counter, the coffee threatening to make a second appearance.

**Baby, please call me. I just want to talk.**

**She didn't mean anything to me.**

Gwen, this is getting ridiculous. Just call me.

I know you're at Ivy's, you don't have any-where else to go. Don't make me come down there.

Gwen, this is ridiculous. Just fucking come home. I'm going to let you throw your little tantrum tonight, but if you aren't home by the morning, I'm coming to get you.

Since you're still ignoring me, I guess I have to come get your ungrateful ass.

Those were just from when I left last night. Presumably, if I listened to the voicemails that followed his visit this morning, they would all be along the same line. Hands shaking, I put my phone down next to my mug, deciding I needed something a little stronger.

Grabbing Ivy's trusty bottle of tequila from the liquor cabinet, I poured myself a shot then put the bottle back on the shelf. The familiar burn did it's job and helped to calm my frayed nerves

I still wanted to scream out my frustrations though. Everything was happening at lightning speed and I just needed a moment to catch my damn breath.

Deciding not to let the building anxiety win, I headed for the bathroom to take that shower I so desperately needed. I let the water warm up while I queued some of my favorite angry songs.

I had never understood people who took showers without music. Even in college, I had a portable speaker so I could jam out. Something about the hot water paired with a good playlist could make even the worst days better.

The mix of water and music worked its magic. By the time I got out of the shower, the water had started running cold. Wiping the fog away from the mirror, I scrunched my hair to keep the curls decent as I sang along to the Charlie Daniels Band. I was a country girl at heart, growing up in a small town in Pennsylvania before heading off to Pittsburgh for college, so there were still a few things here and there that brought me back to my roots.

Just as I finished my impromptu karaoke session, I heard the front door open and close. Assuming Ivy had gotten home, I wrapped my towel around me before popping my head out of the bathroom.

"Hey, Ivy, what are your thoughts on pasta for dinner?"

My stomach had started growling while I was in the shower, and all I could think about was spaghetti and meatballs from the family-owned Italian place down the road. Hearing a chair scrap from the kitchen, I stepped out of the bathroom thinking maybe she hadn't heard me.

"Ivy, wanna go to—" I froze in my tracks. Matt was standing by the front door, turning the deadbolt and tucking the chair under the handle. "Matt, what the hell?"

He turned toward me, and I could feel his eyes roam up and down my body. The smile that stretched across his face made my skin crawl.

The tiny towel no longer covered me enough, and I attempted to wrap it around my body tighter. Fear coursed through me. The man I once knew was nowhere to be seen. The one in front of me had a look in his eye that told me I needed to run.

If I could just make it to the bedroom...

My first mistake was turning my back to him. Matt crossed the small space before I could take more than a few steps. His calloused hand gripped my upper arm tight enough to leave a bruise and pulled me toward him until my back slammed against his chest.

"Now, now, Gwen. There's no reason we can't have a little fun before I take you home."

# Chapter Three

## *Gwen*

"**M**att, please." My words came out in a sob as one of his arms wrapped tightly around my waist, keeping me flush against him as he walked us to the middle of the living room. Stopping next to the couch, he pressed his dick into my back, making bile rise up the back of my throat. "Please, I don't want this."

His hand covered my mouth, using it as leverage to pull my head to the side.

"Don't lie to me, Gwen. We both know you love this." His voice was like nails on a chalkboard. I shook my head against his hand, the motion making him hold on tighter and forcing my neck backwards into a painful position. "Stop playing hard to get, baby. We both know you're going to let this all go and come home with me. Just like you always do. You're nothing without me."

Matt's arm on my waist loosened as he snaked his hand down my body to the bottom of my towel. His hands on my body felt wrong, but his words played on repeat in my head.

*"You're nothing without me."*

He was right... I didn't know who I was anymore without Matt in my life. I *was* nothing, and fighting it was useless. Maybe, if I go back with him now, he would forgive me for leaving.

Matt dug his fingers into my thigh, and the hot tears building at the back of my eyes spilled over. The pain cleared the fog that settled in my mind.

*He would never stop hurting me.*

I started fighting, again. Matt's grip on my tightened even as I scratched as his forearms. I refused to roll over like a trained dog performing for the chance of treats.

Suddenly, I remembered the one self-defense class Ivy had dragged me. The instructor's words blared in my mind. *"Women have a lower center of gravity. If you're pressed against someone, your back to their front, drop your body weight and lean forward. Easiest way to use the attacker's own weight against them. Throw them off balance first if you can. Remember to SING. Solar plexus, instep, nose, and groin."*

If I could get Matt on his back, I probably had an actual chance of getting away. The bedroom locked from the inside, and was closer than the front door. Praying Ivy would be home soon, I made my choice.

Picking up my foot, I stomped down hard on top of Matt's as my fist made contact with the sensitive spot between his legs.

"Fuck!" he yelled, his grip on me loosening. I grabbed his forearm with mine, mimicked Ivy's stance from this morning, and leaned for-ward.

Matt's feet left the floor, his body weight on mine for a split second before I bent forward completely and threw him over my shoulder. He landed with a thud in front of me, and a small smile formed on my lips at the sight of him lying flat on his back for the second time today.

He groaned as he curled into the fetal position, cradling his bruised manhood in his hand. I took the opportunity to run past him to the bedroom, just barely missing his outstretched arm as he attempted to grab my ankle, snagging the edge of the towel instead. Letting the towel go, I looked over my shoulder once I reached the door.

Matt stumbled to his feet, and I quickly shut the door. The lock on the handle clicked into place easily.

"You stupid fucking bitch!" The banging of his fists shook the door frame. I looked around the room for something heavy I could put in front of it.

Matt wasn't exactly a big man, but I had no doubt he could find his way into the room if he wanted.

Seeing nothing that I could easily move in front of the door, I quickly realized I backed myself into a corner. There was no escaping if Matt made it into the room.

I ran to the far side of Ivy's bed, and sank to my knees. From outside the door, I heard a loud thud that vibrated the floor underneath me. A buzzing in my ears drowned out the yells from the other side of the door as someone tried to desperately get through.

It was silent for a moment, but then the door swung open. I wrapped my arms around my knees, and buried my face down.

"Oh, sweet pea…" *That's not Matt.*

Looking up, I saw Ivy crouching before me, her hands settling on top of mine. A small flat-head screwdriver stuck out from underneath her fingers, presumably what she had used to unlock the door. I looked over the bed to see Matt lying face down on the floor with my dad's baseball bat next to him.

My attention went back to Ivy, my brain registering her saying my name. "Gwen? Are you okay?"

I nodded my head and watched as she rose, grabbing her robe from inside her closet before she wrapped it around my shoulders. My legs shook as I stood, and Ivy helped me put my arms through the sleeves of the robe, securing the tie around my waist. I barely had a chance to glance at Ivy before she was pulling me against her for a hug. The panic that had been coursing through my veins slowly melted away.

A knock coming from the front of the apartment had us pulling apart. We sidestepped Matt's unconscious body and made our way into the open living area. Two uniformed police officers with confused looks on their faces stood in the doorway.

Several hours later, Ivy and I were seated in front of the coffee table with to-go containers of spaghetti and meatballs. Somehow, Ivy had convinced the owners of the Italian restaurant to deliver dinner to us, and I swear I saw her slip the delivery person a $50 bill.

Honestly, she could have flashed her boobs and I wouldn't have questioned it. The fact that I was eating my favorite pasta in the comfort of Ivy's home was all I needed.

After the officers had called for an ambulance, one of them put Matt in handcuffs while the other took Ivy and my statements. I learned she had checked her security camera after a dozen unanswered phone calls, and saw Matt in the apartment. She had called 9-1-1, but was already on her way home. I recounted everything that had happened after I had gotten out of the shower while Ivy downloaded some of the images from her camera to send to the officer, corroborating my side of the story. There wouldn't be any way for Matt to twist this in his favor.

The officer assured me that Matt wouldn't be getting out on bail anytime soon, as all but one of the judges were taking vacations. With the backlog of cases, he would be lucky to see the inside of a courtroom for several months. That information should have brought me a sense of relief.

But all I felt was dread.

I still had no idea where to go from here.

"Alright, babes, before we watch our favorite morally gray man, we gotta talk about next steps." Ivy took a large drink of her wine before sitting it down next to her food. "I told you my couch is always yours, and that hasn't changed. But I also know you, and you're already stressing about what to do next."

Ivy was a mind reader.

"I guess…" I looked down at my hand as I spoke. The stupid engagement ring was still on my finger and out of habit, I was fiddling with it. Why was I even still wearing the damn thing? "I should decide what I want to do with this."

I pulled the ring off my finger and put it into Ivy's waiting hand. She examined it for a second then tossed it onto the coffee table. It bounced off the smooth wood with a soft *clink* and landed on the rug on the opposite side.

She looked at me and shrugged, "Pawn it."

"I can't do that, Ivy!"

"And why not?"

*Wait, why couldn't I?* It wasn't a family heirloom or anything. It was simply a piece of gaudy jewelry that Matt had probably put minimum effort into picking out for me.

"You could use the money to start fresh somewhere," Ivy encouraged.

The money would be nice. I didn't have much saved up, and if I wanted to be able to get an apartment soon, I would need money for a deposit and first month's rent.

Ivy was right.

"Okay. Step one, pawn my engagement ring. What next?" I asked. It was a question I should answer for myself, but knowing Ivy, she probably already had a plan put together in her head as we spoke.

"Well, I have a friend in Chicago who runs a nanny agency. Her name's Carol. I reached out to her today before my meeting started and raved about you. She'd love to meet with you, and then help you find a family that could be a good fit."

"Chicago?" The thought of moving to a new state made the bottom of my stomach drop.

"Gwen, I think it would do you some good to get out of this state. I know you feel some kind of moral obligation to stay because of your parents, but I know they would have wanted you to go out and live your best life. You can't do that here. Not with all the trauma you have experienced. It's time to do something for you."

My chest tightened at the mention of my parents. After the car accident that took both of them from me, I was a wreck. I did some really stupid shit and almost flunked out of college, but somehow, Ivy helped me snap out of it.

Since then, I felt like I was always making decisions based on what I thought would make them happiest, not myself. Matt came into my life, and was my first long-term relationship. He proposed early on in our relationship which gave me pause, but I convinced myself they would have wanted to see their little girl married. So I said yes.

We see where that big life decision led me...

Now, what Ivy was saying had my heart doing somersaults. *Could I possibly make a choice that would benefit me whether or not I thought it would have made my parents happy?* I wanted to believe I had the strength and confidence.

Ivy believed in me... and if she did, so could I.

"Okay," I whispered.

"Okay?" Ivy seemed surprised.

"Yes. You're right. Maybe it's time I start living the life I want to have, not the life I think my parents wanted me to have. So let's talk to your friend."

Ivy jumped up and ran to her bedroom. She ran back, stopping in front of me and bouncing on her heels while handing me an envelope.

Taking it from her, I opened it as she sat down next to me. Inside was a printed copy of an email confirmation for two plane tickets to Chicago for this weekend. Confused, I met Ivy's enthusiastic gaze.

"What are these?" I had expected a video call with her friend, not whatever this was.

"I bought them last night after you went to bed. I had hoped I could whisk you off to Chicago for the weekend, so it would be easier to convince you to leave Matt. I didn't anticipate him going psycho and doing all the hard work for me. Plus, when I talked to Carol today, she told me she had a couple leads for some jobs and could meet us for drinks Friday night and talk logistics. Plus, I don't have any contracts keeping me in Pittsburgh. If you find a job, we can both move!" She paused, taking a second to breathe.

"Ivy, I don't know what to say," I hesitated, wanting to agree but still feeling unsure.

"You don't have to say anything, babe. Even if Carol's leads don't work out, we can still have a fun weekend away from this mess."

I launched myself at her, nearly knocking both of us over with the force as I hugged her tight.

"Thank you. Thank you, thank you, thank you." I was grateful for my best friend and I needed her to know that. Ivy hugged me back, and for the first time in a long time, I actually had hope for the future.

Two days later, Ivy and I boarded a plane to Chicago and were sitting at a high top waiting for Carol in one of the bars near the Airbnb we were staying in. Picking at my cuticles under the table, I took a minute to look around the bar. As my eyes moved past the front door, it opened and in walked a woman who looked a little out of place.

Dressed in a light blue tennis skirt with a matching quarter zip, she looked like she was in her late-30s. Her light brown hair was up in a high pony with a pair of sunglasses on top of her head. Ivy waved from her chair next to me, and the woman walked our way.

"Carol! It's so good to see you!" Jumping down, Ivy greeted the woman with a hug.

"Ivy! It's been too long. I'm so glad you two decided to make a trip out here." Carol seemed to be a genuinely happy person, offering me her hand with a wide smile on her face. "I'm Carol. You must be Gwendalyn."

"Yes, but everyone calls me Gwen." Taking her hand, I shook it while offering a small smile of my own.

"It's so great to meet you. Sorry for the less than professional attire. I had a tennis lesson right before this, and it was easier to come straight here than to go home and change." She offered up a small laugh while releasing my hand.

"I appreciate you taking the time to chat with me."

"Of course! Let's get straight to business so that we can enjoy ourselves afterward. Ivy filled me in on the basics of your situation. Are you hoping to start immediately, or do you want a little time to adjust first?"

"I can be flexible. Though, honestly, sooner would be better than later. There are some thing…"

Ivy's phone went off, interrupting me, and she quickly answered it. "This is Ivy." Someone on the other end talked as she slid down from her stool and whispered, "Work."

I offered a thumbs up, and a small nod before she headed outside to take her call.

Carol didn't miss a beat, picking up right where we left off. "Well, depending on what you're looking for in terms of number of children and ages plus benefits, I have a few families on the hunt right now. One of them is a single dad who is a bit desperate for help. He's got a two-year-old boy, who is just the sweetest thing. I could probably get you an interview tomorrow while you are in town. If the meeting goes well, we can talk about logistics regarding background checks and everything afterward."

"I would love that. Are you sure?" I was surprised by Carol's relaxed approach toward placing nannies with families. A first time meeting in a bar didn't scream the most professional of interviews.

"Absolutely. I've known Ivy since we were kids. Any friend of hers is good in my book. Plus, I've been where you are." Reaching out, she placed her hand on top of mine. "We've got to stick together. So, however I can help, I will."

"Thank you." The words barely came out with all the emotions clogging my throat. In a matter of minutes, I formed a deeper connection with her than most people I've known my entire lifetime.

"I'm going to reach out to him real quick." She gave my hand a squeeze before pulling out her phone and typing away. I was about to get up to check on Ivy when she walked back inside.

"Everything okay?" I asked as she reached the table.

"Yeah, just my boss. Nothing crazy." She waved her hand dismissively, but I didn't believe her. There was something in the way she was holding herself that told me she wasn't telling me the whole truth..

"Good news!" Carol enthusiastically put her phone down on the table. The small object made too loud of a noise, startling me. I jumped in my seat. Carol mouthed a quick "Sorry" before sharing her news. "It's done! Four o'clock tomorrow. His name is Anthony Marino. I'll send you all the details."

Carol waved down a waitress as I stared at her, bewildered by the entire exchange. Or really the lack of one. Ivy just chuckled next to me.

Given their history, it would make sense that she was used to this kind of behavior from Carol. When the waitress came over, she ordered a bottle of house red and the waitress happily obliged. Soon, we each had a glass of wine in our hand.

"It can't be this easy, can it?" I took a sip of wine, hoping that the anxiety I was feeling would settle with the alcohol. "Starting new? Finding myself again?"

"It can be if you let it," Ivy said before taking her own drink.

*I guess we were about to find out.*

# Chapter Four

# Anthony

"**D**id you seriously think you could get away with it? That you could touch a woman without her consent and there wouldn't be consequences? Just because she didn't want to file charges doesn't mean we don't have all the fucking details."

My partner was angry.

Actually, angry wasn't a strong enough word. Jason was enraged.

The man tied to a chair in front of us struggled against his restraints. Blood dripped from his nose, and his lip was split in several places. His left eye was already starting to swell, the skin various shades of purple. He was basically a human punching bag for Jason the last fifteen minutes.

But Mr. Dickhead here still wouldn't admit what he did.

His girlfriend was currently admitted to the hospital with a concussion and several broken ribs. When we had been called in, it was because of the suspected sexual abuse. She had let us take her statement and informed us her boyfriend was actually the one responsible, but ended up not wanting to press charges.

She said it was her fault, that she shouldn't have tried to tell him no while he was drunk.

*Fucking bullshit.*

Her unwillingness to put his ass in jail didn't matter, though. We had gotten everything we needed.

"I don't know what you're talking about," the man snarled. They always snarled.

"Come on, man," I said, straightening from my place against the door frame. "Tell us what we want to hear and we'll cut you a deal."

It was our routine. Jason played bad cop and got them sweating, or bleeding. I played good cop and told them we would make a deal. We had been doing this longer than I could remember.

"Fuck. You." He spat at Jason, who turned away a second too late. Bright crimson liquid painted his cheek and neck. When he turned back to the asshole, a devilish smile spread across his face.

In a blur, Jason had a knife sticking out of the dude's shoulder. His screams filled the warehouse room we were in and *oscurità mia* got excited. *Time to play.*

Jason stepped to the side, giving me a turn to torture the fucker. I walked up to the man, twisting the knife sticking out of his shoulder and pushing it in further.

"Fuck, man. Stop! Please—"

"Too late," I cut him off. "Did she ask you to stop? Did she say please? Did you fucking listen?" I pulled my own knife out from my belt, the knife my father gave to me when I was old enough to learn how to wield it. The handle was wrapped in leather that was worn and blood-stained, but the blade was sharp. It had to be in order to teach these assholes a lesson.

Without hesitation, I stabbed my knife into his hand, embedding the tip into the wood underneath. Leaving it there, I took several steps back so Jason could land another punch to the man's ribs, cutting off the line of expletives coming out of his mouth. By this point, there was no way he didn't have a broken rib or two of his own.

He coughed up blood, confirming my suspicions, and I couldn't help the smile that tugged on my lips as he groaned.

Jason leaned in close to the fucker so he was inches away from his face. "Here's the thing, Mr. Williams. Whether you admit to it or not, we still know what you did. It stops today. You won't be laying another hand on any woman, least of all your girlfriend."

At the mention of his name, it was like a switch flipped.

"That bitch got what she deserved." His demeanor changed, no longer pretending to be innocent.

Jason pulled his knife from the fucker's shoulder, then moved behind the chair. My partner's free hand fisted his hair, yanking his head back. "She deserved a concussion and broken ribs?"

"She deserved a lot more than that," he sneered, trying to shake his head free, but Jason held steady. "You should've seen the things that woman was sending me all day. Then I get home, and it's like she's not even the same person. She's a fucking tease." Every word this man said made me sick. He treated women like objects, only good for sex and nothing else.

"You can't blame a man for getting pissed when he's been hard as a rock all day. If she didn't want me to stick my dick in her pussy, the least she could have done was use her mouth to get me off instead of constantly nagging me. That woman doesn't know when to shut up. Doesn't matter." I saw a smile threatening his lips. "She'll think twice before saying no to me again. I made sure—"

Jason heard enough and he silenced the dumbass with a knife pressed against his throat.

This dude had officially pissed me off. Walking up, I pulled my knife from the dumb fuck's hand and the darkness inside me smiled from the involuntary grunt that came from him. "You won't be going anywhere near that woman, with your dick or otherwise, ever again."

"And what makes you so sure of that?"

I answered his question by shoving my knife in between his legs, aiming for his dick. A blood-curdling scream filled the small space, letting me know I hit my mark.

"That's how," I muttered, smiling down at my handiwork.

Jason continued holding onto the asshole's head, but pulled back his knife slightly as the dude thrashed in his chair. We wouldn't want the asshole to accidentally cut his own throat, essentially putting himself out of the misery he was currently experiencing.

It was only a couple more seconds before he passed out and his body went limp. Grabbing my knife, I wiped it off with one of the bloody towels nearby and inspected it for any damage.

Jason released the asshole's head, shoving it forward so the first thing he saw when he came to was his own bleeding dick.

Walking back around the chair, Jason looked down at the asshole before turning to me. "Honestly, Tony, why do you have to cut our fun short every single time?"

"At least I made him suffer." Shrugging my shoulders, I put my knife back on my belt and gave my clothes a once over. Not finding any evidence of the last hour on me, I looked to Jason, who was watching me with consideration. He wanted to say something more, I just knew it. "What?"

"How's Ollie?" Jason finally asked. He knew I hated when he checked in on me, but I couldn't fault him for asking about my son.

He wasn't exactly a kid person, though. Other detectives, their partners were pseudo aunts or uncles. Not Jason, though.

"Surprisingly, okay," I sighed. "Or at least from what I can tell. He's always been a bit of a quiet kid." I leaned against the wall, crossed my arms over my chest, and stared at the asshole slumped over in his chair.

"What about *her*?" Jason came to stand next to me. Of course, I knew who he was talking about.

Kimberly, Oliver's mom and my ex-wife.

I *really* fucking hated even thinking about that woman.

"Still haven't heard a peep. I have no idea where she is, but wherever it is, she can stay there. After everything she put Oliver and me through..." I trailed off, not wanting to think about the past right now.

"How's the whole childcare search going? Didn't your neighbor Katie have her baby?" Jason quickly changed the subject, and I released yet another frustrated sigh.

Because it wasn't going. It had been almost a month of searching. I was running out of time.

"Yeah, Katie's little girl is almost one now, I think. I know between that and watching Oliver, she's gotta be exhausted. She'd never tell me, though. She and her husband both give me those looks of pity whenever we cross paths." I chuckled, thinking about how they'd look at me if they knew what I actually did with my evenings.

After Kimberly, the darkness that I always tried to keep hidden refused to be pushed down.

My mom used to call it *oscurità mia*. She would tell me stories about how my father once had his own and how much it controlled his life. When I was old enough to understand, I learned the story of how she wanted a better life for me, convincing my father to move from Italy to the States before I was born and cutting ties with the syndicate.

It was hard, but they were happy. They made sure I went to the best schools and learned about my heritage, including the language. I was never fluent, but I knew enough to get by.

Ultimately, I was grateful my parents made the tough choice to leave everything behind. But in those organizations, you don't get to just walk away.

The day before my nineteenth birthday, my parents paid the ultimate price for leaving. They found us. I was forced to watch as they assaulted my mother and tortured my father. Then three bullets were fired, one meant for each of us.

But I survived.

I built a life I knew my parents would be proud of.

I became a cop.

I started a family.

I kept the darkness inside me under control... Until I couldn't.

That's when I joined Jason in his "passion project."

He knew the system didn't always get it right. Too many times abusers and rapists got away because of the fear they instilled. He wanted them to understand how it felt to have the control ripped away. So inside this abandoned warehouse, Jason and I did just that.

"Have you heard anything from that nanny agency? Carol's Caregivers or whatever?" Jason pushed off the wall, walking over to the fucker still passed out and kicking his foot.

"I have a meeting with one today. Carol said she seems like the perfect fit. I'm just glad that they handle all the business side of things and all I have to do is say yes or no to candidates as they come along. These last few, though," I rolled my eyes, "I'm not sure where they came from, but now I'm getting desperate."

"When are you meeting this new one?"

"Four o'clock."

"Um, Tony? It's four now." Jason chuckled as I frantically looked at my watch.

"Fuck!" I quickly grabbed my badge and gun from a beat up filing cabinet near the door before running out.

As I made it to the back door of the warehouse, I heard Jason shout after me. "Good luck! You're gonna need it!"

# Chapter Five

## Gwen

Carol came over a bit before my interview with a bottle of wine and a wide smile. She handing me her car keys, wished me good luck, then plopped down on the couch next to Ivy. The nerves I felt only moments before were washed away by the gratitude I had for the two women in front of me.

I left before the tears could fall. I was tired of crying, even if it was for happy reasons.

Pulling up outside of the two-story brick house, I put the car in park as I double checked the house number. The clock on the dashboard let me know it wasn't quite four yet, but it was better to be early than late. I slung my bag over my shoulder, took a fortifying breath, then made my way up the walkway.

The address Carol gave me was in a little suburb just outside of Chicago. It didn't take long to get here, and there are so many kid-friendly activities in the area. The house itself was two stories with a brick exterior and a porch that ran the entirety of the front side. It was exactly the kind of home I wish I could have.

Climbing the few steps up, I gave the doorbell a quick ring before stepping back. It didn't take long for the door to open, a woman who looked to be in her late thirties holding a crying toddler on her hip coming into view. The woman looked relieved to see me, and the toddler instantly stopped crying, more interested in the stranger standing in front of her.

"Can I help you?" The lady's eyes were red rimmed with dark purple bags under them. Her hair was in a bun, but several pieces were falling out. The ends were laying in what appeared to be spit up on her shoulder.

"Uh.. Hi, I'm Gwen. Gwendalyn, but everyone calls me Gwen." My answer didn't seem to clear any confusion. "Umm, I'm here for an interview... with Mr. Marino."

"Oh, thank heavens. Come in, please." The woman stepped aside, letting me in, while awkwardly adjusting the little one from one side to the other. "I'm Katie, and this is Lucy. My husband and I live next door. Anthony told me he had an interview today and would be back in time, but here we are. If you don't mind, Lucy here is running a fever and just can't seem to get comfortable. Oliver is watching TV in the living room with a snack. Phone numbers are on the fridge if there is an emergency."

Before I could say anything, Katie had her bag slung over her shoulder and was out the door, the soft click of the lock quickly following. If it hadn't already been the weirdest week of my life, I may have actually been surprised about what just happened.

Following the sounds of a children's show, I found a little boy with brown curly hair sitting cross-legged on the couch with a bright orange bowl nestled in his lap. Every couple of minutes, his little hand would reach in and grab a goldfish, all while his eyes stayed glued to whatever was on the TV.

I wasn't sure what to do. Approaching him seemed to be a bad idea, because what if I scared him? Hopefully, his father would come home before Oliver realized there was someone new.

That plan was quickly thrown out the window when he reached into his howl, and upon not feeling any goldfish, jumped off the couch. Oliver stopped in his tracks when he noticed me standing in the doorway. His little body tensed up as he clung to his bowl.

Immediately, I got down on my knees. "Hi, Oliver, I'm Gwen," I began in a calm voice. "Miss Katie had to go home." As he hesitantly began walking toward me, my mind swam with uncertainty. The normal reaction to a stranger being in your home would be to scream, yet he seemed more curious. The sound of his little feet padding across the carpet stopped directly in front of me.

"More, peas," he said, holding out his empty bowl while looking up at me with wide eyes.

I was speechless. I had never met a two-year-old who was unfazed by a complete stranger being in their house, yet here he was, more upset he was out of goldfish than me being here.

"Um, sure. Can you show me where they are?" He nodded before toddling off toward what I assumed to be the kitchen.

Taking in my surroundings as we went, I followed along while he carried his bowl in his hand. The house felt bigger on the inside than it looked. Mr. Marino didn't seem to be the decorating type–the walls blank, void of photos or decor. Wondering how long he had been doing this single dad thing, my heart broke a little for him and the boy in front of me.

When we made it to the kitchen, I sat my bag on an empty bar stool. Oliver  pointed to a cabinet near the fridge as he offered me the bowl. I took the bowl from his outstretched hand, and opened the cabinet turned into a makeshift snack pantry. It was stuffed full of goldfish, fruit snacks, and applesauce pouches.

This dad had reached survival mode a long time ago, by the looks of it. I pulled out a bag of goldfish, filling up Oliver's bowl before handing it to him.

"Tank you!" He grabbed a handful before shoving them into his mouth greedily. I chuckled as I watched him. He looked at me with curiosity in his eyes, as if wondering what would come next. "Trains?"

"Sure! I would love to play trains." A smile spread across his face as he put his bowl down on the floor and ran off. I bent down, picking up his bowl and putting it on the counter, then followed the sounds of toys hitting the floor.

Oliver was leaning over a toy box that I hadn't noticed earlier, tucked against the side of the simple gray couch. As I sat down next to him, he triumphantly pulled out a shiny black engine and held it out to me. There was nothing but pure joy written across this boy's face as he dug out a second train, bright red in color.

His excitement over the little things made me happy. Maybe the cruelty of the world hadn't gotten to him yet. I didn't know what had happened to his mom, but I did know that whatever it was, this sweet boy didn't deserve it.

I wasn't sure how long we sat there playing with his trains. I had found a container of train tracks, and we built an elaborate track that ran the entirety of the living room. Oliver was sitting on my lap, laughing as I narrated the train's path in my best conductor voice, as if we were inside the train watching out the window.

"Now, if you look to your left, you can see the giant orange chair statue. The wooden legs are solid oak and can withstand even the strongest of hits. The upcoming couch tunnel is the first of its kind. Built in 1753, this gorgeous piece of architecture is one of a kind. You will never find another tunnel like this." Oliver giggled from my lap. "Oh, no. Folks, it appears we're experiencing some strong trackulence. Please hold on!" I made my legs jump, causing Oliver to bump around, and his giggles turned into laughs. It was contagious, and it didn't take long before I was laughing with him.

In the middle of our laughing fit, I heard the front door open. Unsure of who it was, I stood up, putting Oliver on my hip. Before I could decide what to do next, a voice came from the front door.

"Katie, you here? Oliver?" A man dressed in black slacks and a gray button-down shirt turned the corner, freezing in the doorway after making eye contact with me.

My breath hitched as I stared into his hazel eyes, a few stray pieces of his brown hair falling in front of them. His beard was neatly trimmed and very short.

My eyes involuntarily roamed down his body. He was tall, and even from a distance, I could tell he had at least a foot on me. My heart skipped a beat as I once again met his gaze.

His face hardened.

"Who are you?" he snarled, his lip curling with anger as his eyes darkened. His hand twitched toward the gun attached to his belt. My heart jumped into my throat, and my stomach clenched in fear.

"I-I-I'm Gwen," I quickly responded, my eyes darting to his hand that was hovering above the weapon. "Um, Gwendalyn. We had an interview scheduled today." His eyes continued to burrow holes into me, the tension between us almost palpable. Slowly, the creases between his brows loosened and his hand relaxed at his side. Oxygen rushed back to my lungs as Oliver wriggled down from my arms.

"Daddy!" Oliver ran to Mr. Marino, his chubby hands stretched wide to the man who seemed to melt before my eyes. He squatted down, and scooped Oliver into his muscular arms.

"*Figlio mio,* how's my sweet boy?" Standing up, he pressed a kiss in his son's hair while Oliver threw his arms around his father's neck.

Mr. Marino held onto him tightly, the veins on his forearms more prominent from the action. If I hadn't already known they were related, there would be no doubt after seeing the two of them together. Oliver was a miniature copy of his dad, his wild curls and brown eyes an identical match. They also both had small dimples that formed when they smiled.

"Play trains, Daddy! Trains!" Oliver pointed to the elaborate track set up covering the floor, and I did my best to keep my composure as Mr. Marino walked further into the room, carefully stepping over the tracks in his path.

"This looks amazing, Oliver. Did you have a fun day?" Oliver nodded his head and Mr. Marino sat him down on the floor. Oliver started running along the track, following its twists and turns while giggling. Mr. Marino turned to me, reaching his hand out to me.

"Hello, Gwendalyn. I'm Anthony. I apologize for being late." The softness of his face while interacting with his son was gone, replaced by the less than inviting scowl that seemed to be his natural state. His lips were pulled into a thin line as he looked down at me. Hesitantly, I accepted his hand, giving it a small shake.

"No apologies needed," I mumbled. "Um, Katie had to leave. Her daughter was sick. I just assumed she let you know." He pulled out his phone, tapping on it and letting out a sigh.

"Apparently she did." I heard him mutter curse words under his breath, looking toward his son as Oliver grabbed one of his engines to run along the track.

"It really is okay. Um, do you still want to do the interview? I understand if things are a little hectic right now."

He met my eyes just as Oliver ran up between his dad's knees, knocking him off balance. Reaching out, Mr. Marino grabbed my arm to keep from stepping on his son. The touch sent electricity through my body and goose bumps formed on the skin beneath his calloused fingers. My eyes darted to the connection, shocked by the reaction, then up to find his eyes wide.

He quickly released my arm, shaking his hand as if trying to rid it of pain. He took with him an unexpected warmth that had me questioning my own sanity for a minute. After everything that had happened the last week, I shouldn't be any type of okay with the touch of a man, let alone one who looked as if he could snap me in half like a twig.

"Hey, little buddy, you must be hungry. Why don't we get some dinner started, yeah?" He turned away from me, grabbing hold of Oliver's hand and leading him out of the room. I stared after them, unsure of what to do.

"Um, Mr. Marino?" I cleared my throat. He looked over his shoulder at me.

"Anthony, please. Mr. Marino was my dad."

"It was a... pleasure meeting you. Maybe you can reach out to Carol and we can reschedule?"

"Shit, the interview." He ran his hand over his face, then realized his mistake. Glancing down at Oliver, he put his finger to his lips. "Don't repeat that, little man." Turning back to me, I could see the wheels turning inside his head, trying to come up with a solution. "Would you like to stay for dinner?"

I was seconds away from politely declining when Oliver let go of his dad's hand, bounding toward me. Grabbing my hand, he pulled me forward while looking up at me with perfected puppy dog eyes. "Miss Gen stay?"

I couldn't say no.

Allowing him to pull me along to the kitchen, I glanced at the clock in the hallway, making a mental note that it was nearly five in the evening now and that I should update Ivy. Though by that point, she and Carol may have been working on a second bottle of wine, and not even realized what time it is.

When we reached the kitchen, Oliver let go of my hand and climbed up onto one of the stools at the kitchen island. Anthony rummaged through the freezer, pulling out a bag of chicken nuggets shaped like dinosaurs.

Oliver was sitting on his knees, wiggling in his chair and clapping his hands. I quietly shuffled behind Oliver to make sure he didn't fall off while Anthony placed the nuggets onto a baking tray and slipped them into the oven. Once he did, he returned to the fridge and pulled out a large orange and a bag of carrots.

"So, Gwendalyn, how long have you lived in Chicago?" he asked while making quick work of the fruit and vegetables in front of him. I was mesmerized by the action, the movement of the knife in his hand making me pause before I answered his question.

"Well, actually, I don't live in Chicago. I live in Pittsburgh. Born and raised in Pennsylvania."

"What brings you to the city then?"

"Hopefully accepting a new job," I answered. He stopped chopping, intently staring at me as if waiting for me to elaborate. Trying to keep my answers vague, I decided to offer him a small version of the truth. "I'm looking for a fresh start somewhere new."

Confusion flashed across his face, and I could only imagine how many questions must be going through his mind. A ringtone filled the kitchen, interrupting Anthony before he could speak. He pulled out his phone, and answered without looking at the caller ID.

"Marino." His face tensed. "Sir, can Kruegler handle this by himself? I'm in the middle of something." A pause, presumably as he waited for the response on the other end. "Of course, sir." Hanging up, he shoved his phone back in his pocket, frustration lacing his features.

"Anthony, is there anything I can do?" It had only been a few hours, and I already felt a pull toward this family.

"I hate to ask, but that was my boss. I'm being called in for a case." He must have noticed the confusion on my face, so he continued. "I'm a detective, Special Victims Unit. We got a call for an interview. I'm not sure how long it will take, but would you be able to stay with Oliver? If Katie's daughter is sick, I'd hate to ask her, and I don't have any family nearby. I wouldn't ask if I had other options. I—"

"Anthony, I can stay." Interrupting his rambling, I looked down at Oliver. "As long as it's cool with you, buddy."

Oliver nodded his head, reaching with his whole body on the island to get the cut up orange in front of him. Anthony chuckled, grabbing the knife before pushing them closer to him. "Only if you're sure. Let me write down my number in case there is an emergency." I nodded my head, reassuring him of my decision, as he scribbled down his number.

Once finished, he walked around the counter, planting a kiss on his son's head before giving him a hug. "Be good, *figlio mio*. I love you."

Oliver had a mouthful of orange, and the juice dripped down his chin as he tried to respond to his dad. Quickly, I reached for a paper towel from the roll sitting in the middle of the island to wipe it.

Anthony was out of the kitchen before I could finish the task. I exhaled, making a mental note to text Ivy once I got Oliver settled with dinner.

"Well, kiddo, looks like it's just you and me again. Let's see what kind of trouble we can get into." I smiled at him and he gave me a cute, toothy grin of his own.

# Chapter Six

## Anthony

I put my truck in park in the hospital lot and lessened my grip on the steering wheel as I looked around for Jason. It wasn't often we drove separate when we went to do interviews, but we also didn't usually get called in on a night off. It was happening more often though, and I felt I had my partner's temper to blame.

My mind wandered as I waited, and the first thing I thought about the feeling of Gwendalyn's arm under my hand. The electricity I felt when our skin made contact had my body responding in ways it hadn't in years, long before my ex-wife.

When I had opened the front door to the house and heard my son's laughter, I swore I was hallucinating. I could count on one hand the number of times I have heard that laugh. There was a serious lack of joy in my son's life, and I hated that.

Oliver was an easy-going boy, friendly to a fault with everyone he had ever met, as if his little brain never truly understood the trauma he had gone through at an early age. But what I walked into this afternoon was different. Oliver clung to her, trusting her completely.

If I was being honest with myself, I felt the same way, and I barely spent any time with her.

She stood behind Oliver protectively at the kitchen island, and talked to him at his level. None of the other applicants had done that.

They had a connection.

But there was something else, too. I had no doubt she was leaving to get a fresh start, but there was more to her story than she was telling me. The hesitation when she answered my question and the way she tensed up as she talked told me everything I needed to know.

There was a chance my sudden departure was not going to work in my favor tonight. Though, Gwendalyn seemed more than comfortable staying. I needed someone who understood that working for me wasn't going to be easy. Calls like tonight were only the tip of the iceberg if our string of bad luck with calls kept up.

Jason's car driving through the lot toward me pulled me from my thoughts. I turned off my truck as he parked next to me then jumped out and slipped on my suit jacket that was in my car from earlier today. Instinctively, my hand ran over my badge and gun where they were attached to my belt. Jason unfolded himself from his car and I chuckled as I waited for him.

"Shut up, asshole." Jason shot me a look.

He hated having to drive his car, typically opting to ride his beloved 1959 Harley Davidson Sportster motorcycle whenever possible. He had helped his uncle restore it long before Jason even had his license.

I knew how to ride, but hadn't in years. It was something my ex hated, and I gave up for her and Oliver.

"Where's your Harley?" I asked.

"She was already locked up for the day. There have been too many lowlifes wandering around my apartment complex lately, and I couldn't risk someone getting to her while I was at the warehouse." He shrugged as he walked around his car with a large cup of coffee in one hand while his other pulled a notepad from his back pocket, already turned to a page covered in his chicken scratch. I never understood how that man could read his own handwriting.

"You know what we're walking into?" I pulled my own notepad from my back pocket. The worn pages threatened to fall apart with every use. Flipping through countless pages of assault interviews, I found a blank sheet and pulled out a pen from my inside jacket pocket.

"Female, twenty-nine. She was admitted a few hours ago." He deciphered his notes as I took down my own, making them legible for when we would ultimately need them later. "They've already done a rape kit, and she's agreed to talk to us. Not sure why *we* got called in instead of the on-shift detectives, though." He flipped his notebook closed with a flick of his wrist before shoving it into his pocket as he led the way through the doors into the hospital lobby.

"Probably because you've pissed off the captain one too many times," I said under my breath, but Jason shot a smirk over his shoulder toward me. My partner really needed to learn how to keep his smartass remarks to himself during roll call.

Jason strolled through the front doors of the hospital and up to the lobby desk. I followed after him, keeping my notepad and pen clutched in my hand. Typically, I took notes during interviews while Jason gave the survivors his full attention.

When we reached the nurse sitting behind the desk, Jason flashed her a smile. The same one that tended to get him anything he wanted. He set the coffee cup on the desk before sliding it toward her. "Hello, my sweet Samantha. How are you doing this fine evening?"

Grabbing the coffee, she took a long sip before setting it down. "Detective Kreugler, a pleasure under normal circumstances. I'm relieved they actually sent you two. I had asked the dispatcher to assign y'all, but they mentioned you were off duty."

The playfulness in her expression melted away as she typed away at her computer. Jason looked back at me over his shoulder, and I nodded my understanding.

We had gained a reputation around the station as the gentlest of the detectives in our unit. The irony of that superlative wasn't lost on me.

"Anyone sitting with her?" Jason turned his attention back to Samantha.

"One of my nurses," she responded as she wrote the room number on a post-it note. "Her name is Sophie Brown. She lives alone and doesn't have family nearby. She's still pretty shaken."

"Thanks, Samantha. Have a good night." Jason nodded to her, then glanced down at the number and headed toward the room. Before following after my partner, I offered a nod of my own. She flashed a sad smile from behind the coffee cup she had brought back to her mouth.

Jogging after Jason, I caught up to him as he stopped in front of a door. Double checking the room number, he shoved the post-it into his pocket as he turned to me.

"Ready?" he asked, gesturing to the room with his head.

"Yeah," I grunted.

He knocked and waited for the soft, *"Come in,"* from the other side before he opened the door. As we walked in, I took in the room. Miss Brown was sitting in a recliner chair in the far corner with a blanket wrapped around her shoulders and one tucked across her lap.

A nurse was sitting beside her on a stool, holding her hand and whispering to her. Miss Brown kept her focus on her lap, not making eye contact as we silently made our way across the space. The nurse stood up and offered her stool to Jason. He took it from her with a whispered "Thanks," and sat down, a soft squeak filling the otherwise quiet room.

"Miss Brown, I'm Detective Jason Kreugler," he began in a soft voice. "You can call me Jason, though. This is my partner, Detective Anthony Marino. Are you comfortable telling us about what happened to you?"

Miss Brown nervously nodded her head, a tear escaping down her cheek. "Ye-yes. Um, you can call me Sophie."

I reached for the box of tissues next to the bed and handed it to the nurse to offer it to Sophie, then stepped back to where I was standing. Jason and I had been at this long enough to know that most survivors at this point were still pretty apprehensive around men. We typically tried to reduce contact and keep as much distance as possible.

"Alright, Sophie. Take your time; as much as you need. Whenever you're ready, start from wherever you feel most comfortable," Jason spoke, his hands clenched together in front of him, ready to listen to whatever she was able to give us.

The door closed behind Jason with a soft click as he joined me in the hallway. We left Sophie with the nurse to talk about next steps, including helping her find resources for navigating the inevitable emotions she would have to navigate. I had put our cards on the table near the bed, letting her know if she thought of anything else to not hesitate to reach out.

Looking down at my watch, I groaned at the time and checked my phone for any messages or missed calls. It was close to 8 p.m., which meant Oliver needed to be in bed soon. I didn't expect Gwendalyn to know that, or even attempt a bedtime routine. But Jason and I still needed to write up our report, as well as debrief with the captain.

All I wanted was to get back to my house, so Gwendalyn and I could have a conversation.

Making my way out to the parking lot, I was so focused on getting to my truck that I didn't realize Jason was hot on my heels.

"Hey, Tony, wait up a second!" Only Jason called me that. He knew I hated it, and using the unwelcome nickname was his way of getting my attention. I stopped in my tracks, just outside the hospital doors, as Jason walked up behind me. "How'd the nanny interrogation go? Is she hot?"

I spun around, my fist connecting with Jason's jaw. Disbelief flashed across his features, mirroring my own surprise, as he cupped his chin. Shaking out my hand, I grimaced. "Shit, I'm—"

"What the fuck, man?" he cut me off. I had no clue what had come over me, but my body was shaking with fury.

"I'm sorry. I just..." Nothing made sense right now. Fifteen minutes in the same room as Gwendalyn, and already my brain was claiming her in some possessive way. We hadn't even been alone. My partner's brows raised in silent question as he rubbed his jaw and waited for some kind of explanation.

"Oliver was laughing, Jason." Heat rose in my chest, trying to make sense of what was happening as my voice grew louder. "I can count on one hand the number of times I've heard that little boy laugh!" I yelled, somehow mere inches away from my partner's chest.

Jason grabbed my upper arms, dragging me away from the doors. I jerked out of his grasp, annoyed–at myself, not him–but he didn't need to know that. His hands shot in the air in a defensive stance. "Shit. Okay, I get it."

I scrubbed a hand down my face and forced air into my lungs, willing the darkness that blurred the edges of my vision back down.

I needed to regain control.

"Anthony, go home and straighten all of this out. I'll handle the paperwork and captain tonight." Jason clasped a hand on my shoulder as he finished.

"Thanks," I muttered. Grateful for my partner, I walked to my truck.

The drive back to my house flew by in silence. I parked in the garage and took a minute to fully get my shit together.

As I opened up the door from the garage to the house, I fully expected to hear the sounds of playing. Instead, quiet filled the house.

Gwendalyn sat at the kitchen island with a book, and the baby monitor in front of her. Her body was relaxed, a stark contrast to how she appeared earlier. I cleared my throat to make my presence known in hopes she wouldn't be startled. Gwendalyn snapped her head toward me, jumping in her seat.

"Hi," she exclaimed, a little louder than she probably intended. I was distracted by her hand on her chest, the loose flowy shirt she was wearing doing very little to hide her curves. She grabbed a bookmark from the counter and stuck it in her book. "So sorry. I guess I didn't hear the garage door. Let me put these last few things away for you."

I shrugged off my jacket and laid it on the back of one of the island chairs while I continued watching her, letting my mind wonder.

She slid from the stool, shoving the book into a bag that I hadn't noticed earlier. My eyes drifted further down her body. The pants she had on clung to her legs like a second skin, the round globes of her ass begging to be cupped and kneaded by my hands. She looked at home in my kitchen, her movements natural as she moved around the kitchen and put away the few things still out on the counters.

Her hair was down, and fell in soft waves down her shoulders. I wanted to run my fingers through the strands, imagining the softness. She stepped in front of me, and her closeness stirred some primal instinct from deep within as she offered me the monitor from the island.

The smell of citrus invaded my nose. The urge to pull her against me, and bury my face into her was overwhelming. I forced my eyes off her body and shook the thoughts from my head, mentally scolding myself.

I accepted the monitor, seeing Oliver curled up in his crib fast asleep with his favorite stuffed animal.

*She put him to bed?*

"Anthony, is everything okay?" Gwendalyn asked quietly, pulling my attention away from the monitor.

"Oliver is asleep?" The intended statement came out as a question as I blinked down at her.

"Oh, yeah. He started getting sleepy, so I asked if he wanted to put on comfy clothes and snuggle on the couch with books. He fell asleep pretty quickly after that and I carried him up to bed as she talked." My eyes slipped back to the monitor as she talked, unable to fathom that she had gotten my master negotiator toddler to bed without a fight. "I'm sorry, Mr. Marino. If I did something—"

"You're hired," I cut her off, making my decision final.

"I'm sorry?" She froze, confusion covering her face, and it hit me that I sounded like a crazy person.

"The job, being Oliver's nanny. If you want the job, you're hired." *That was not coherent, either.*

"I'm… We've… Are you sure?" She was surprised, her wide blue eyes staring up at me as she picked at the skin around her nails.

"I was prepared to offer you the job when I walked into the house this afternoon and heard Oliver laughing. He's a sweet boy…" My voice trailed off, as the sound of his giggling danced once more through my mind.

Her face softened, and I tore my gaze away and spun around. Marching to the fridge, I pulled out a beer from the top shelf. I needed something to do with my hands before I did something I would regret.

Silence filled the kitchen once more. I glanced over my shoulder, fully expecting Gwendalyn to be nowhere in sight. But there she was.

Her eyes met mine, and she gave me a soft smile. Her cheeks turned a little red, warmth rising in her that was mirrored in the brightness coming from her eyes.

So gentle, so kind.

"Do you want the job?" I turned fully and took a swig of beer, waiting for her answer.

She hesitated, but only for a moment.

"Yes. When can I start?" Her eyes brightened even more somehow as she answered, the swirls of blue shifting like the waves of an ocean. There was a tightness in my chest that made it hard to breath as I stared into them.

I was drowning, and I couldn't care less. Just as long as I got to look into these eyes every day.

"Mr. Marino?" Her soft voice pierced through the thread that was weaving a dangerous web between us. It sounded as if she was scared, and I realized I had stepped toward her.

Not just a single step. No, I was close enough to her now that I could feel her breath as she exhaled. It danced across my skin, and sent a shiver down my spine.

Swallowing stiffly, my eyes scanned her body. Her muscles tensed as I did, her shoulders lifting toward her ears. My hands twitched to touch her.

"Anthony?" It was breathy, a single word portraying more emotion than an entire conversation ever could.

I had to resist the urge to pull her into my arms, because my name coming from her beautiful lips had my body responding in a purely primal way.

Putting much needed space between us, I stepped back, and quickly rounded the counter once more. Her shoulders relaxed as I picked up my beer bottle, and her gaze left mine.

I hated that. I wanted her to look at me.

Fuck, this was going to be an issue, this lure between us. It was something that I needed to keep in check if I wanted her to be here for Oliver.

I still needed to answer her question. "Monday. I'm off and can help you move your stuff in."

With her bag on her shoulder, she froze. That was not the reaction I was expecting.

"Why—Why would I need to move my stuff in?" Her voice was barely above a whisper. Avoiding my gaze still, she picked at the skin of her nails.

"I assumed Carol shared all the details with you," I started, wishing she would look at me. "I believed she called the position a 'live-in.' I work weird hours and need someone to basically be on call, just like tonight. You'd have your own space in the basement with it's own entrance."

"I know I just accepted, but could I have some time to think about this? The live-in aspect changes things for me a little..." She winced, a bead of blood gathering on the nail she had just been picking at.

She made a fist to hide the injury, then tightened the grip on her bag before lifting her gaze to mine. The lightness in her eyes had shifted, the sadness washing over them darkening her irises.

"Of course," I answered. "I'll get your email from Carol and send you the contract. Take tomorrow and think about it. If you have any questions, just let me know." Hesitantly, she nodded her head.

"Thank you. I will definitely keep in touch. If there isn't anything else?"

"Let me get you some cash for tonight." I grabbed my wallet from my back pocket as I stepped around the island, and pulled out several twenty dollar bills.

"You don't have to do that!"

"Yes, I do. You saved my ass." I stopped with plenty of space between us, not wanting to push boundaries yet again. Her eyes bounced between mine and the cash from my extended hand.

"Please," I insisted, pushing my hand forward an inch.

"Thank you," she whispered.

Our fingers brushed, only for a second, but the small goosebumps that formed up her arm told me she felt the same thing I had in the kitchen.

"Let me walk you out," I offered, needing a reason to stay in her presence just a little while longer.

"Thank you, again, for all your help tonight," I say as we reach the front door. Opening it, I looked to Gwendalyn and she met my gaze. "I hope to hear from you soon."

"Of course." She forced a smile, and I hated that I caused her this discomfort.

I tracked her all the way to her care, the tension in her body never leaving. I continued watching as she climbed in, and then slowly pulled away.

There was no doubt in my mind now. Gwendalyn was running. Whether it was from something or someone, I was going to find out.

She was going to accept this job. I would make sure of it.

# Chapter Seven

## Gwen

Sitting in the quiet car outside of the Airbnb, the events of the last few hours weighed heavy on my mind.

This job was exactly what I wanted. Oliver was the sweetest boy, genuinely happy and so clever. It would be a dream to take care of him. But his father?

My heart still raced from my interactions with Anthony. I could feel his gaze on me even now, his eyes darkening as he stalked toward me. Something about that man pulled me in and I wanted to let it.

I took a deep breath, closing my eyes and letting my head fall back onto the headrest. *Could I do this?*

There was no way I could rely on my own thoughts and feelings to make this decision. I needed Ivy's opinion.

Walking into the house, I found Carol and Ivy sat on the floor of the living room. They each had a wine glass in their hands, and an open bottle sat nearly empty on the coffee table. Laughter filled the small living room as the pair pressed their shoulders together.

Seemingly sensing my presence, Ivy looked over her shoulder and smiled as I made my way to the kitchen to grab a glass. I dropped my bag and Carol's car key on the counter before joining them on the floor. Plopping down next to Ivy, I emptied the bottle into my glass then took a long drink.

"I'm not sure if that means things went well or bad," Carol whispered to Ivy over her wine, avoiding my gaze. Ivy chuckled at her words, and the tension in my shoulders that built up during my drive slowly melted away.

"He offered me the job," I whispered, looking down at my glass of wine as if it was the most interesting thing in the room.

Out of the corner of my eye, I caught the excitement that spread across both of their faces. Ivy set down her empty glass before clapping her hands excitedly like a child on their birthday. *This probably wasn't the first bottle of wine they had tonight.*

"Gwen, that's amazing! You really won him over, didn't you?" Looking up at my best friend, her happiness was contagious. I couldn't help feeling a bit excited for the opportunity and found myself smiling, too.

"There's just one thing..." I paused, taking a breath to gather myself. "It's a live-in position, Ivy. And after everything that happened with Matt, I don't know if I can do it." I could feel the tears building, and attempted to push them down with another drink of wine.

"Shit," Carol muttered from the other side of Ivy. "Forgot about that part..."

I didn't blame Carol. Even if she had remembered the whole live-in part of the job, Ivy probably would have still pushed me to do the interview.

"Sweet pea." Ivy rested her hand on my knee, giving it a gentle squeeze. "What do you want to do?"

"I'm not sure. On one hand, everything just felt so right. Oliver is the sweetest kid and we had a connection and Anthony... It just felt right." I stopped myself before I could spill my guts completely about the attraction to Anthony.

"On the other hand, the thought of living in his house has my stomach in knots. I don't want to be put in another situation like I was with Matt, dependent on him to support me." After emptying my glass of the remaining wine, I set it down on the table before letting out a small scream of frustration. A few stray tears had slipped past the walls and I quickly wiped them away.

"I'm so tired of crying! I want to punch something, or someone," I yelled, clenching my hands into fists.

Ivy reached onto the couch, pulled a large pillow into her arms and offered it to me. I grabbed it, settled it on my lap, then pictured Matt's stupid face as I jabbed my fist into the middle. It did little to alleviate my building frustration, so instead, I leaned down into the fabric and let out the loudest scream possible.

The fabric seemed to absorb most of the sound, though all I could truly hear was the pounding of my heart. Sitting up, I discarded the pillow behind me with a toss and hoped I wouldn't hit anything fragile.

"What if I talk to Anthony?" Ivy and I both turned to Carol, who was sipping her wine without much expression, even though she just witnessed me fully in the middle of an emotional spiral. "I could explain to him the situation–with minimal details–and let him know you aren't currently comfortable with the idea of living in his house. I could help you find a nearby apartment. You may have to negotiate some kind of on-call schedule, but it's not completely unheard of."

"I don't think I could afford an apartment on my own. My savings would barely cover a deposit, let alone first month's rent. Matt's engagement ring was as fake as he was, so that didn't help," I mumbled.

"Well, what about Ivy?" Carol looked toward her as I turned my head. I could feel myself gaining some hope. Ivy had said she would go wherever I was, and even though I always protested, at that moment I knew I needed my best friend.

"There's something I need to tell you," she sheepishly replied and hung her head, refusing to meet either of our gazes. The little bit of hope I felt moments ago quickly disappeared. After a minute, Ivy looked up at me. "Remember the call from last night when we were at the bar? That was the manager of the biggest event center in Pittsburgh. They want to offer me a six-month contract for their wedding and holiday season. It's an amazing opportunity." I could see the guilt in her eyes as she said it.

My heart hurt for my friend. Ivy stayed in Pittsburgh to offer me support when I needed it the most. She would never admit to being unhappy, but I knew she wanted to do more with her life.

I knew I would always be able to count on her, but right now, I wanted to give her the opportunity to find the happiness she deserved.

Even if that meant we would be in different states.

"You should accept their offer," I blurted. Ivy blinked at me, nearly speechless from my statement.

"Gwen—" she tried to argue with me.

"No," I cut her off, giving her a look as I took her hand. "It's about time you did something for yourself instead of following your damsel in distress best friend everywhere. Maybe accepting this job, and moving on my own, will be good for me."

Ivy threw herself at me, enveloping me in a hug tight enough to break a rib or two. We nearly toppled over, and in the process of trying to stay upright, I heard a chime and watched Carol fish out her phone from her pocket.

"I'm so proud of you," she whispered quietly enough for only me to hear. I squeezed Ivy as hard as I could, silently thanking her for everything she did to get me to that point.

Ivy pulled away, grabbing my hands in hers with a smile beaming on her face. "Okay, I'll accept the job, but as soon as this contract is up, I'm coming to Chicago. Plus, I'm only a phone call away if something happens. I won't hesitate to jump in my car or book the next flight. I'll always have your back." She released my hands and pulled me in for another quick hug, before Carol cleared her throat next to us, effectively getting our attention.

"I have your back now, too, ya know?" She finished typing away on her phone before looking up and waving her phone toward me. "That was Anthony emailing me about wanting you and only you. He's willing to do whatever it takes for you to accept the position, including doubling the pay, if that's what it takes."

My jaw fell open. He wants *me*? And only *me*?

Carol raised her brows, shrugging as if this was an everyday occurrence.

Looking at Ivy, she nodded her head at me, her way of silently encouraging me to do what felt right. There was still a part of me that hesitated.

For so long, my own happiness relied on making other people happy. I didn't need to do that anymore. Matt was in jail, and he was no longer able to hold me back. Ivy would always support me no matter how far apart we lived.

It was time to do something simply because I wanted to, and tell my fears to fuck off.

"So what do you think? Do you want the job?" Carol interrupted my inner pep talk and I turned toward her.

"Yes." A smile tugged at the corner of my lips.

"Yay! This calls for a celebratory drink!" Ivy squealed, jumping up from her spot on the floor, and I heard her bare feet on the floor of the kitchen. Carol started typing away on her phone again as mine alerted me to a notification.

"That'll be your contract. Give it a once over some time tonight before you sign it and send it back to me. I'll let Anthony know you've accepted and are going to review the contract," she said without looking up from her phone, still typing away when Ivy came back with a bottle of champagne.

"I had a feeling my best friend would find herself a new job while we were here. I had to buy the good stuff, just in case," Ivy said. She shot me a wink while popping the cork off the bottle.

More tears threatened to make their escape. Unlike earlier, these tears were from pure happiness, and a gut feeling that everything was going to be okay.

The rest of the weekend went by too fast.

Carol stayed the night on Saturday after we finished the bottle of champagne, and an additional bottle of wine. In the morning, the three of us went to brunch at one of Carol's favorite spots. Afterward, she insisted on taking Ivy and me to all the best shops nearby. It turned into an impromptu, but much needed, shopping trip.

I had decided there was no point in trying to get my things from Matt's house. Ivy told me she'd hire movers to go get my stuff if I wanted, but it didn't feel worth it. Clothing was replaceable, and anything of value was in his name. I refused to waste my energy fighting him for any kind of ownership.

The best thing for me to do was move forward and not look back.

Early Monday morning, the three of us drove to the airport. After several dozen hugs and promises of *"I'll visit soon,"* Carol and I waved as Ivy went through TSA. Afterwards, the two of us went out for lunch before she drove me to Anthony's house.

We parked outside his house, and I did my best to shove down the building anxiety. My fingers mindlessly worked at my already shredded cuticles while Carol assured me that my contract and payroll were all squared away.

I looked down at my hands cupped in my lap, and saw blood quickly pooling at the base of my nail from the picking. She wordlessly passed me a bandage from her center console. I quickly wrapped my finger while taking a deep breath, then turned to look at Carol.

"Thank you. For everything," I leaned over to give her a hug.

"You've got this," she whispered, giving me a small squeeze.

The back of my throat burned with an overflow of emotions. When we pulled apart, a stray tear fell onto my cheek and I quickly wiped it away before Carol could see it.

"I'll call you at the end of the week to check in, but do not hesitate to reach out if you need absolutely anything before then," she said as I got out of the car.

I offered her a smile, not trusting my voice. If I talked, I might start crying for real.

I grabbed my suitcase from the trunk then stepped onto the sidewalk. Ivy leant me one of hers when we made the trip to Chicago, and insisted I keep it. The wheels rolled smoothly up the driveway as I made my way to the front porch.

Pausing by the steps, I turned and waved to Carol as she drove away. Her car disappeared around the corner, and I took a minute to gather myself. Butterflies fluttered in my stomach.

I was a strong, independent woman. I had this.

Reaching out to ring the doorbell, I paused when I heard a tiny voice coming from the other side, followed by what sounded like tiny feet shuffling. "Daddy, daddy! Miss Gen?"

"She will be here any minute, *figlio mio*. Patience." I could only imagine the two of them on the other side of the door, his dad crouching next to him and Oliver bouncing on his toes.

"Ow-sigh, Daddy. Peas!" Oliver's excited voice filled my heart with joy, and I knew I made the right choice by accepting the job.

"Alright, little man," Anthony sighed. "We will wait outside for Miss Gwendalyn."

The click of the front door opening was my only warning before Oliver bolted out. I stepped sideways too quickly in an attempt to avoid a head-on collision with him, and ended up tripping over the suitcase at my side.

My arms flailed, trying to find something to grab onto for balance, but it was a lost cause. I landed with a thud on my ass, a dull pain radiating through my lower back as a groan escaped my lips.

Anthony's shoes came into view, and I quickly tried to scramble to my feet. The attempt was unsuccessful. My suitcase was on my legs, and I struggled to get myself free.

Without saying a word, Anthony picked up my suitcase and sat it next to him. He offered me his hand, and I did my best to avoid his gaze while taking it. The warmth in my cheeks continued to grow in intensity as I stood.

"Are you okay?" He released my hand as he spoke. His low voice awakened something inside me, and I couldn't help but look up at him.

His eyes were intense as they looked into mine, filled with a heat that should have had me wanting to pull away. Instead, I felt safe, safer than I had in a long time. As I continued staring into his eyes, heat traveled down my body and settled in my stomach. All common sense left my brain as I thought about his hand on other parts of my body.

"Gwendalyn?" His voice was deeper this time, concern lacing every syllable of my name.

Mentally, I splashed myself in cold water. *Pull yourself together, Gwen. You need this job, not dick.*

"I'm okay." Trying to laugh off the embarrassing moment, I forced a smile as I brushed the dirt off my pants. I broke eye contact with Anthony, and turned around in time to see Oliver running back up onto the porch.

"Miss Gen! Trains!" He held out a black engine twice the size of his hand for me to see after climbing the small step that led up to the porch. Ignoring the feeling of Anthony's continued gaze on me, I crouched down in front of Oliver. The train engine looked brand new, as if it had just come out of its packaging.

"That is such a cool train, Oliver."

"Tunnel, peas?"

"Not right now, *figlio mio,*" Anthony cut in. He leaned down and offered open arms to Oliver, who ran the few steps so his dad could pick him up. I stood quickly, suddenly feeling like I was an intruder. "How about we show Miss Gwendalyn her room?"

"I show, Daddy." Oliver wiggled in his dad's arms in an attempt to get down. Chuckling, Anthony leaned forward and opened the door before setting him down.

Oliver took off into the house, and I caught a glimpse of a smile forming on Anthony's face as he watched his son. I reached out to grab my suitcase that he had set upright in between us, but his hand beat mine, grasping the handle.

Stepping forward, he leaned against the open door, stopping to look back and motioning with his head for me to go on. My eyes widened, blinking in shock as it hit me that he was essentially holding it open for me. Two chivalrous acts within the span of a few seconds, all without what seemed to be a second thought from the man doing them, was not something I was used to.

I made my way inside, following the sound of little feet down the hallway that went past the kitchen. Oliver was excitedly standing at a door that I could only assume led down to the basement.

Pulling it open himself, Oliver plopped down on the top step, and flipped over onto his belly to slide down the steps. I covered my mouth with my hand to help hide the laugh that escaped out of me.

Anthony walked up behind me. The warmth radiating from his body sent a shiver down my spine, and a breath caught in my chest. I looked over my shoulder, not expecting the smile that was plastered on his face.

"I have no idea where he learned to do that, but he's been doing it since before he started walking," he muttered. Shaking his head, he gestured for me to lead the way.

Carefully making my way down the stairs, I turned down a short hallway that opened into a room with a bed and dresser on opposite walls. Oliver was happily jumping on the bed.

"Oliver, please get down." Anthony walked past me, set my suitcase next to the dresser, then scooped Oliver back up into his arms. I watched the two of them for a moment, soaking in the love that Anthony had for his son.

Carol shared with me the few details Anthony gave her about the situation with Oliver's mother, how she left one day and hadn't asked for any kind of visitation or custody. It broke my heart thinking about a mother being able to just leave her child behind without a second thought.

Oliver's giggles filled the room as Anthony tossed him into the air. After a moment, he stopped and Oliver snuggled into his dad's shoulder. "I think Oliver is ready for a nap, so I will let you get settled. There is a full bathroom through that door," he paused and pointed toward a door I hadn't noticed until now. Then continued, "and if you need anything, do not hesitate to ask."

"Thank you." I smiled, feeling nervous, but somehow at home.

"No, thank you," Anthony whispered, tucking a now quiet Oliver onto his shoulder. I nodded my head. "Come up whenever, but no pressure. We'll see you in the morning otherwise."

He nodded his head and turned, padding quietly out of the room with a now dozing Oliver cradled in his arms. Once I heard the door at the top of the steps close, I sat down on the bed and looked around the room.

Soft afternoon light filtered through sliding glass door opposite the hallway. My new room overlooked the small backyard, a small wooden play set situated in the back corner. As I looked out, a cardinal lands on top of the beam. The universe was sending a happy little nod my way.

My new beginning started today.

# Chapter Eight

## Gwen

Day turned into night quicker than I thought. I had resigned myself to staying in my room until morning, not feeling particularly hungry while I focused on unpacking. Now, I found myself sitting on the bed and looking at the bare room around me. Hot tears burned the back of my eyes as I thought about all the little things I left behind in Pennsylvania.

Photos, momentos... All gone.

Taking a deep breath, I laid down and closed my eyes, wanting to think of anything else. That's when images of Anthony standing over top of me flashed in my mind. The way his hand felt on my skin and how I wanted to know how it felt on other places of my body.

I forced my eyes open, sitting up and groaning as I ran a hand down my face. This wonderful new opportunity was going to be ruined very quickly if my brain didn't stop thinking about Anthony as anything but my boss.

As I sat there continuing to berate myself, the smell of baked lasagna somehow found its way downstairs. I tried to ignore the way my stomach growled but when my mouth started watering, I gave in.

I wasn't sure what to expect when I got upstairs, but it definitely wasn't Oliver running circles around his dad while he tried to plate dinner. Anthony looked exhausted. There were dark circles under his eyes that I could have sworn were not there when I got here just a few hours ago. He looked like a sleep walking version of the man I met this afternoon.

My chest tightened watching the pair. Underneath the obvious exhaustion was a dad who was just trying his best. It was clear he loved Oliver very much. I just hoped I would be enough to help the two of them.

Oliver was babbling about trains as Anthony finished putting lasagna onto two plates. The anxious part of my brain yelled at me that I was intruding and should leave them to eat dinner together. Before I could turn tail and run back to my room, Oliver spotted me.

"Miss Gen!" He ran towards me with open arms. I crouched down and he threw his little arms around my neck. Standing carefully, Oliver wrapped his legs around my waist as I held him up.

"Hey, little man. What are you up to?" I asked. Oliver started going on about his trains. I only caught about half of what he was saying, but I smiled down at him anyway.

Anthony cleared his throat. I glanced past Oliver who now had both hands planted firmly on my cheeks as if he was telling me secrets of grave importance. Oliver continued on as I met Anthony's tired gaze.

He had a plate of food in each hand and I realized I was blocking his access to the table. I stepped out of his way, doing my best not to trip over my own two feet while holding Oliver. He was still babbling away about something, but I didn't understand any of it.

I was too focused on his dad.

Anthony changed his clothes since this afternoon. My eyes were fixed on the black shirt that stretched to accommodate his biceps, and the grey sweatpants that sat low on his hips had me thinking inappropriate things. I wanted to lick the veins that ran so prominently up his forearms while my hands explored the hair that I knew had to be covering his chest.

*Pull yourself together, Gwen.*

When I pulled my gaze away from his body, I found Anthony watching me with one raised brow from beside the table. There was a tiny glint in his eyes that disappeared when I blinked. His face was neutral, not even a hint of amusement, and I wondered if I had imagined it.

I offered a small smile in hopes it would cover up the fact that I was just ogling him. His continued blank expression sent a wave of unease through me causing my muscles to tense.

Anthony stepped toward me, and the breath caught in my lungs. I stood there frozen, staring at his chest. Then he stopped in front of me and I prepared myself to be berated.

Instead, Anthony cleared his throat which grabbed Oliver's attention. He turned to his dad and flung himself out of my hold into Anthony's waiting arms.

Too many feelings fought for control. My heart pounded in my chest as the world around me went out of focus, like I was viewing everything from too large of a distance. The voice in my head was telling me to run, to hide in my bedroom until morning.

I was frozen to the spot though as I watched Anthony get Oliver settled in a booster seat that was strapped to one of the chairs. Everything around me was happening in slow motion.

Panic seized my body, and I felt trapped.

"Gwendalyn?" Anthony's voice broke through the mental fog. The He was standing behind Oliver who had already begun picking at his dinner. Green beans fell off the side of his plate as he attempted to pick up a piece of lasagna with his fork.

"Sorry?" My gaze met Anthony's who was watching me with worry in his eyes. It was obvious I had been standing there unresponsive for longer than I imagined.

"Are you okay?" he asked, the concern apparent in his voice. He shifted where he stood as if he wanted to be closer to me but decided against it. Something inside me wanted to go to him, to find comfort in arms I knew could hurt me all too easily.

None of it made any sense.

"Yeah, I'm good." The tightness in my chest lessened as I took several deep breaths. "I'm okay." That one was more for myself than Anthony. I had been through a lot in the last week and if there is one thing Ivy has drilled into my head, it was to give myself grace.

"Alright," Anthony nodded. His eyes flicked down to my hands, and I realized I was picking at my cuticles. I glanced down at my fingers to make sure I wasn't bleeding then clasped them together behind my back. Anthony cleared his throat again, and I met his eyes. "Would you like to join us for dinner?"

I hesitated, but the hungry growl that came from deep inside answered for me. Oliver giggled from next to Anthony as he offered me a toothy grin.

"Sit." Anthony grabbed the plate that he had sat in front of the chair next to Oliver and placed it down across from him instead.

"Oh no," I tried to object, not wanting to take his plate of food. "I can get my own, but I don't want to interrupt. I can just…"

"Gwendalyn," he interrupted. The gravelly tone he used to say my name had me clamping my mouth shut. "Sit." He said it a little more forcefully the second time and pointed to the chair.

It wasn't a request, but something told me that Anthony wouldn't push it if I said no.

His shoulders were relaxed and even his raised arm wasn't tense. The veins that I had wanted to lick earlier weren't even showing. This wasn't the body language of a man who was going to put up a fight if I didn't do what he wanted. This was a man who could see my hesitation and didn't want me thinking I wasn't welcome.

I moved slowly and just as I broke eye contact with him, the corners of his lips ticked upward. My cheeks flushed feeling Anthony's heated gaze on me all the way around the table. Sliding into the chair as gracefully as possible, my mouth watered as I stared down at the plate in front of me. It looked amazing and I was starving.

"You should eat before it gets cold." I looked up to find Anthony standing at the kitchen island, pointing a spatula in my direction. A shadow of a smile flashed across his face, and he narrowed his eyes as if in a silent dare to challenge him. I grabbed my fork, and he turned his attention to making himself a new plate of food.

My gaze went to Oliver who had successfully gotten several bites of lasagna into his mouth, and was now intentionally pushing the vegetables off of his plate. I couldn't help the smile that pulled at my lips or the tears that burned in the corners of my eyes.

For the first time in a while, I genuinely felt happy without any *what if* scenarios threatening to take it away.

"Miss Gen sad?" Oliver asked. He now had the entirety of his vegetables hiding under the rim of his plate.

"No, buddy. Just happy." I blinked away the tears and continued to smile at him. Oliver looked to his dad, who had just sat down at the table next to him. Anthony pushed a glass of water toward me and I thanked him quietly.

"Sometimes, people cry when they're really happy, *figlio mio*. Tears can happen with any big feelings." Anthony took a bite of his food while Oliver thought it over. He seemed to accept the answer because seconds later, he was knuckles deep in pasta sauce again.

I watched the two Marino men between bites of my own dinner. Oliver babbled about whatever came to his mind while Anthony practically inhaled his food. The reason was clear when Oliver suddenly declared he was suddenly all done.

Anthony was anticipating his son's inability to sit still, and wanted to finish his own food before things got chaotic.

Oliver not so gracefully tried to climb out of his seat. His tiny hand landed on the edge of his plate, nearly catapulting what was left of his food all over his dad.

A deafening squish seemed to echo through the small space as Anthony reached out to keep the plate from leaving the table. He lifted his hand and flattened green beans fell from his skin, landing in a pile on the table. I had to stifle a laugh behind my hand as Anthony let out a sigh.

Oliver seemed oblivious to the entire thing, and had one leg swung over his booster seat. Anthony quickly grabbed him, muttering under his breath about forgetting to buckle him in. I felt a ping of guilt and wanted to apologize for distracting him. I quickly stood up to offer help in some form. But when Anthony turned to me, the words got stuck in the back of my throat.

I had expected his face to be screwed up in anger or frustration. Instead, he was smiling down at me as he put Oliver on his hip. I quickly looked away and started to grab our plates, wanting to distract myself in some way.

"Don't worry about the mess," he said, then turned to Oliver. "I'll get everything sorted once I get *little man* in bed." Oliver giggled as his dad tickled his stomach. He wiggled for a moment then threw his arms around his dad's neck. Anthony started to leave the kitchen when Oliver turned in his hold.

"Night, Miss Gen," Oliver yelled to me.

"Night, buddy," I said while trying to hide my laugh. "I'll see you in the morning."

Anthony's gaze met mine over his son's head. His face was relaxed but there was something hidden behind his eyes—a flicker of something raw and unguarded. Lips parted as if he wanted to say something but was holding himself back.

"Good night, Gwendalyn," he whispered.

I was having a Pavlovian response to the way he said my name and I had to remind my body that Anthony was my boss. It didn't matter though; I couldn't look away. The breath in my lungs was stuck and the longer we stood there, the weaker my knees felt. We were caught in a game of chicken waiting for the other to be the first to look away.

Heat crept up my neck and my cheeks warmed. I was seconds away from saying or doing something I would regret when Oliver interrupted the moment. He pulled his dad's attention away with a sneeze to the face. Anthony broke eye contact and used his free hand to wipe away the snot that had landed on his cheek all while Oliver laughed.

"Good night, Anthony," I forced out. He offered me a quick nod then turned to Oliver.

I sat down before my legs could give out on me as I watched the two of them head upstairs, dirty plates still in hand. It wasn't until I heard a door shut that I was finally able to take a deep breath again.

*He is your boss.*

I was just touch starved and desperate for attention that didn't lead to arguing or being grabbed. All of this was in my imagination. At least that was what I kept telling myself as I cleaned up the table.

I repeated it over and over again while I put things in the dishwasher and put away the leftover lasagna. By the time I was done and heading downstairs again, I started to believe it.

Because I couldn't lose this job. I deserved a fresh start and I couldn't have that if I kept thinking with my vagina.

*God, that sounded like something Ivy would say.*

I missed my best friend already. It wasn't the same not having her in the same city. Wanting to call her, I picked up my phone that I had left on my nightstand, but my blood ran cold when I saw the dozen missed calls from unknown numbers and several voicemails. It only took listening to a few seconds of the first message to have my stomach in knots.

I turned off my phone and set it down as if it was a bomb ready to explode.

I wanted to scream.

Matt was supposed to be in jail. Even so, I changed my number so he wouldn't have a way to get a hold of me. Yet, the proof was right there on my phone that he had found it anyway.

I crawled into bed, all the fight leaving me when my head hit the pillow. Silent tears slid down my cheeks as I curled into myself.

None of this was supposed to happen.

"Miss Gen?" A tiny voice near my ear interrupted my not so dreamless sleep. I hadn't even remembered falling asleep last night, but knew I must have been dreaming the moment Anthony stood in front of me in nothing but those grey sweatpants.

My boss frequented the starring role in my dreams the last few weeks more than he should have. Especially after I spent all that time trying to convince myself to stop thinking about him in that way. It was obvious that all the self-talk made very little impact on my subconscious.

For the most part, I was able to establish clear professional boundaries, if only in my own mind. It was made easy by the fact that Anthony was so trusting when it came to me taking over Ollie's routine.

The first few days were exhausting trying to figure out what worked and what didn't all on my own. In general though, Ollie was an easy going kid and we found our rhythm. But alongside finding a routine that worked for us, I had to navigate Anthony and his work schedule.

It was a lot of mental juggling.

"Miss Gen?" Something wet pushed into my cheek and pulled me from my thoughts. My eyes flew open.

A small figure sat on the bed next to me. I rolled over to flick on the bedside light and check the time, not surprised at all when my phone told me it was barely three in the morning.

I turned back to my mystery visitor, and saw Ollie next to me clutching a teddy bear. The smell of sour dairy hit my nose as I spotted the vomit that covered the stuffie and part of his shirt. I pushed aside the question of how he got out of his crib and scooped him up, taking him into my ensuite bathroom.

"Oh buddy, did you get sick?" I whispered, doing my best to keep my cool. Oliver nodded his head and curled into me. He pressed his head into my neck and I shivered from the sudden heat on my skin. There was no doubt he had a fever.

It was going to be a long day.

# Chapter Nine

## *Anthony*

Jason's ringtone echoed from my bedroom into the bathroom. I groaned to myself, my head lulling to the side as it rested on top of the toilet seat.

I had bolted out of bed and ran to the bathroom just a few minutes ago, last night's dinner making a reappearance. I had yet to find the energy to get up. But if Jason was calling, it meant there was a case.

Pushing myself up to my knees, I used my bathroom vanity as support to stand. My phone stopped ringing from my nightstand, and I took the moment of silence to pull myself together. I grabbed the hand towel from its holder to wipe away the sweat that gathered on the back of my neck from purging the contents of my stomach.

Whatever caused all this in the first place was not going down without a fight. My throat burned as vomit crawled up. I squeezed my eyes shut as I gripped the edge of the marble counter. Air filled my lungs as I forced deep breaths through my nose.

I refused to throw up again.

The feeling passed moments later and I was determined to make it out of this bathroom without further incident. Dinner just upset my stomach, nothing more. I ignored the shaking in my hands as I turned off the bathroom light, and made my way to my phone. Just as I picked it up, a text notification came through from Jason.

> Interview at Grace General. On my way there now.

> Meet you there in 20

Pulling work clothes out of the closet, I sat on the edge of my bed to put them on. A chill ran down my spine, and I cursed myself for not turning off the fan before sitting down. The central air in the house was always hit or miss, especially in my room. It was nearly impossible to fall asleep unless I had my tower fan on, but it definitely worked a little too well during brisk mornings.

My hands still shook as I slid my socks on my feet and when I stood up, my muscles ached in protest. I chalked it up to the fact that work has been physically brutal recently. Jason had to have pissed off someone important because we were being thrown shit cases that required too many foot chases. Why do the assholes always run when they've been caught with their pants around their ankle?

I headed downstairs as quietly as possible, not wanting to wake up Oliver, but when I rounded the corner of the staircase, I was surprised to see him on the couch curled up under a blanket with his eyes shut. One of his shows was playing on the TV, as if he had fallen asleep while watching it.

I discussed with Gwendalyn the desire for Oliver to cut back on the screen time as much as possible during her first week here, and she had agreed. This was the first time I had seen him in front of the TV since she started, but I also wasn't normally up this early.

Our cases had been keeping me at the station late into the night so most mornings, I slept in. By the time I headed out for the day, Oliver and Gwendalyn were gone from the house.

Was she just letting him watch TV when she thought I wouldn't know?

Grabbing the remote off the end table, I turned off Oliver's show. My already aching muscles tightened even more as frustration crawled across my skin. The voice in the back of my mind told me to talk to her and get an explanation before getting upset.

*No, it was obvious I trusted her too quickly.*

Noise from the kitchen told me Gwendalyn was most likely in there. My feet led me to her of their own accord, fueled by the flashes of memory from when I found Oliver crying in the corner when my ex-wife was supposed to be watching him.

I rounded the corner to the kitchen with a few choice words on the tip of my tongue, but froze in the doorway and clamped my mouth shut as I took in the scene in front of me.

Laundry was piled on the kitchen island and looked to contain Oliver's sheets and several pairs of pajamas. Gwendalyn was leaning back against the kitchen counter, her typical leggings and flowy t-shirt outfit replaced by a grungy pair of sweats and bleach stained oversized shirt. Her hair was up in a bun on top of her head and there was something on her shoulder.

She was unaware of my presence, the phone in her hands having her complete attention. Tears ran down her cheeks and snot gathered just below her nose as if she had been crying for a while. *Oscurità mia* screamed to fix whatever was causing her to be this upset.

I stepped into the kitchen, wanting to ask what was wrong, when the smell of vomit made my stomach turn. It stopped me mid step and I forced a deep breath through my nose to keep myself from hurling.

The feeling passed and I cleared my throat, inadvertently scaring Gwendalyn. She jumped and her phone slipped out of her hands. The clattering echoed through the otherwise quiet room as it hit the floor.

"Cheese and crackers, Anthony," she whispered as she squatted down. She quickly wiped her eyes before grabbing her phone. "I wasn't expecting you to be awake this early." Her voice wavered slightly as she spoke.

"That's obvious." The words came out harsher than I planned, the earlier frustration making its way back to the surface. Her shoulders tensed as she stood and avoided my gaze as she looked around at the disarray surrounding us.

Immediately, I felt like a jackass.

Her cheeks were splotchy and I noticed a bit of snot under her nose that she missed. I wanted to wipe it away, but I didn't know how to do it without disregarding the very obvious boundaries we needed to keep in place.

"I'm so sorry things are a mess," Gwendalyn interrupted my thoughts. She walked up to the kitchen island, and began sorting through the laundry. "Oliver threw up at some point in the middle of the night and somehow climbed out of his crib to come get me so I got him cleaned up then let him watch a show so I could start a load of laundry with his stuff and mine and I thought he was okay but then he threw up again a little bit ago so I have more laundry going now and I just needed a minute. I'm sorry. Let me get things cleaned up. You probably want to get ready for work."

Her hands shook as she picked up one of Oliver's crib sheets to fold. My stomach dropped. Whatever she had been looking at on her phone when I walked in obviously had her rattled. I didn't know her backstory, our conversations lacking since our paths barely crossed. But all the signs were there that told me whatever she ran away from had chipped away at her confidence.

And I wasn't helping.

*Yulp, absolute jackass.*

Gwendalyn had my complete confidence for a reason and I should be the one apologizing for ever doubting her, even if it had all been only in my head.

She was nothing like my ex-wife, and it was obvious how much Oliver adored her, something his deadbeat of a mother could never say. Anger pulsed through me at even the thought of my ex-wife. My hands clenched into fists as I shoved down the darkness that threatened to ruin my day.

This wasn't the time or place.

"Anthony, are you okay?" Gwendalyn's soft voice broke through the haze that had settled over my mind.

My jaw hurt from how tightly it was clenched. There was a layer of sweat formed along the back of my neck and every muscle in my body ached.

"Anthony?" Gwendalyn was in front of me now. I couldn't trust my voice. My heart raced, pounding against my tightening chest.

The longer we stood there, the more it seemed she consumed me. The way she looked up at me with her brows raised, as if in concern, had me forgetting about our professional relationship.

Her scent wrapped around me, calming the rage that had built in my chest. The tension in my body loosened. I wanted to know how she felt in my arms, to have my nose pressed against the column of her neck.

She lifted her hand and rested the back of her palm on my forehead. A chill ran down my spine at the contact. Her chest brushed against mine. My hand twitched to wrap it around her waist. That closeness felt too nice and I took a step back before I could do something stupid.

"You are burning up," she whispered, hurt flashing across her face. I blinked and the softness returned to her eyes. "I bet you're sick with whatever Oliver has. You should rest."

I shook my head and wiped my clammy palms on my pants as I spoke. "I don't do sick."

"Being sick isn't exactly something you get to choose. It's going to happen whether or not you want it to."

"I have a case." I was frozen to the spot, unable to move as I tried to force all the inappropriate thoughts from moments ago out of my head.

She sighed and I watched as she went to the corner cabinet where I kept basic medicines for when I didn't want to walk about to my bathroom. She pulled out the bottle of Tylenol, palmed a few, then filled a glass with water. When she returned to the spot in front of me, she offered me both the medicine and the glass. I took them with a grunted thank you and downed both in a matter of seconds.

"You're a grown man which means I can't force you to, but I think you should call into work." Gwendalyn left it at that and returned to her previous task. Obviously, she was right. I was certain if I told her about the need to vomit that woke me up in the first place, she would find a way to force me back into bed.

Pulling out my phone, I sent Jason a quick text then pulled up my email to let my boss know I wouldn't be in today. Over the tiny screen, I caught the corner of Gwendalyn's lips turning up. A silent *told you so.*

Jason quickly replied with a thumbs up, and I rolled my eyes as I pocketed my phone. He knew I hated when he used those stupid emojis, but he did it anyway. That dude loved getting under my skin whenever possible, just for the fun of it.

Letting out a deep breath, my aching muscles begged me to go lay down. I knew I should head up to bed, but I caught myself watching Gwendalyn finish the laundry. The shakiness in her hands was gone, and she seemed to be standing a little taller. She moved around the space like she belonged here.

Because she did.

"Miss Gen!" Oliver's tired voice carried through the house.

"Coming, buddy!" Gwendalyn called out. She quickly worked to finish folding the piece of laundry in her hands, then added it to the pile. I couldn't believe how quickly she got through everything. Or maybe I stood there longer than I thought.

I needed to do something other than stare at my nanny.

"I'll get him," I said. Gwendalyn turned to me, her brows pinched together.

"No, you should go get some rest."

"I'm sick, not dying." My attempt at a chuckle turned into a cough. I turned my face into my elbow, and waved her off as she took a step toward me. "I can take care of my own son. No reason for all of us to be sick."

My words came out harsher than I meant. She froze in place, her eyes down at her feet. That far too familiar feeling of guilt had me rushing to apologize.

"Gwendalyn, I'm sorry," I said softly, and she lifted her gaze to meet mine. "We're good. Take the day off."

"Alright, but only if you're sure." Her hand twisted together in front of her. Now that I was really looking at her, she looked a little pale.

"Very." I stepped out of the kitchen, giving her space to leave. "Go."

She nodded and her shoulders visibly relaxed as she scooped up a pile of clothes that appeared to be hers. When she slipped past me, it took every ounce of self-control not to pull her against me. I stayed frozen to my spot, hands clinched into fists while I watched her disappear downstairs.

When the door closed behind her, a sudden heaviness settled in my bones. My body screamed for rest, and I wanted nothing more than to lay down with Gwendalyn next to me. Her hand on my forehead, her chest against mine, all of it opened up a part of me that I closed off long ago.

Feelings that I thought I would never experience again bubbled to the surface. Every part of me wanted to dive in head first. But being drawn to the woman who lived in my home and took care of my son was completely inappropriate.

I forced those desires deep down, locking them up next to *oscurità mia.*

"Daddy?" Oliver's voice came from behind me. Turning, I looked down at my son. His little face was pale, and his eyes were rimmed in red. He coughed openly into the air, not even attempting to cover his mouth. His favorite stuffie was gripped tightly in his little fist at his side.

"Come here, *figlio mio,*" I whispered, bending down. Oliver shuffled into my open arms, and curled up against my chest with his head tucked into my neck.

My heart squeezed in my chest as I hugged him close. My son was the most important person in my life, and I needed to remember that.

# Chapter Ten

## *Gwen*

"A s soon as things slow down here, I'm flying out for a visit. It's been months and I miss you, babe," Ivy whined and stuck out her bottom lip, pouting at me over our video call. I chuckled at the absurdity of this grown woman making the same face that Ollie does when he wants a sweet treat too close to dinner time.

But she wasn't wrong. It was months since we'd seen each other in person. Over three months, actually. I really missed her hugs. That whole thing about time flying by when you stay busy was definitely a true statement.

"I miss you, too," I acknowledged, blowing her a kiss, and her fake pout disappeared.

We both laughed, and for a second, I forgot Ivy was a time zone away from me. It felt weird not having my best friend living in the same state, but this move had been good for me. Ivy reminded me of that every chance she got.

As she put it, I had my sparkle back.

"Ollie should be up from his nap soon. There's a small farmer's market starting soon a few minutes from here, and I'm hoping I can get my hands on some fresh flowers to brighten up this place." I pushed my laptop back before leaning against the kitchen island so I could still see Ivy, but relieve some of the pressure from my aching feet.

"How're things with Anthony going?" She gave me a knowing look, and I shook my head. I was not going to give her what she so desperately wanted.

"I barely see the man, let alone interact with him." I rolled my eyes and heard her chuckling as I pushed myself off the counter top. I busied myself with prepping our bag for the day. "Whenever he's home in time for dinner or bedtime with Ollie, I tend to give them space. Ollie doesn't see him often, and I want them to have their special time without my hovering."

There was a shift that happened after he and Ollie were sick. Anthony avoided being in the same space as me for too long and while that wasn't much different than before, it seemed he actively avoided being alone with me.

I did my best to not make things weird. He was my boss, and I needed to keep this job.

I refused to lose it because my vibrator was having a hard time keeping up.

"Has he made eyes at you again?" Ivy pushed, refusing to let this go. I stopped in front of the screen, covering my face and groaning.

Why had I told her about that moment after dinner on my first night here? I should have kept it to myself, because knowing my best friend, Ivy was bound to use it against me. That moment just so happened to be right now.

"Ivy, I have thus far been able to keep things extremely professional between us." My voice was muffled behind my hands and I swore I could hear muted giggles coming from the screen. "He won't make eyes at me again. If he even made eyes at me the first time." The last part was more for me than her. I had to remind myself that I was his nanny.

"Who won't be making eyes at you?" Startled, I jumped up straight, and turned toward the familiar voice. Anthony was standing in the doorway to the kitchen, his button-down and dress slacks looking as if he had just run a marathon. I was caught in the gaze of his brown eyes, like a magnetic field pulling me in.

Ivy cleared her throat, causing me to jump yet again. She managed to shoot me a quick wink just as I gushed out a quick goodbye and slammed the laptop closed.

Warmth rose into my cheeks, and my stomach tightened. I closed my eyes and took a breath, before turning back to Anthony.

"I'm sorry. I didn't expect you to be home so early," I said, turning back to Anthony and ignoring his question. He raised a brow at me, but thankfully didn't comment any further on what he had walked in on.

"I wasn't supposed to be, so no need to apologize. I needed a quick shower." His gaze flicked down his clothes as if the damp patches were all the explanation I needed.

Silence filled the air between us. I was finding it hard to formulate a coherent response when his shirt was clinging to his body, exposing the clear outline of his abs. This time I cleared my throat, forcing my eyes to stop roaming his body.

"Well, Ollie should be up soon, and I had planned on us heading to a farmer's market. Nothing is set in stone, if you want us to stick around," I said, going back to organizing the bag.

"No," he said. "I have to head back to the station to finish paperwork after I shower. As long as we don't get called out into the field again, I should be back by dinner."

I nodded my head in understanding before looking anywhere, but at him as I gathered everything in my arms to leave the kitchen.

Anthony hadn't budged from his position in the doorway. As I made my way toward him, I refused to make eye contact, not wanting him to see the embarrassment written all over my face from the events of the last few minutes. I cleared my throat, not trusting my voice at that moment.

"Something you'd like to say?" he asked.

I shook my head.

No matter how hard I had tried to ignore it, my body felt things that it shouldn't. His voice alone had me clenching my thighs together in an attempt to alleviate some of the pressure between my legs. My heart was beating so frantically that I swore Anthony could hear it.

He tilted his head down, his warm breath dancing across my skin, goosebumps quickly forming. My nose filled with a scent I had come to associate with him, pine and bourbon. Where is came from, I had no idea. He never drank hard liquor in front of me or Ollie.

I chanced a glance, and the darkness that danced in his eyes had my legs nearly collapsing underneath me. His lips were inches away from me. All it would take was me standing on my tip toes…

"Words, Gwendalyn," he growled.

Silently, I begged him to put me out of my misery. I needed his hands on me, to feel that rush of electricity again from my first night.

No. What I needed was to get out of here. Now.

"Excuse me?" I forced out the words on a squeak.

Anthony continued to hold my gaze, but stepped to the side just enough to allow me through.

His body heat cocooned me as I tried to squeeze past, doing everything in my power to not let a single centimeter of my body brush against his.

When I made it through, I continued down the hallway toward the basement door, resisting the urge to look over my shoulder to see if Anthony was still leaning against the door frame.

*What just happened?*

I quickly forgot about Anthony, and the confusing interaction once Ollie and I ventured out for the day. The farmer's market was bustling with vendors, including several fresh flower stands, and Ollie insisted we check out every single one.

We came home with more than I had anticipated, and I was now attempting to balance the full bags and several bouquets of daisies in one hand while guiding Ollie inside with the other. Surprisingly, we made it inside without incident, and I watched Ollie run to the playroom to start setting up his trains with the brand new wooden tunnel he'd seen at the market.

He had insisted on needing it, and I had been unable to resist. He had carried it around proudly as we finished weaving our way through people, and would not let me put it in any of the bags with our other things when we got home. He carefully placed the tunnel over a part of the tracks he had still set up from this morning and pushed his train through. The smile that spread across his face was contagious and I took a few more minutes to watch him before I went to the kitchen to start dinner.

Slowly pulling things out of the bags, I sat aside what I planned on using for dinner and put the rest away. After that was done, I got a pot of water on the stove to start boiling before turning my attention to searching for something to hold the flowers I got.

I found a vase that looked to have seen better days hidden in the back of the cabinet above the refrigerator. Pulling it down, I gave it a quick wash, then set it down by the flowers as I began stripping and arranging a couple of the daisies into the vase. My heart was happy, and I found myself smiling down at the little arrangement.

Matt had never let me have flowers in the house. He argued they were a waste of money and space. I got the memo to stop bringing them into the house when I found the vase my grandma had left me smashed into pieces on the floor.

The irony of the situation was he always brought home a fresh bouquet of roses after every fight. Even though I was allergic, I would keep them out on the counter for a few days, suffering through the inevitable migraines from my itchy eyes and throat.

I continued working on the flowers until it was time to start dinner. Ollie was still happily playing with his trains and dinner was going in the oven when I heard the front door open and close.

Anthony was home.

My body warmed at the feeling of his eyes on me. Glancing over my shoulder, Anthony was standing in the doorway with his arms crossed. His gaze wandered up and down my body. I looked down at my outfit, wondering if maybe he thought something was wrong with my leggings. They were dirty and not the most flattering thing, but comfort over style was my motto.

When I looked up again to meet his eyes, they were filled with an intensity that made me want to run and hide. Unease settled in my bones as a sudden tension settled in the air. I turned my attention back to cleaning up the dinner prep mess.

Anthony came up behind me, the heat radiating from his body sending a shiver down my spine. My heart pounded in my chest as my stomach did flip after flip.

"What are those?" he muttered. His words were clipped, like he was trying to hold himself back from saying more.

I peeked over my shoulder to see what he was talking about. My mind spiraled into a panic when I realized he was gesturing toward the daisies still scattered on the kitchen island.

Shit, I should have asked first.

Anthony was upset.

"I'm so sorry." I scooped everything up into a pile as quickly as possible. Several flowers fell off the counter top in my hurry to clean it all up. I grabbed what I could in my hands, and stepped toward the trash can. "I got them from the farmer's market and thought they would brighten up the space. I can get rid of them…"

A hand on my shoulder stopped me just as I was about to drop them into the open bag, and I froze. My body reacted on instinct, my muscles tensing as my jaw clenched close.

I braced myself for the harsh words, being called stupid for wasting money usually the first thing to be said. Instead, I was stunned when Anthony released my shoulder, letting his hand linger on my upper arm as it fell to his side. He stepped in front of me, and gently pulled the daisies out of my hands.

"I never said you had to get rid of them," he started, "let alone throw them away. I apologize for making it sound like I wanted you to." I spun to watch him as he walked back to the island, and put the daisies down in a tidy pile. When he turned back to me, a soft smile played across his lips, and I relaxed a bit.

"I was just surprised by the flower choice. Most women tend to get arrangements with roses."

Finding my voice, I said the first thing that came to mind. "I'm allergic to roses."

"That is good to know," he said, stepping up to the fridge. He pulled out a bottle of water, finished half of its contents in a few long swallows, then directed his attention back to me. "Did you and Oliver have a good day?"

"We did. Did he show you his new train tunnel? He's obsessed with it and has been playing with it the entire time I was making dinner."

"His lack of enthusiasm toward my arrival home makes more sense now," he said, sounding annoyed but understanding.

"My bad." I offered him a smile as an apology, but was met with an intense gaze that made me wonder if I had offended him. The playfulness he had toward me just a few hours ago seemed to have disappeared. "I'll go get him," I quickly added.

This back and forth, hot and cold routine was getting to be too much. The anxiety that had slowly been building was threatening to take over as I desperately tried to shove it back down.

*Focus on Ollie.*

I found Ollie down on the floor of the living room, pushing his train through the tunnel. Leaning down, I scooped him up, and threw him over my shoulder while I tickled his sides. He laughed and wiggled in my arms until he was nearly pushing himself out of my hold.

"Your dad is home, buddy," I said. Setting him down on his feet, Ollie ran toward his dad.

As Anthony picked him up, Oliver grabbed onto his dad's face to make sure he had his full attention. "Daddy, new tunnel!"

"Did you tell Miss Gwendalyn 'thank you' for the tunnel?"

"Yes," he nodded his head in tandem with his reply. "She best, Daddy." Anthony looked toward me, and I saw a glint in his eyes again for just a second before it disappeared. He returned his attention to Ollie before I was able to say or do anything.

"I am so glad you had a good day, *figlio mio.* How about we—" His sentence was cut off by the ringing of his cell phone, and I knew immediately he was being called into work. Pulling out his phone, he offered Ollie to me and I took him out of his arms.

"Marino." He gave Ollie a kiss on the head.

I had gotten used to this happening, as Anthony frequently got called into work at weird times. Ollie normally never seemed to mind, but for whatever reason, tears began welling up in his eyes as Anthony turned his back to us and left the room.

After a few moments of muffled conversation, the front door closed. The muted thunk echoed Anthony's departure throughout the house.

"Daddy leave?" Oliver whimpered, and my heart shattered. I wrapped my arms around him tighter while he laid his head on my shoulder.

"Yeah, little man. I'm sorry. How about we have some ice cream after dinner, though? Since it'll just be you and me."

"Yes!" His tears instantly dried up as he sat up in my arms.

Chuckling, I planted a kiss of my own on his head before putting him in his chair at the dining table, making sure he was properly buckled in.

# Chapter Eleven

## Anthony

Doing my best to be quiet, I took my boots off at the front door, and made my way through the house to the kitchen. My stomach had been growling at me for the last few hours since I had to skip dinner. I was still fuming over the fact that I had to leave like that, even though I knew Gwendalyn understood.

But she wasn't my main concern. It was Oliver.

Giving up time with my son hurt, and I only hoped he was never too upset by my departure when it happened. It wasn't fair to her to have to deal with the fallout of my own actions.

Standing in front of the refrigerator, I noticed a note in Gwendalyn's handwriting stuck to the fridge.

*Left you a plate in the fridge. -G*

I opened the fridge door to see the plastic wrapped plate she left piled with what looks to be some kind of pasta.

My mouth watered at the thought of devouring it as I removed the plastic and warmed it up in the microwave. As I waited for it, I couldn't stop the way my mind wandered back to Gwendalyn leaning against the counter this morning.

I wanted to know how it felt to have her underneath me, for her scent to consume me.

I wanted to run my nose along her jaw and press my lips to her skin, to run my tongue along the goosebumps that would form.

I wanted to hear my name from her lips as my hand slipped beneath the waistband of her leggings.

The beeping of the microwave completely jolted me out of my fantasy.

*Fucking hell.*

I welcomed the sting that came from handling the hot plate. No matter how much distance I put between us, it didn't seem to matter. This wasn't the first time my damn dick had done all the thinking in the last few months and it was turning into a problem.

This afternoon was a brief lapse in judgment. She was my employee, and thinking about her in any other way was extremely unethical, even if the path of ethical righteousness wasn't one I regularly followed.

There was something about her that made me want to be better, like a guiding light.

*Luce mia.*

I couldn't lose her. Oliver couldn't lose her.

She was the best thing to have happened to us in a long time.

Pasta danced across my taste buds as I shoveled it into my mouth, needing to end this night and crawl into bed. Moments later, the plate was empty, and I left it in the sink.

The house was quiet like always, but somehow it felt different. It felt lighter. These walls had seen happy moments and heard laughter these last several months, and it showed.

White noise came from Oliver's room as I passed it, and I slipped into mine as quietly as possible. I changed into a pair of sweatpants, and was about to collapse into bed, when a sudden pull to check on my son had me silently moving through the hallways once more.

When he was a baby, I used to sit by his bassinet for hours every night just watching him sleep. Now, I did it on occasion to remind myself of the innocence I strived to protect every day.

Cracking open Oliver's door, I took a step in and froze when I saw a sleeping figure on the floor next to his crib. Even in the soft glow of the night light, I could still make out Gwendalyn's features.

Her hair was twisted up in one of her signature messy buns on top of her head, and the oversized shirt paired with sleep pants did little to hide her body from my wandering eyes as she lay on her side. She had one hand under her head while the other was in between the slats at the far end of the crib.

Presumably, it was holding onto Oliver at one point, but he had long since migrated to the other end and was currently curled up with a stuffed bear.

Without thinking, I quietly stepped further into the room until I was standing behind Gwendalyn. After gently pulling her hand out of the crib, I did my best to lift her into my arms without waking her.

She curled into me, her head resting on my shoulder. Her warm breath on my shirtless chest sent chills down my back, and I relished in the way her body fit against mine. A soft hum came from her throat, and I thought I had succeeded in my mission to keep her asleep until I heard her mumble. "I didn't mean to fall asleep."

"Shhh. It's okay, *luce mia*," I whispered. She sank further into my arms as I walked out of Oliver's room and across the hall back to mine.

Would it have been a better idea to take her down to her own bed? Yes, absolutely.

But the thought of her sleeping in my bed, even without me next to her, sparked something inside of me. A primal need to claim her as mine, even if I had no right to. Call me selfish, but I wanted to hang onto that feeling for as long as possible.

Thankfully, I was not someone who regularly made the bed.

After gently laying her down, a content sigh left her lips as she curled up on her side. I lifted the blankets over her body, draping them carefully around her shoulder, before tucking behind the loose strands of hair that had fallen out of her bun.

The sight of her in my bed made my heart skip a beat, something I didn't know it could still do after everything it had been put through.

I forced myself to leave the room, not wanting to do something I would regret in the morning.

Heading downstairs, I threw one of my extra pillows I grabbed from my bed on the couch before flopping down on top of it and throwing my arm over my eyes. I hated myself for wanting to go back upstairs, and lay in bed with Gwendalyn.

She was too tempting, calling to a part of me that I hadn't remembered was there, and she didn't even know it.

*Walking in the front door, I heard laughter coming from the kitchen. The sound pulled me toward the two most important people in my life.*

*I stopped in the doorway, leaning against it as I watched Gwendalyn with Oliver on her hip dancing around the kitchen island. Before they could notice me, I snuck up behind them and pulled them both into my arms.*

*"Daddy!" Oliver exclaimed as he attempted to wiggle out of Gwendalyn's arms and into mine. Laughing, she let him go, and I grabbed him, settling him in the crook of my arm.*

*"Hello, figlio mio." I planted a kiss on the top of his head before turning my attention to Gwendalyn.*

*My arm was still wrapped around her waist from my earlier embrace, and I took a moment to admire her ocean blue eyes. Little specks of green appeared around the edges of her irises when she was happy, and I couldn't help but get lost in them. Gently tugging her toward me, she continued laughing as she softly collided with my chest.*

*"Hello, luce mia." Leaning forward, I captured her lips with mine, the simple greeting quickly deepening with lust as we continued our embrace. One of her hands found the back of my neck and continued upwards as her fingers ran through my hair. I gripped her tighter against me, my fingers digging into her waist as the softest moan escaped her throat.*

*Every kiss felt like the first with her. Her body fit against mine like a puzzle piece and I felt complete. My heart was finally full of pure love instead of hate. Our tongues danced, and I swallowed every moan. We were lost in the moment, in each other. I wanted it to last forever.*

*"Ewww, Daddy kiss Mommy," Oliver interrupted us and Gwendalyn pulled away giggling. I reluctantly let her. She turned to Oliver, giving him a quick peck on his cheek.*

*"I'll let my boys spend some time together. Dinner is almost ready." She smiled up at me, making my heart soar. I released her waist, watch-*

*ing as she made her way to the stove. For just a moment, everything was right. Oliver was happy. I was happy.*

*"Daddy, we play?" Tiny hands on my face, but I didn't want to take my eyes off Gwendalyn. "Daddy?" I closed my eyes.*

*"Daddy?" Oliver's call for me was muffled.*

*"Daddy?" he shouted again, as if from a distance. As if he was far away and I couldn't seem to reach him.*

*"DADDY?"*

My eyes snapped open.

I wasn't standing in the kitchen. I wasn't holding Oliver. Gwendalyn wasn't just in my arms.

Oliver was on top of my chest, his face inches away from mine, as I laid on the couch. Realizing none of it was real, the heart that felt so full only a few seconds ago slowly drained.

I sat up with a groan, lifting Oliver off of me and onto the couch. I was about to stand up when it hit me. "Oliver, how did you get out of your crib?"

"I climb Daddy. I strong." He looked up at me as if I should have known the answer already. And I absolutely should have. The dad-guilt hit hard as I wondered what else I had missed.

*Had she said something to me about Oliver climbing out of his crib? Had I been so distracted by my thoughts of her that I couldn't even process the information she told me about my own son?*

"Daddy, where Miss Gen? I hungry," Oliver whined while shifting on my lap.

"How about we make breakfast today?" The words were out of my mouth before I could even process them.

I hadn't cooked a full meal by myself since long before Oliver was born, let alone *with* him. We survived on casseroles from neighbors and a lot of boxed pasta when it became just the two of us. Boiling water had always been simple enough.

Surely I could find my way around the kitchen again if only to spend some quality time with my son, right?

"Pantats, Daddy!" Oliver's face brightened, the joy apparent on his face of getting to help me.

"Of course, *figlio mio*." Scooping him into my arms, I walked to the kitchen and put him on his feet by the fridge. He ran around the island, coming back with a step stool I had never noticed before, and placed it in front of the counter.

Distancing myself from Gwendalyn had backfired. I was basically a stranger in my own home.

Pulling out all the needed ingredients for breakfast and placing them on the counter in front of Oliver, I looked down at him. He was bouncing on his feet as he happily waited for a task. He grew up right in front of my eyes, and I never noticed.

Mentally kicking myself, I determined it was time to get my head out of my ass and stop acting like a lovesick teenager. I was a grown ass adult who could control his feelings and his dick.

"Alright, little man. Let's get breakfast going." Oliver clapped his hands, then excitedly reached for the eggs I had set out. Before I could stop him, he had them crushed against the counter, shell pieces and yolk flying everywhere.

*I may have overestimated my abilities.*

# Chapter Twelve

## *Gwen*

Rolling over in bed, I readjusted the pillow beneath my head and pulled my blankets tighter around myself. Though slightly confused by the lack of softness to them, I decided it wasn't important enough to warrant getting up.

Yawning, I breathed in the most intoxicating mix of pine and bourbon. My body relaxed further into the mattress, but then... it hit me.

My eyes flew open.

This was *not* my bed.

I nearly fell on my face trying to rid myself of the sheet tangled in between my legs when a photo of Ollie and his dad caught my attention. Freezing, I looked around the room and recognized all of Anthony's things.

*Shit, how did I end up in his bed?*

A loud beep interrupted the growing anxiety, and it took me longer than it should have to recognize it was the smoke alarm.

Rushing out of the room, I crossed the hallway to find Ollie's door wide open with him not inside. Frantically searching the closet, I called out to him, wondering if he climbed out of his crib and then hid when the alarm went off.

"Ollie! Oliver!" Panic set in when I couldn't find him. I continued calling for him as I ran down the steps, angry at myself for not talking about fire safety with Ollie.

A familiar sound broke through the panic as I reached the bottom step. Ollie's giggles came from the back of the house and I sprinted to the kitchen. I was preparing myself to have to scoop him up and make a run for it.

But when I rounded the corner into the kitchen, my feet stopped dead in their tracks.

On the stove was a tray of something burnt beyond recognition that I assumed used to be bacon by the smell in the air. Next to it was the stove top griddle, which had a half melted spatula on it, covered in a wet baking mix. There were eggshells scattered on the floor and a bowl filled with more of the wet mix

Even with his back turned to me, there was no hiding that Ollie was covered head to toe with flour. He had his little hands up in the air mimicking his dad, who was using a kitchen towel to try to fan smoke away from the alarm.

Anthony was shirtless under the kitchen apron he had on, and I couldn't help myself as I admired the detailed lines of his arm muscles and noticed he, too, was covered in flour. Trying to hold in my laughter, I slapped my hand over my mouth, muffling the chuckle that escaped.

I was unsuccessful, tears springing to my eyes as a full laugh came out of me, and I leaned on the doorway for support.

Ollie noticed me first, turning and running toward me while laughing. Picking him up and putting him on my hip, I wiped some of the mix off his face.

"Miss Gen, I make bakefest wif Daddy!" he shouted over the alarm.

I looked at Anthony. He stopped fanning the smoke, and turned to me with a pleading look on his face. Not bothering to hide my smile, I walked past him and opened the window nearest the alarm. It didn't take long for the alarm to stop blaring, and I accessed the mess that was the kitchen.

"How about we let your dad go get cleaned up while we handle all this? Then we can see what can be saved for breakfast." Oliver twisted in my arms, and I held on tighter so he couldn't get into anything else.

Anthony stood still under the fire alarm with wide eyes as if he was something was stopping him from moving.

"Go, I've got this." I gestured with my head as a small smile spread across my lips in silent reassurance.

"Thank you," he mouthed, barely meeting my eyes before leaving the kitchen.

I ignored the disappointment that squeezed at my heart, turning my attention to Ollie who was still trying to wiggle out of my arms. I sat him on his feet then worked on getting some of the loose mix off him.

This wasn't exactly the wake up I expected, but if there was one thing I learned recently, it was to stay on my toes where the Marino men were involved.

"I think this is as good as it's going to get, buddy. We'll get you changed after breakfast," I said.

"Cean now?" he asked, continuing to smile up at me.

"Yeah, let's get things cleaned. Wanna go get the broom and dustpan?" Without answering, Ollie grabbed it and began haphazardly sweeping the floor.

Even though I knew he was going to end up making a bigger mess, all that mattered was he was kept busy. This way, I could focus on cleaning up everything else.

Twenty minutes later, the kitchen was returned to order and Ollie was watching a cartoon in the living room with a bowl of dry cereal. He had quickly lost interest in helping clean, which I didn't blame the poor guy, and nothing was very salvageable from the breakfast disaster.

I was starting the dishes when a knock on the front door echoed through the house, startling me. Drying off my hands, I made my way to the front door, and peeked in on Ollie. He was still hypnotized by the talking tiger who was now singing about going potty.

Whoever was at the door grew impatient. They were now pounding on the door, causing the door to rattle on its hinges. Without looking through the peephole, I swung open the door and my heart dropped into my stomach.

Standing on the porch was Matt, holding a single rose in his hand. I froze.

He must have thought it was an invitation; he tried to walk into the house. Panic coursed through me. I threw a look over my shoulder to make sure Ollie was still in the living room and Anthony was upstairs. The sound of water running told me he was still in the shower.

Shoving Matt back onto the porch with a hand on his chest, I stepped outside with him and closed the door softly behind me.

"Matt, what are you doing here?" He tried to push the flower toward me and I pressed my back against the door, putting as much distance between us as possible.

He pulled away, looking almost hurt that I wouldn't accept his gift. There were so many questions running through my head right now.

"How did you find me? How did you get out of jail?" The unknown phone calls had been less frequent, but they hadn't stopped. Ivy wanted me to change my number again. I was too worried Anthony would ask too many questions.

So, I just dealt with it.

"I called in a favor. I know you didn't mean to have me arrested," he chuckled, as if this was all some kind of game that he was obviously winning. "I had to call in another favor so I could find you. I know you feel guilty about having me arrested. That's why you haven't answered my calls."

"Why would I feel guilty, Matt? You tried to force yourself on me." I was trying to stay calm, but I was failing. Matt needed to leave so I could get back inside before Anthony came downstairs and discovered I was gone.

"If Ivy hadn't shown up, you would be back with me, where you belong." His jaw set as he spoke, his fists balling at his sides. He leaned forward, and I reached for the doorknob behind me, my flight instinct setting in.

My chest rose rapidly, trying to figure out if I could make it inside before Matt could react. I would deal with Anthony's unfortunate opinion of me later. I just needed to get away.

He lifted his hands defensively, the crumpled flower dangling between his fingers. "Okay, fine. I'm sorry. We've been engaged for over a year, baby. Just come home where you believe and we can figure this out."

"I don't belong with you, Matt," I lashed out, a wave of confidence washing over me.

Anger twisted his features as Matt realized I wasn't going to make this easy. He lurched forward, throwing the rose on the porch and grabbing my wrist. I tripped over my feet as he yanked me against him.

"It's time for you to stop playing house with some stranger," he spat out. I flinched as spit landed on my cheek, and an involuntary whimper left my throat.

I pushed my hand against his chest, tears springing to the corners of my eyes. He laughed, and the fight drained from me.

An engrained response to keep from getting hurt.

"Can I help you?" The unmistakable voice came from behind me.

I didn't need to look to know that Anthony was behind me somewhere. His presence alone wrapped me in a blanket of security, easing the fear that was making knots in my stomach.

"Nope. Just talking to my fiancé. In private, if you don't mind," Matt snarled through gritted teeth. His grip on my wrist tightened as he swung me around to stand next to him, and I fought back the tears that stung my eyes.

Meeting Anthony's gaze, I silently pleaded for help, not caring that it may mean the end of my employment with him. He stepped out onto the porch, his hand hovering above his gun.

Matt tensed next to me. His grip on my wrist tightened as he undoubtedly saw the weapon.

"She won't be leaving with you," Anthony asserted confidently.

Matt tried to interrupt, but stopped when Anthony took a step toward him. Matt let go of my wrist and I inched behind Anthony, who was continuing his advance toward Matt.

"I know your type. Men who think they can intimidate women. That's not how this is going to work. So I suggest you get off my property before I make sure you never step foot within spitting distance of Gwendalyn again."

Without him realizing it, Matt had been backed to the edge of the porch. He took one last step back and proceeded to fall flat on his ass.

Anthony continued towering over him as I peeked out from behind him. As Matt got up, Anthony's left arm settled against my side and his right hand hovered above his gun.

"This isn't over," Matt spat, then turned and headed down the street. I stayed behind Anthony as I watched him leave, knowing his threat wasn't an empty one.

He would find a way to ruin everything.

Anthony turned around, and there was a softness in his eyes as he looked down at me.

"Gwendalyn?" The way he said my name sounded unnatural after all these months, soft and full of concern.

"I just... I need a minute." I took a step back and turned back to the house, vaguely hearing my name being called again.

Ollie was asleep on the couch, a blanket tucked around his tiny frame. I headed straight to the kitchen and set to finishing the dishes.

I focused on the task in front of me, ignoring the burning behind my eyes. Until the redness of my wrist caught my eye.

My hand flew to my mouth, muting the small gasp that escaped as silent tears ran down my cheeks.

"Gwendalyn?"

I spun on my heel and collided with a hard chest. Through the haze of tears, the recognizable flash of anger on Anthony's face made my heart pound.

*I was about to get fired.*

He took my wrist in his hand, his rough fingers sliding across my inflamed skin as he inspected it closely. A heat settled across my skin at his gentleness and I realized I wasn't the target of his frustration.

Suddenly, I was pressed against him with his arms wrapped around me. My body tensed with uncertainty, but Anthony didn't let go.

"Are you okay?" he asked quietly.

I didn't know how to answer him.

Because Matt found me.

He found me, and I was about to lose my job, and everything was falling apart again.

A sob escaped as I pressed my face into Anthony's shirt and my hands fisted the fabric. One of his hands rubbed small circles on my back as my body shook.

"Shhh, I got you," he whispered into my hair, his chin resting on top of my head. "Just breathe."

There was a small voice telling me that this wasn't right. But I couldn't force myself to pull away.

I couldn't bring myself to care about how far beyond the professional boundary we were right now.

Matt found me.

Anthony didn't move, as if content to wait as long as it took for my body to calm and the tears to dry. My fists slowly relaxed, dropping the balled up fabric. Anthony loosened his grip, and I tilted my head back to look up at him.

His gaze found mine, and for a split second, I stopped breathing. The way his eyes shined caused my heart to skip. He cupped my jaw and brushed his thumb along my lower lip. There was something in his expression, a silent question.

All rational thoughts went out the window as I pushed up on my tiptoes and pressed my lips to his.

His hand went to the back of my head, gently holding it as he steadied me. My body melted into his and for a second, I was lighter than I've ever been. My heart was beating in my chest so fast that I was afraid Anthony could hear it.

Then the rational part of my brain came back online. I jerked away with such force that Anthony's hands were frozen in the air.

Frustration once again pinched his brows together as he dropped his hands.

This time, it *was* aimed at me.

"Anthony, I'm so sorry. I didn't–" I stepped backward as I spoke, trying to put distance between us when my back hit the wall.

Anthony rushed forward with his hand out and I flinched away, pressing myself into the wall. My legs no longer wanted to support me as I slid completely to the floor, my back against the wall as I pulled my knees to my chest.

"Gwendalyn?" Anthony squatted down in front of me.

His hands twitched, as if he wanted to reach out and comfort me, but I was thankful for his restraint. My mind and body needed space.

Between Matt showing up and Anthony letting me kiss him... it was all too much.

I laid my forehead on my knees, attempting to take a deep breath to re-center myself.

"Gwendalyn?" His voice sounded a million miles away.

I struggled to get air into my lungs, and my body began to shake with the exertion as my anxiety grew with every passing second.

"Gwendalyn, you need to focus on breathing, okay?" Anthony's voice was still soft as I nodded my head but didn't look up.

I did what he asked, and after a few minutes, it became easier. My heart stopped racing. Slowly, I lifted my head and found Anthony still in front of me.

After a few minutes of focusing, my heart stopped racing, and it became easier to take in air. Slowly, I lifted my head and looked up at Anthony. He hadn't moved.

"Will you talk to me?" The gentleness in his words gave me the courage to nod my head.

He deserved an explanation, even if I was scared of what would come next.

Anthony sat down on the floor in front of me, taking a deep breath before asking his first question. "Who was he?"

"Matt, my ex-fiancé," I started. "The week before my interview with you, we had gotten into a… disagreement. I had walked in on him… with another woman… I got upset, and when I tried to leave, he…" I trailed off, not sure how to put what had happened that night into words.

"Was he physical with you?" Anthony didn't hesitate with his question, as if he already knew the answer. All I could do was nod my head.

I didn't want to give Anthony all the details about my relationship with Matt. The slaps when I said something he didn't like. The grabbing when I tried to walk away.

But he needed to know that what happened on his porch was not a one off. Matt wasn't a good guy.

Anthony continued looking at me, urging me with his eyes to tell him as much as I wanted.

"When I left that night, I went to Ivy's place… He showed up the next morning, but she kicked him out…" I focused on my hands as I spoke, the healed skin around my nails now torn to shreds once again. "It wasn't enough, though… She left, and he broke in… He tried to…" I stopped, trying to decide how much to say. "He said he wanted to have fun… before he took me home."

Looking up, I caught Anthony's eyes, anger flashing across them before he blinked and it was gone. If it weren't for the fists he was making, I would have told myself I imagined it.

"Anthony, I'm so sorry. This wasn't supposed to happen. He wasn't supposed to find me. I don't know how he found me," I rambled defensively, the fact that he had been carefully listening to me this entire time without judgment lost on me.

Anthony reached out, hesitating at first before gently placing his hand on top of mine. His thumb made small circles on my hand. I focused on the movement, using it as a grounding point to keep myself from spinning.

When Anthony spoke, I continued my fixation on our hands. "Gwendalyn, none of this is your fault. You don't need to apologize, okay?" I nodded my head, but there was always going to be a part of me that would blame myself.

"If I can just have a little bit, I'll get all my stuff packed up," I whispered the words as my heart shattered into a million pieces at the thought of leaving.

But Anthony needed to do what was best for Ollie. I loved that little boy with every fiber of my being, but if Matt was trying to lay some twisted claim on me, there was no way I could keep him safe.

"What?" He sounded surprised, as if I just said something completely absurd.

"You want me to leave…"

"No, absolutely not."

"But Ollie? You have to put him first…" I trailed off, his hand on top of mine squeezing gently.

"I am putting him first, Gwendalyn. He's done nothing but flourish since you arrived. If you left, he'd be heartbroken." Fingers under my chin tilted back my head until my eyes met his. "You're a part of our little family now, like it or not. We'll figure this out, together."

Panic was quickly replaced by hope. Before I could respond, the sound of little footsteps came into the kitchen. "Daddy, snack?"

Anthony dropped his hand from my chin, looking over his shoulder at Ollie. "Of course, *figlio mio*. Give me one minute." He turned his attention back to me. "Why don't you go take a shower and I'll spend some time with Oliver?"

Not giving me a chance to fight him on it, he stood up then offered me his hand to help me off the floor. Once I was standing, he ran his fingers up my arm, tucking a stray piece of hair behind my ear.

His touch lingered as his eyes searched mine before he let his hand fall.

He turned, scooping up Oliver and tickling his sides as he made his way to the back door. Ollie's giggles trailed them and I could just make out Anthony's words as I walked out of the kitchen to the basement door. "How about ice cream?"

I smiled to myself, knowing Ollie was going to love every moment of this unexpected time with his dad.

Once downstairs, I found myself standing in front of the bathroom mirror after going through the motions, getting everything I needed for a shower.

The woman looking back at me was not someone I recognized. She was a little beaten and bruised around the edges, but there was something growing in the middle.

A feeling of freedom and safety that hadn't been there in a long time.

# Chapter Thirteen

## *Anthony*

I made the executive decision that everything would be easiest if Gwendalyn's ex-fiance simply disappeared by my or Jason's hands.

But the fucker was smarter than he looked. It was like he fell off the face of the Earth. Months passed, and none of our usual means of tracking yielded any sort of result.

I stared at my computer screen at the station, hoping some new information would just appear out of nowhere. That asshole needed to be found.

Gwendalyn hadn't been the same. She never showed it in front of Ollie, but I saw the way her smile didn't quite reach her eyes.

I needed to do something.

Oliver's third birthday was coming up, so I asked Gwendalyn if she would be up for planning something. It seemed like a good way to take her mind off things.

Within days, she had an entire schedule for his birthday written out and had even made up invitations for me to give to coworkers.

The plan was to host a barbeque at the house, complete with everything to make a three-year-old's birthday dreams come true. Which essentially meant Gwendalyn had him pick out whatever cake he wanted and she had ordered it.

Oliver was ecstatic to show off a picture of the dinosaur cake he picked, complete with dirt and volcano. There was no doubt in my mind the two of them had an entire array of dinosaur decor picked out for the party to compliment it.

"How're things at home, Tony?" Jason pulled me out of my thoughts. I looked up to find him leaning against my desk with a shit-eating grin on his face.

It fucking annoyed me.

"Why do you ask?" Giving my attention to the scattered papers on my desk, I sifted through them, and hoped Jason would take my obvious disinterest in the conversation as a hint to go away.

"Oh, no reason. Just wondering if you've finally broken down and admitted to yourself those true feelings you have for our dear Gwen."

I narrowed my eyes, refusing to give him the satisfaction of an answer.

In a moment of weakness, I confided in Jason about everything that happened with Gwendalyn and immediately regretted it.

*"I think it's time you take that woman to bed,"* he had told me.

Gwendalyn was my nanny.

Not only that, but no matter how much I cared for her, I wasn't sure I could ever trust my heart to fall for another woman after what happened with my ex-wife.

Jason chuckled as he pushed himself off my desk. "Boss man wants to see us. You good?"

Straightening up the papers in front of me, I added them to the growing stack on the corner of my chaotic desk. Sometimes I wished Gwendalyn could organize every aspect of my life.

Life was so much easier since she came into our home. Oliver was happier too, getting the one-on-one attention he deserved. Gwendalyn may not believe me, but I was serious when I said we would figure this out together.

She was a part of our family.

Grunting as I stood, Jason released my shoulders after giving them a squeeze. Turning to him, I motioned with my head for him to lead the way. "Let's go."

Following behind Jason, we made our way through the maze of desks in the bullpen to the captain's office. Sitting behind his desk, Captain David Barlowe was flipping through a file when we entered.

He was a quiet leader, only involving himself in our cases when absolutely necessary. Although Jason and I have never involved anyone else with our extracurricular activities, the worst cases always seemed to fall in our laps, as if our captain somehow knew.

We never tested the theory.

"Sir, you wanted to see us?" Jason dropped into one of the chairs opposite our boss, stretching out his legs as he leaned back. He always was the one to make an entrance.

Choosing to remain standing, I stood behind the other chair, and gripped the back of it with my hands.

Captain cleared his throat while closing the file he was looking at, then offered it to Jason. "I have a case for you."

Stepping behind my partner, I peered over his shoulder at the police reports as he handed me a stack of photographs. Flipping through them, each photo displayed a different woman with varying degrees of bruising. I started to notice a similarity to the bruising, as if the same hand was the cause of each one.

Making eye contact with our boss, he nodded, his voice strained as he spoke what I had been thinking, "A serial rapist."

"How do we know they're for sure all connected?" I asked, my eyes flicking back to the file in Jason's hand.

"We're not. But during the interview process, every woman described the exact same assailant. Male, late 30s, average height and build, black ski mask. He attacked them in parking lots at night outside of bars and clubs. The asshole also said the exact same thing to each woman. 'You're not her but you'll do.'"

"Fuck," Jason muttered under his breath. "These police reports are a mess, sir. It's like these dumbasses have never interviewed someone before."

He offered me a police report that was covered in chicken scratch. There was no way anyone would be able to decipher it.

"I know. All of the assaults happened outside our jurisdiction, so nothing I can do about it."

"Wait," I paused, peering over the reports at the captain. "How did we catch the case then?"

"A detective who was investigating one of the assaults noticed the similaities between all the cases. He took his suspicions to his captain. It became high profile after that, and the chief decided it needed to be reassigned to more *experienced* detectives. So here we are."

"I agree with Jason. These reports are a mess, sir." I tried to keep the edge out of my voice. Jason handed me several more papers, each worse than the last somehow. "Even if we had a suspect, there's no evidence. No prosecutor would take this to trial."

"Unfortunately, you're right," the captain said. "Which means..."

He didn't have to finish his sentence. Jason and I exchanged a knowing look.

In order to catch this guy, we had to hope another woman was assaulted and came forward so we could do things the right way.

*Fuck, I hated this.*

Sighing, I gave Jason back what I had in my hands and he took them, tucking everything back into the file.

Jason then stood, nodding to our boss. "We'll start putting together a profile based on what information we do have and reaching out to see who would be comfortable talking to us. Hopefully, it'll help make sure if he does this shit again, it'll be the last time."

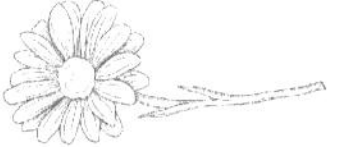

After some profiling and a few interviews scheduled, Jason and I went to a coffee shop down the street from the station to grab a bite to eat. Walking in, the smell of coffee beans hit me and I could feel the energy immediately course through my veins.

We ordered our things, then stepped aside to grab a table and wait. I pulled out my phone, checking to make sure there were no messages from Gwendalyn. Even though I knew she had everything under control and was putting space between us, I could still hope.

"Tony?" My head snapped up at Jason's voice. The concern on his face was genuine. "In all seriousness, how is she?"

"I don't know." Putting my phone back in my pocket, I tried to keep the frustration out of my voice as I replied, but Jason has always been able to read my body language. My nerves were on edge and it was evident by my bouncing leg.

I hadn't been able to sit still since comforting Gwendalyn on the kitchen floor. She was scared, which meant I wasn't doing my job. Add to that the fact that a trip to the warehouse hadn't happened since the day I hired her, and I was wound tighter than a Jack in the Box ready to pop open.

"Have you found the guy?" Jason asked.

"No. It's like he fell off the face of the planet," I groaned. "He hasn't used any credit cards and he must have a burner phone because finding a way to track him has been impossible. I had watched him leave that day, thinking I would be able to get a license plate, but all he did was walk." Bringing my hands up, I scrubbed my face, shoving down the darkness that was threatening to surface at the mention of this fucker.

At that moment, our names were called. Jason jumped up, mumbling he would get everything before walking away. I tracked him as he flashed the barista a wink before returning with our food and drinks, putting everything down on the table.

"The bright side is, Oliver's birthday has been a good distraction," I muttered, reaching for my coffee.

"Oh shit, I completely forgot about the little man's birthday! When is his party again?" Jason asked, inhaling his food.

"Saturday. Gwendalyn has the entire day planned, right down to the minute that I need to start cooking. Though I'm surprised she's letting me after the breakfast fiasco." I stared at my partner over my coffee cup. He laughed through the too large bite he had taken.

"Hey, I'd like to see you try to survive the hand I've been dealt, asshole," I scoffed at Jason, setting down my coffee and shooting daggers at him.

"I'd love to show you how it's done," he winked. "If I was pining over a woman like that and knew she had even a sliver of the same feelings toward me, I'd be claiming her."

"Well it's a good thing you are in fact not in my shoes right now."

"Maybe, but I may just have to shoot a shot with her on Saturday."

"You wouldn't dare." I narrowed my eyes at him, unsure if he was just messing with me  or not.

"Wouldn't I?" There was that shit-eating grin again. I swear...

I was about to respond when our phones went off simultaneously. Knowing fully well what the notifications meant, we grabbed our food boxes and coffee before heading out the door. Our phones rarely got notified at the same time unless we were on a case.

That meant the fucker had hurt someone... again.

# Chapter Fourteen

## Gwen

I was on edge for weeks after Matt's unwelcome visit, constantly waiting for the other shoe to drop. The texts, phone calls, and voicemails were constant for several days, and Ivy wanted me to file for a restraining order.

She also tried to get me to talk to Anthony, but I couldn't do it. Even though his reaction that day was full of genuine concern and him wanting to help, the anxiety that this fresh start could easily be taken away kept me from confiding in him.

I did my best to keep up happy appearances, especially in front of Ollie. It wasn't fair to him to let my own problems get in the way of my job, but I didn't want to potentially put him in danger. I focused on having playdates with other nannies in the area that Carol connected me with.

Katie, the next for neighbor who I met for a brief moment that day I "interviewed," introduced herself properly. I wasn't sure if Anthony said something to her, or if she witnessed what went down on the porch, but the day after everything happened, she came over with a plate of cookies and her little one on her hip. Katie was only a few years older than me, and we clicked instantly. We met up almost daily after that, and it helped my anxiety so much.

But I still had this feeling that I was being watched, and I hated it.

When Anthony asked me if I would want to plan Ollie's birthday party, I jumped at the opportunity to distract myself with something as joyful as celebrating the sweet boy who brought so much happiness in my life again.

Making my way up to Ollie's room, I carefully carried a large bag of balloons up the stairs. I spent most of last night and all this morning blowing them up. Today was all about Ollie, not all the crazy things that happened. The little man was turning three, and I was going to make it special.

He was still fast asleep when I slipped into his room. I was excited to see the joy on his face when he woke up to all the balloons. Silently, I began scattering the balloons around his room, keeping a few to toss into his crib with him once I woke him up. I couldn't help pausing the morning celebrations to watch him sleep for a few more minutes. The peaceful nature of toddlers when they slept was unmatched.

My heart hurt for Anthony as I looked down at his son. Our paths crossed a few hours ago when he got called in for a witness interview. He took the day off but that doesn't stop bad people from breaking the rules.

Curiosity had painted his features this morning as he gathered his things while I sat in the living room blowing up Ollie's balloons. I told him what I was doing with them, and that I had planned on including him once I got everything ready.

Guilt had flashed across his face, and I knew it was because he was missing out on these special moments with his son. I rushed to reassure

Anthony that this afternoon would be even more amazing and fun for Oliver.

He left without saying anything after that, and I did my best not to take it personally. Anthony had a lot on his mind.

Deciding it was time to wake Ollie, I tossed the last few balloons into the crib with him before rubbing his back to wake him up. "Ollie. Wake up, buddy."

Slowly, he turned over, colliding with a balloon that was bouncing around behind him. His eyes shot open and a huge smile spread across his face.

"Balloons!" Ollie grabbed one that had settled next to him and gave it a squeeze.

"Happy birthday, buddy!" Leaning over his crib, I lifted up him and his balloon, putting him on the floor amongst the dozens of others. Ollie's laughter filled the room as he began tossing one after another into the air. I joined in, sitting on the ground next to him as I grabbed a balloon nearby and tapped it with an open palm.

For just a moment, the world stopped turning. A perfect bubble of safety and love surrounded us. Something in my gut told me this was the first time either of us felt this way in a long time.

Gathering him up in my arms, I couldn't help but want to snuggle him, even with his protests of wanting to get back to the balloons. My gut twisted, remembering the countless number of fights I had with Matt about wanting to start a family, but I quickly pushed it down.

Today was Ollie's day, and I refused to let it be haunted by my past.

"Are you sure you have everything handled?" Standing on my tiptoes, I tried to peer over Anthony to see how everything was cooking. I was barely tall enough to see over his shoulder, my flats that I had paired with my short sleeve sundress not helping matters.

The weather ended up being the most perfect spring day, and I wanted to look nice. I had added leggings since chasing the tiny humans would be my main job today. Though now I was regretting the extra layer as a bead of sweat ran down my back. We were slightly behind according to the schedule I had made because of Anthony's late return home, but I reassured myself it would be okay.

I made sure to invite everyone on the street as well as many of the children and their families that Ollie and I saw on the regular. Anthony even invited some of his co-workers, especially ones with kids around Ollie's age. I wanted this party to be perfect in every way.

The little man deserves to feel celebrated and loved.

"Gwendalyn, I promise I have it handled." The frustration in his voice had me pulling away.

"I'm sorry. I know I'm being a nag," I mumbled. Turning around, I spotted Ollie playing with Katie's daughter and took a step to walk away when a hand grasped my upper arm.

My body went still, my heart racing as I slowly turned my head toward Anthony. He immediately released my arm, dropping his hand. My fingers twitched, wanting to reach out and hold it.

"I'm sorry," he offered, his eyes softening.

"It's okay." I tried to add reassurance to my words with a small smile.

"I know you want things to be perfect. Trust me when I say Oliver has not been this happy ever." He pointed to where Ollie was running around the yard laughing, a large smile on his face, when he stopped and waved to us. "You did that, Gwendalyn. None of this would have been possible without you. Our little family would not be complete without you."

His fingers interlocked with mine, giving my hand a quick squeeze before he released it and turned back to the grill. "Now, I need to make sure these burgers and hot dogs don't burn, or there may be a riot."

I chuckled as I walked away. Smiling at guests as I made my way through the yard, I tried to shove down the uneasy feeling rising from my stomach.

There was still so much anxiety surrounding Matt's sudden disappearance. I was on edge, waiting for him to do something. For so many years, I was convinced that what Matt had to offer was the best I could do. It was like I had been an observer of my own life.

Now, everything that I worked so hard to create for myself since I left was being threatened. I couldn't let this new life be ripped away from me.

Lost in my thoughts, I ran into a hard chest, and my body tensed as hands grabbed my upper arms and steadied me. Immediately, I pushed away, my chest rapidly rising and falling.

*So much for being able to keep my anxiety under wraps.*

"Easy there," he said. "I'm Jason, Anthony's partner." My eyes flew up, landing on the chiseled jawline of a man nearly twice my size.

His dark brown hair was pulled back into a small man bun, while the sides were shaven. His lips were formed into an easy smile. Movement caught my eye, and I followed it, finding his hand outstretched between us.

Taking it, I was caught off guard by the tattoos littering his forearm, my eyes drawn to a black and white vine of ivy. The leaves were weaved expertly around the other designs.

"You good?" he asked and I returned my gaze to his face.

"Oh, yeah," I gulped, releasing his hand and taking a step back. Jason rocked on his heels, tucking both of his hands into his pockets, looking down at me. "Sorry for my clumsiness. I'm Gwendalyn, but everyone calls me Gwen."

"Oh, I know who you are," he chuckled, adding a wink. My stomach fluttered, thinking about Anthony talking about me to his partner. It no longer felt like an elephant was sitting on my chest, knowing there was no way Anthony would invite him if he wasn't completely trustworthy. "Thanks for taking care of our guy. We both know he was a mess before you came into the picture."

My head turned, looking over my shoulder to eye Anthony still standing by the grill. He had taken off his apron and I could fully appreciate the way he looked in his tight-fitting polo and jeans. I had to force the drool to stay in my mouth.

As if sensing my eyes on him, he turned and his eyes searched the crowd until they landed on me. Jason and I were underneath the big tree that sat towards the middle of the yard near the fence line. I could just make out the corner of his mouth curling into a smile. My cheeks warmed and I swallowed, before shifting my gaze back to Jason.

"Well, someone had to do it," I laughed, thinking back to the frantic man I met a few months ago.

"Jason." Anthony's deep voice startled me, causing me to jump back into him. His hands came up to rest on my upper arms. His grip was gentle, just barely pressing into my skin.

*How the hell had he gotten over here so quietly? And quickly?*

Jason put up his hands in a defensive motion, putting even more space between us. "I was just introducing myself to your girl," Jason said, keeping his eyes on me. "It was great meeting you, Gwen. Hope we can chat more soon."

He looked over my shoulder, a silent communication going on between Anthony and him, before he turned and walked away.

I spun in Anthony's arms, ready to tell him off for whatever just happened, but was immediately distracted by his eyes burning into me. One of his hands rested on my cheek and I leaned into him. My skin warmed from his touch. His fingers trailed up and down my arm, and I practically melted.

Our embrace was intimate and my mind screamed at me to walk away, but my body wouldn't let me. We were avoiding each other, putting physical distance between us since that day in the kitchen.

But his was what I wanted and trying to deny myself this little pleasure was torture. His eyes softened, his lips parting as if he wanted to say something.

"Gwendalyn, I need to–" Anthony started, but our bubble was burst by the overexcited shriek of a woman's voice.

"Ollie, baby, come see mommy!" The shrill voice carried across the yard, silencing nearby conversations. Everyone turned their attention to the women standing over a frozen Ollie. Anthony's body tensed up, and I pulled my gaze away from the scene unfolding behind us to look up at him. His eyes darkened, his hand on my arm tightening.

"Anthony." I let out a strangled gasp as tears formed in the corner of my eyes.

Anthony's eyes were still on me, but it was like he was looking through me, not seeing what was right in front of me.

Before I could say anything else, he let go of my arm. The skin stung as I knew there would be evidence of this later. It didn't matter though.

Anthony ran toward the woman, who was now holding a fearful Ollie in her arms. I followed behind, reaching them just as Anthony pulled Ollie away from the woman. He pressed his trembling son into my arms with a look that told me everything I needed to know.

This wasn't going to end well.

I tucked Ollie in my arms, and backed up until I hit a hard chest. Jason stood behind me, his gaze trained on Anthony. He rested his hands on my shoulders, and I wanted to thank him.

"What the hell are you doing here, Kimberly?" Anthony's loud voice had me whipping my head back.

He was livid. The anger coming off him was palpable in the air. My heart rate increased, wanting to shrink and hide behind Jason.

Ollie's shaking body grounded me, and I squeezed him tighter as he buried his face into my neck. A sudden wetness on my neck told me he was crying. I debated if I should take him into the house when the woman Anthony referred to as Kimberly started screaming.

"It's my baby boy's birthday party! I'm his mother and I'm allowed to be here!" she screamed.

"You certainly are not! We haven't heard from you in two years. You need to leave now." Anthony placed himself between her and us, blocking my ability to see anything that was happening in front of him. Several of the cops in attendance stepped forward, everyone preparing to back up Anthony.

"No! I want to see my baby!" Kimberly shouted as she tried to get around him. Anthony put out his arm, blocking her attempt to get near us. She snapped, slapping Anthony across the face. Jason quickly shifted around me, rushing forward and grabbing her by the arm.

"Let go of me!" Kimberly's screams of protest were ignored as Jason dragged her toward the gate that led to the backyard. She wasn't going without a fit, kicking and slapping Jason wherever she could.

They paused and Jason looked down at her, his face hard and unwavering.

"There are about a dozen cops in this backyard alone and you just assaulted two of their fellow officers," Jason hissed. "Get back in your car and leave before one of them decides to arrest you." Her protests were muffled as Jason continued pulling her through the gate and out of view. Whispers filled the air, the tension slowly draining from everyone in the aftermath of what had happened.

Anthony had yet to turn around, still looking at the spot where Kimberly had been standing. I wanted to go to him, to wrap my arms around his waist. I could only imagine what was going through his mind right now, and I couldn't help feeling partially responsible for everything that just happened.

If I had walked away, then he wouldn't have been distracted when his ex-wife came into the backyard. Ollie wouldn't be sobbing in my arms right now. The party wouldn't be ruined.

Jason walked back into the yard and right up to Anthony's side, speaking to him in a hushed tone. Anthony turned his head toward Ollie and me, the rage on his face quickly melting away. He started toward us, and I was prepared to beg for forgiveness.

"Anthony, I'm so..." I started, but was quickly silenced when he cupped my face in his hands.

His lips found mine in a searing kiss that burned through my body.

I was too stunned to do anything more than let him in.

I wanted this.

I dreamed of this.

Everything else melted away and my heart hammered in my chest as Anthony deepened the kiss, shoving his tongue into my mouth.

It took every muscle in my legs to stay standing, remembering Ollie was still wrapped in my arms. *God, I needed him.* A rush of warmth settled throughout my body, the intimacy of this moment not lost on me.

Then his teeth caught my bottom lip, and I wanted to moan, to beg for more. I squeaked in surprise when the pleasure quickly turned to pain and I tasted blood. Anthony pulled away too fast, his eyes wide as regret washed over his face.

He dropped his hands, and stepped back. The loss of him against me sent a chill down my back.

Anthony turned, practically running out of the yard away with an intensity that had anyone standing near him to move away quickly.

All I could do was stand there.

"I have to go with him," Jason was standing in front of me, whispering as I blinked away the haze that followed Anthony's leaving.

Unable to form words, I nodded, then watched as he followed the same path Anthony had. Looking around at the guests still in the backyard, I plastered a smile on my face.

Everyone seemed to be politely ignoring the fact that some psycho woman had just crashed the party and the father of the birthday boy had kissed his nanny then made a hasty exit. Katie quickly walked up to me, offering me silent support as I tried to think of a game plan.

Ollie pulled away from me suddenly, his face red from his tears, and my heart broke. He looked at me as if waiting for answers to all the questions running through his little mind. *If only...*

Letting out a frustrated sigh, I wiped his tiny cheeks free of the stray tears and wrapped him up in a big hug.

"How about we pull out the cake and ice cream?" Katie suggested.

At the mention of sweets, Ollie wiggled out of my arms. The last few minutes were seemingly forgotten as he joined his friends in their chants for ice cream.

I turned to go inside to gather everything, but Katie caught me in an embrace of her own, tightly squeezing my arms. I squeezed my eyes shut to keep the tears that burned the back of my eyes from falling.

Katie let me go, turning her attention to the dancing turned mosh pit of tiny humans behind us. I walked inside, grabbing the kitchen island for support as my fingers brushed over my lips and a sob broke free.

# Chapter Fifteen

## Anthony

The darkness retreated when Gwendalyn was in my arms. It felt so natural, her body against mine. The way she melted into me, after everything she had been through. She trusted me...

And I had hurt her. Just like that fucked up ex of hers.

The whimper that escaped from her was burned into my mind, playing on a loop. The taste of her blood still clung to my tongue.

"Fuck!" I screamed, pounding my fists against the wheel of my truck.

The passenger door opened suddenly, and Jason climbed inside, not saying anything.

He didn't need to.

We both knew what was going through my mind right now. I needed to release the anger burning a hole inside me.

"Is there someone I can punch?" I asked him, my own voice foreign to me.

"Yeah." Out of the corner of my eye, I saw him doing something on his phone. Any other time, I would be curious. Not today. Not when I needed to shove *oscurità mia* back into its cage.

There was only one way to do that. I needed to give into the demand for violence, to feel blood on my hands.

I started the truck, and pulled out of the driveway. Jason probably should have driven, but the roads were quiet enough. We sat in silence on the drive.

The warehouse was quiet, and I walked through the halls on auto-pilot, straight to the room where we usually conducted our business. Turning through the doorway, I found a man tied to a chair with a rag shoved into his mouth. I made eye contact with the asshole, and there was fear in his eyes.

Good, he *should* fear me.

I yanked the rag out, and threw it on the ground. He tried to say something, but I landed a right hook to his jaw before any words could come out of his. His head flew to the side, blood instantly dripping from his lip.

Not wanting to give him any time to recover, I balled his shirt in my left hand and slammed my fist into his ribs over and over until the sound of them cracking had *oscurità mia* smiling.

My vision tunneled as I continued landing punches, alternating between his ribs and face, as I finally let the darkness take over. I felt the blood hitting my face and sweat running down my back, but it didn't matter. My focus never left the fucker in front of me.

*He deserved this.*

My knuckles started splitting, my own blood starting to mix with the fuckers in front of me as time slowed down and he became my own personal punching bag.

"Tony." I barely heard my name over the buzzing in my ears. I ignored it, continuing my assault, and landed a punch hard enough to the middle of the guy's chest that the chair tipped backwards. It fell with a deafening thud against the concrete.

Preparing to straddle him and continue, I was caught off guard when a hand on the back of my shirt yanked me backwards. Adrenaline still coursed through me, and my fist took a swing at the body in front of me, indifferent to who it was.

I was a bull loose in a china shop, simply thriving off the chaos around me.

The punch didn't land, so I charged, my body refusing to stop.

I was caught off guard when an arm wrapped around my neck. My chest heaved from the effort it took to take in air, and every hair on my body stood on end. My fingers clawed at skin.

Slowly, the darkness that was in charge retreated back into the recesses of my mind, the fog lifting as I stopped struggling.

Letting one of my hands fall, I slapped Jason's thigh twice. He released me and I stumbled forward, coughing and taking large breaths as my vision cleared.

My eyes followed Jason as he walked over to the asshole in the chair, checking to make sure he was still alive before kicking the chair so it and its occupant were on their side. I stepped backwards until I found myself hitting a wall. My legs unable to support me anymore without the adrenaline coursing through my veins, I sank to the floor.

My forehead rested against my knees, and my bruised hands sat on top of my head.

"You know you're going to have to explain to a lot of people what that kiss was about," Jason said. I lifted my head just enough to find Jason sitting next to me on the ground, his head resting back on the wall with his eyes closed.

"Shit," I mumbled.

Standing up, I paced the length of the room, running my hands through my hair in an attempt to keep them occupied and not throwing punches. The fact we had been standing in the middle of a crowd evaded me when I decided the best course of action would be to kiss Gwendalyn.

"It'll be okay, man. Gwen will understand, especially knowing that Kim is a crazy b…" Stopping in front of him, I looked down and he trailed off, my biggest mistake coming to light. A flicker of recognition crossed his face, and he voiced what I was unable to say. "She doesn't know, does she?"

I shook my head. The topic of Oliver's mom never came up. I gave Carol minimal details when I hired her to find a nanny and it was my assumption she passed those details on.

*What was Gwendalyn thinking right now? Oliver had to be upset that I left, right?*

Rage found its way to the surface again, and my fist made contact with the wall before I registered what I had done. Pain shot through my hand, my already bruised knuckles immediately swelling.

"Fuck!" I shook it, as if the action would magically cure the damage I just caused to my hand.

"Come on," Jason sighed. "I'll drive you to the ER and then home. My bike is still at your place, anyway." He stood up, reaching out his hand toward me. Digging into my pocket with my non-injured hand, I fished out my keys and handed them to him. Jason then walked out of the room and I trailed behind him, my mind flipping through potential stories for the doctor.

On the drive there, Jason broke the silence. "You like her. It's time you admitted it."

There was no use denying the feelings anymore. When I held Gwendalyn in my arms after warding Jason away, something inside me snapped into place. The way her body felt against mine was nothing short of perfection.

"When the divorce was finalized, I thought it would be Oliver and me forever, him and I against the world. Then Gwendalyn showed up, bringing so much love for Oliver and I wanted that for him. Someone to show him how a mother is supposed to love their child." Jason stayed quiet through my confession, giving me the opportunity to get everything off my chest.

"I was determined not to let my heart fall for another woman again. But damn it, Gwendalyn's filled this void inside of me. What if my darkness becomes too much, though? What if I hurt her? That asshole of an ex has already done enough damage. I refuse to do any more." As I finished, Jason pulled into the parking lot of the ER.

Turning off the truck, he paused before turning his head toward me. "You don't get to take the choice away from her because you're the one who's scared. Tell her, then let her decide."

"Oliver can't lose her, Jason. I can't lose her." I lowered my head, nearly accepting defeat.

"Trust me, you won't lose her by telling her what she needs to know. You'll lose her by pushing her away and not trusting her to do what's best for her," Jason said. I let his words sink in. Of course, he was right. Gwendalyn needed to make the choice, and I needed to let her. "Now, let's go get your hand looked at so you can go get your woman." He smirked at me, knowing that I couldn't punch him for his comment.

Jason grabbed my bag from my back seat, the one that held a change of clothes for moments exactly like this. He stepped out of the car, and I quickly stripped out of the blood stained clothes, changing into jeans and black t-shirt. I shoved the old clothes back into the bag to deal with later, then checked my reflection in the visor mirror for any blood on my face.

Satisfied I could pass my hand off as a workout gone wrong, I climbed out of my truck and met Jason by my tailgate. As we walked inside the all too familiar building, a thousand thoughts ran through my head. Each one of them connected to Gwendalyn and how she may react. I had to make peace with the fact that I may lose her after today...

But I sure as hell hoped I wouldn't

# Chapter Sixteen

## *Gwen*

Pulling a mug from the cabinet, I sat it on the counter while I waited for the kettle to boil. Anthony wasn't home yet and my nerves were getting to me. I wanted to finally get some sleep, but at the same time, I was wound too tight.

Oliver had gone to bed a few hours ago, the excitement from the day finally catching up to him. After cake and ice cream, Katie had helped organize presents as I sat with Oliver and helped him open them.

His smile as he ripped apart wrapping paper would forever be ingrained in my mind, the earlier events seeming to have had no lasting effects on him. I made sure to take plenty of photos, knowing Anthony might want to see them.

*Anthony...* My mind drifted to the kiss; the way he held me, and the way my body responded. It was him taking what he needed, and I happily gave it to him.

I had seen a darkness in his eyes, as if something was taking over. It should have scared me, but he had always been gentle with me, protective even.

The whistle of the teakettle pulled me from my thoughts. Grabbing a tea bag, I sat it in the mug before covering it with the hot water. Slowly, the water turned a light brown as I cupped the drink in my hands, letting the warmth flow through my body. Sipping it as I walked to the living room, one of the end table lights cast a soft glow across the space, lighting my way to the couch.

Sitting down, I tucked my feet under me and pulled a blanket over my lap, then exchanged the mug for my book that had been waiting for me next to the lamp. My mind drifted as I got lost in the fictional world. It didn't take long for my eyelids to get heavy, and instead of the characters in my book building a life together, it was Anthony and me.

A heavy warmth fell over my body and it had me relaxing further into the couch. A soft touch on my cheek made my eyes flicker open. My vision was blurry at first but blinking a few times, I saw a figure kneeling in front of me.

"Anthony?" I cleared my throat and noticed his outstretched arm, his hand still placed gently on my cheek.

"I'm so sorry, Gwendalyn." He went to stand, pulling his hand away, but I quickly grabbed it. Shifting up until I was sitting, the blanket that had been pulled up to my shoulders falling down to my lap.

I gently tugged his hand, urging him to sit down next to me. He sat, hanging his head and avoiding eye contact. My heart broke, feeling the sadness radiating from him.

I didn't know what to say, not able to find words good enough to comfort him. Instead, I reached out to grab his other hand when my fingers brushed over a brace.

"Anthony, what happened to your hand?" I questioned, trying not to freak out as I brushed my thumb over the swollen knuckles.

"It's not important," he mumbled, continuing to avoid my gaze.

We sat in silence for a few minutes, his hand still in mine. I wanted to push him for more details, but it seemed like he was working up the nerve to tell me something. His body was tense, and the leg closest to me was bouncing enough that it made my arm move.

"Kimberly and I met a few years after I got out of the police academy," Anthony started, taking a deep breath as if he needed to say everything at once or lose the battle he was fighting with himself. "We had our fights, like any relationship did, but I was in love. I wanted to make it work. We moved in together, got married, then she got pregnant. I thought we were okay.

"After Oliver was born, we were in a good enough place that we decided Kimberly could stay home with him. It had worked out, anyway, since I had just been promoted to detective and it made sense with my hours. I was dedicated to my work and did my best to be present for my wife and kid, but I saw some really awful things the first few months on the job."

I nodded my head in understanding, even though he wasn't looking at me. His focus was still down, staring at a spot on the rug, or maybe even his shoes.

"Kimberly used it as an excuse to constantly pick fights with me, claiming my lack of attention was obviously because I had found someone better to put my dick in. Defusing the situation never worked and at the end of the day, she refused to believe otherwise." He shifted his shoulders uncomfortably.

"Around Oliver's first birthday, I had made it a point to leave work early so I could show her I could be there for her. When I got home, I could hear Oliver screaming and crying from somewhere in the house. I was scared. When I found them, she was passed out on our bed with an empty bottle of vodka and a bag of pills thrown on the nightstand. Oliver was sitting in his crib in the corner of the room.

"Kimberly hid a lot of things from me during our marriage, including her excessive levels of drinking. If I had known, I would have never agreed to her being a stay at home mom. The only thing I ever wanted was the best thing for my family."

Anger was radiating from Anthony again, his body shaking. I should be scared, but he had never given me a reason to be. Not once had he raised his voice or put his hands on my body in any other way besides gentle and caring.

I let go of his hands, leaning forward and wrapping my arms around him from the side as I let my head rest against his shoulder. His shoulders relaxed as he sighed and muttered, "Is this too much?"

"No. I'm here, for as long as you want me to be," I whispered as I tightened my grip, my head never leaving his shoulders. He closed his eyes, his unwrapped hand coming up to hold on to my arm across his chest. The gentle squeeze sent a flutter through my stomach, hoping I was doing enough to help ease the pain he must be feeling.

His entire body rose with his next breath before he continued. "I was furious that Kimberly would be stupid enough to do something like this, but I had made sure she was breathing before I rushed to Oliver. Katie was the only person I thought to call, knowing she was home next door. I quickly found out that Katie had actually been the one watching Oliver all along, agreeing to do it because she and her husband were trying to start a family. Kimberly would call her soon after I left for work. She was never actually home alone with our son."

"Anthony, I'm so sorry. That should have never happened to you," I sighed.

"Instead of calling 9-1-1 like I had originally planned on doing, I woke her up by throwing her in a cold shower, then telling her she had forty-eight hours to get her stuff and leave. When she tried to protest, I told her I would have her arrested for child endangerment if need be. Obviously she was pissed by the entire situation, going so far as contacting my captain at work with made up stories. I served her with divorce papers shortly after and filed a motion with the court for sole custody, with no visitation. She didn't even bother showing up to the hearing, so it was an open and shut case. I hadn't heard a thing from her until today. In all honesty, I had hoped she was dead."

We sat in silence for quite some time following Anthony's confession, his head hanging from the weight of it all.

It broke my heart thinking about a baby Ollie sitting and crying for hours while the woman, who was supposed to love and protect him at all costs, was unconscious a few feet away. I could only imagine the confusion and despair Anthony must have been feeling when he went through all of that.

My own anger was settling in my body, the emotion so intense I thought my stomach was going to explode. I shifted my arms and moved until I was kneeling in front of Anthony, needing to focus on him to keep from letting my own emotions take over.

"Whatever you need, I will be here," I whispered, settling my hands on his knees as his face lifted to meet mine. His eyes were filled with sorrow. The happy man I knew only hours ago replaced by this dejected shell in front of me. "Anthony, we'll figure this out together."

"Gwendalyn, I can't ask you..." he started, but trailed off as my hand rested on his cheek.

"You said so yourself. I'm a part of the family now. Family takes care of one another." His hand found mine, our fingers intertwining. I became lost in his brown eyes, his scent occupying the space around us while my fingers twitched to run through his hair. My body was screaming for his lips to be on mine, for my tongue to dance with his.

"Gwendalyn..." The dark rich bass of his voice had wetness pooling in between my legs. Our bodies gravitated toward each other, his breath dancing across my skin. I was seconds away from climbing up onto his lap, pressing my body against his.

Then the all too familiar ringtone of his phone cut through the air. Immediately, I pulled away, returning to my place on the couch. Anthony kept his eyes on me, not saying a word, as he pulled his phone from his pocket.

"Marino," he gruffly answered. The emotionally vulnerable man that was sitting next to me was now gone, replaced by the professional Anthony ready to jump back into work whenever needed. As I continued holding space next to him, our eyes never leaving one another, his grunted replies and pinched eyebrows brought me comfort that maybe he found this call as ill timed as I did. "Be there in fifteen."

Anthony hung up, shifting to shove the phone back into his pocket. "I'm sorry, I have to go," he mumbled. He hesitated before standing, reaching out toward me with his hand slightly before quickly pulling it back.

The words he had trouble finding earlier still hang between us unsaid.

"I understand," I whispered, tearing my gaze from his, staring down at my hands. This was his job and being called out at the most inconvenient time to handle cases was a part of it. What was not a part of his job was comforting me, even if we were in a gray area with our professional relationship.

"Gwendalyn," Anthony cleared his throat, but I refused to look up at him. I would no longer be able to hold back the tears if I did. Thankfully, he didn't push a response, and I listened to his footsteps as he left the room, the front door closing harshly behind him.

The loss of his body next to mine left me feeling abandoned.

I was struggling to hold back the tears that burned the back of my eyes. As the loneliness set in my body, I knew it was time for bed. Sighing, I stood up, my eyes sweeping the room when they landed on a bouquet of daisies I hadn't noticed until now.

The tears silently fell as I picked them up. My heart pounded in my chest thinking about Anthony buying me these flowers, my favorite flowers.

Not taking my eyes off the petals, I grabbed my forgotten mug off the end table, walking to the kitchen to dump out the now cold contents.

The irony of Anthony doing exactly what Matt used to do was not lost on me.

There was a part of me that wanted to throw away the bouquet. Instead, I pulled the vase from under the sink, placing the daisies in it, then set it on the kitchen island.

Anthony was different. He hadn't come home with empty promises and flowers that I was allergic to. The daisies were a little reminder that even if he couldn't say the words, Anthony cared.

I dragged myself down to my room, wiping my face as I sat on my bed and deciding to see if Ivy was still awake. She always knew exactly what to say. I missed her like crazy, and I wanted to tell her about everything. There had been so much that happened today.

I had left my phone off and in my room this morning to avoid the distraction through the day. Clicking on her contact, she answered quickly, switching over to a video call before I could even greet her. As it opened, I could tell she had her phone propped up on the kitchen counter as the screen showed a view of cooking at her stove. She didn't look at the screen right away, her eyes glued to whatever she was making.

"Hey babe! How was the little man's party?" She glanced at the screen and her face lit up with a smile.

"The party was so much fun. Ollie crashed hard tonight," I laughed, thinking about how he had barely kept his eyes open through bath time. He was curled up with his stuffed bear and snoring before I had even shut the door. "How's everything going there?"

"Oh, you know," she said, waving around the spoon in her hand when she replied. "Same old, same old. Nothing new or exciting happening here. How about you?"

"Well, Anthony may have kissed me...?" I whispered.

"I'm sorry, what?" Ivy's screech echoed through the phone. She dropped the utensil and snatched up her phone, holding it in front of her face. "I need details, babe!"

"I don't know where to start..."

"Um, at the beginning? Duh!"

"His non-invited ex-wife showed up to the party," I started, "and Anthony was livid. It caused a whole scene. His partner dragged the ex-wife out before things went too far south, but Anthony wasn't okay. There was just something in his eyes I can't explain. But then he kissed me, and it was like I could feel it draining out of him. I mean, that kiss was..." My voice softened, disappearing entirely as I recalled the way my body lit up when his teeth sank into my lip.

The emotional high I felt was addictive. I had been surprised by my body's reaction, but Anthony must have taken it as a rejection from me. The remorse in his eyes when he pulled away shattered me.

"Gwen?" Ivy pulled me from my thoughts. I ran my finger along my bottom lip

"He didn't stick around. He left and his partner went with him. I'm not sure where, but when he came home a bit ago, he had a brace on his hand and a bouquet of daisies. We sat on the couch and he told me what had happened with his ex-wife. It felt like there had been more he wanted to tell me, but then he got called into work."

"Are you okay?"

"I'm so confused, Ivy," I sighed. "This man is infuriating most times and when he's not, my mind can't stop picturing the things he'd do with that mouth. But what if I'm not good enough? What if I end right back at square one?"

"Bullshit. That man lives for you," Ivy said. I scuffed, but she continued. "Talk to him. Tell him how you feel. Or I will hop on the first flight there and force you two to have a conversation."

"Fine," I muttered, curling up on my bed. I faced my nightstand, propping my phone up against the lamp.

Ivy's features softened, giving me a second to settle before she talked again. "Everything will be okay. Even if it doesn't seem like it now. Do you want me to stay on until you fall asleep? I need to finish making my late-night snack." All I could do was nod my head as I grabbed a pillow to hold against my chest and pulled my bedding over me.

Ivy sat her phone down and went back to cooking. I watched her moving around her kitchen as my eyelids started getting heavy. Letting them fall, I hoped that when I woke up in the morning, everything would have magically fixed itself.

# Chapter Seventeen

## Anthony

"Here you go, man." Jason offered me a mug of black coffee courtesy of the ancient coffee pot from the break room. It produced the worst tasting coffee known to man, but, at this point, all I cared about was the caffeine content.

I took the mug from him, chugging nearly half of the scalding liquid before sitting it down. After we met at the hospital and found the survivor was not awake, we gathered what we needed from the staff to start our report before heading to the station.

It was the middle of the night, so most of the other detectives were home. There were a few unlucky ones like us who were still here, flipping through case files and trying to find leads.

"Whoever this guy is, he's escalating." Jason sat his own mug down on his desk across from me before lowering himself into his chair.

I grunted a response, and ignored his eyes on me as I flipped through the case file in front of me. I flexed the fingers of my bruised hand, thankful the bones weren't broken. The doctor wanted me to wear a brace for a few weeks, but gave me the okay to take it off as needed for hygiene purposes.

As if I needed one more thing added to my list of shit to deal with.

We needed to catch the asshole responsible for terrorizing all these women. The case constantly pulled me away from Oliver and Gwendalyn. I promised her we would deal with her past together, but so far, she was handling everything alone.

At the very least, she deserved a night off.

"Shit Tony, did she reject you?" he asked.

That caught my attention, my head snapping up to glare at him from across our desks.

Jason didn't back off, though. He continued to look at me with a smirk on his face as he leaned back in his chair, putting his hands behind his head. Jason was a cocky asshole when he wanted to be, and right now, he wanted to rub my inability to tell a woman how I felt in my face.

"For your information, we were in the middle of talking when I got the call. The only thing I was able to tell her about was Kimberly," I said with annoyance.

"You chickened out." Jason laughed, and I talked myself out of chucking my stapler at his head, choosing to instead move my focus back to the file.

It was always easiest to ignore Jason's childish taunting, even if he *was* right.

I should have been able to tell her. But there was something about the way she was kneeling in front of me, the sadness in her eyes. No woman had ever looked at me that way.

It scared the shit out of me.

The words got stuck as I second guessed myself. What if I said the wrong thing and scared her off?

"Let me scour through the case file, man. You need to go home and beg for forgiveness after the shit you put her through today. I'm tired of working with your lovesick ass, especially when all of this could be easily solved by you just telling her how you feel."

"Fine," I grumbled. Standing, I gathered what I needed to head out without looking in Jason's direction. Whatever look he had on his face would make me want to punch him, and I needed to stay focused.

When I finally made my way home, the house was dark. No doubt Gwendalyn went to bed long ago. Before I could talk myself into going back to the station, I forced myself to go inside. At the very least I could grab a shower after the shit storm of a day.

But I couldn't get my feet to take me upstairs.

I needed to at least see her.

A million thoughts were running through my head, my nerves standing on edge as I treaded lightly down the stairs. I made my way down the hallway, but froze before I could step into the room.

*What the fuck am I doing? This is creepy as hell.*

Not caring, I took a few steps forward, but stayed near the edge of the room. My heart skipped a beat when I saw her curled up under the blankets, clutching a pillow to her chest. Her phone was propped up on the nightstand and I wondered what she was doing before she fell asleep.

"No... please..." she whimpered softly in her sleep, and it took every ounce of control to not immediately rush forward to comfort her. I held my breath as she turned over in her sleep, only releasing it when she settled back into sleep. My arms ached to hold her, to chase away whatever was haunting her dreams, but I forced myself to walk away.

*Oscurità mia* wanted to play and if I lost control, there was no telling what would happen.

On autopilot, I made my way up to my bathroom, and turned on the shower. My clothes ended up in a pile on the tile and I tossed the brace for my hand next to the sink. Hot water hit the muscles on my back as I stepped under the stream of water. The warmth relieved some of the tension as I ran my fingers through my hair, pushing the wet strands back and out of my face.

Frustration bubbled to the surface as I tried to sort through the countless emotions going through my head. Mostly guilt for not setting expectations with Gwendalyn earlier.

I was playing with her emotions by not telling her how I feel and not allowing her to actually decide. Just because she kissed me in a moment of weakness doesn't mean I get to take advantage and push myself on her. My dick had been doing all the thinking lately, and that needed to change.

She deserved better.

I couldn't deny the way she made me feel, though. Just the thought of her drove the darkness inside of me wild with lust. The way her body felt pressed up against mine was imprinted in my mind.

But I wanted to know what it would feel like to have her body underneath me in my bed. Her hand wrapped around my cock while my hands explored every inch of her body.

My uninjured hand traveled down to my stiffening cock before I registered what was happening. I was fisting it and pumping harshly while I thought about how it would feel to have *luce mia* under me.

The soft flush of her skin.

Her breathy moans.

Her eyes burrowing into my soul.

My motions became desperate, and leaned on my forearm to stay upright.

I was a teenager again, being touched for the first time, unable to hold back my release.

My head fell forward as I coated my hand. My heart pounded in my chest, and I squeezed my eyes shut.

*Fucking hell.*

Pushing off the wall, I turned the water as cold as it would go and punished myself with a freezing shower for what I just did.

I needed to stop.

Gwendalyn deserved more than what I had to offer her. It wasn't fair of me to drag her into my life. There was a piece of me that knew she had every right to make that choice on her own. But if she decided she didn't want me, would I actually be able to let her go?

"Fuck!" Jason swiped his desk and sent files flying into the air. His outburst hadn't surprised me in the least.

He never was the level-headed one in this partnership, and frustration with hard cases became much more apparent when he didn't have the time to teach dirtbags lessons.

Over the last two weeks, the assailant had escalated out of control. Since the first survivor that was found unconscious, we've had to interview half a dozen more, each one with increasing signs of abuse. The one we talked to just a few hours ago had been found in the parking lot of Debbie's, a local bar, a little after sunrise. She had been drugged, horribly beaten, and sexually assaulted.

Jason had done his best to make her comfortable in our presence, but ultimately, we had to have a female detective gather a statement from her. There was no way I could blame her after everything she went through.

The asshole doing all this was smarter than we originally thought. He had yet to leave behind any fingerprints and must be using condoms, because we never find DNA evidence with the rape kits.

I watched Jason collect the discarded files before tossing them haphazardly onto his desk. Putting on his leather jacket from the back of his chair, he pulled his bike helmet out of a drawer in his desk before leaving without a word to me.

I knew where he was going.

Even though I wanted to follow, Gwendalyn texted me this morning and asked if I would be home this evening so she could make plans with a friend. She deserved the break, and I couldn't deny her wanting to spend time with someone other than Oliver, so I told her I would be home before dinner. Looking at my watch, I noticed it was quarter-after-four, so I gathered my own things and headed home.

As I walked through the garage door, I hadn't expected the kitchen to be filled with the wonderful smell of a baked lasagna. It was cooling on the stovetop, and I could hear Oliver laughing.

Following the sound to the living room, Gwendalyn was sitting crossed legged with her back to me, her hair flowing down her back. The urge to fist those waves in my hands, and claim her mouth for the first time since Oliver's party, was getting harder and harder to ignore.

The decision to revisit this attraction after this case was solved and the dust settled was a solo one. It only made it harder on myself to stay away.

There was no denying my body's reaction to her.

Torture. This was absolute torture.

Watching for a few minutes more, a soft giggle came from her as Oliver chased down one of his trains that had gone off track. My heart nearly beat out of my chest at the sound. I would dedicate my entire life to hearing her laugh more often. As Oliver finally caught his train and Gwendalyn relaxed again, I cleared my throat, causing her to jump and whip her head around to face me.

"Cheese and crackers, Anthony. You gave me a heart attack." Gwendalyn pressed a hand against her chest as she stood. "Ollie, your dad is home!"

Oliver quickly abandoned his train, running toward me at full force. I easily caught him, and lifted him up so he could throw his arms around my neck.

"Daddy, I helped make dinner. I spread sauce and sprinkled cheese." His pride was evident in his wide eyes as he smiled at me.

"That's amazing, *figlio mio*. Why don't you go get cleaned up for dinner?" I squeezed him a little tighter before releasing him and letting him run off.

"Dinner is ready," Gwendalyn started. I tried to focus on the words coming out of her mouth, but my dick was doing all the thinking. As I stared at her lips, I wanted to know how they would feel wrapped around my cock. She kept talking as I shifted, hoping she wouldn't notice my growing erection. "I blended a bunch of veggies to add to the sauce, so it should be a relatively balanced meal, if that's all he eats. There's some garlic bread in the freezer that shouldn't take more than a few minutes to cook. I didn't want them to get cold before you got home."

"Thank you," I said. I wanted to reach out and touch her, my hand almost acting of its own free will as she made her way toward me. At the last moment, I shoved my hands into my pockets and moved out of her way. As she started gathering her things, I followed behind her, wanting to enjoy her presence for a little longer. "So, um, where are you going?"

She stopped near the front door and turned, her mouth opened slightly as if she was thinking about what to say. "Oh, um, I'm meeting a friend at a bar. I think it's called Debbie's."

My stomach dropped at that name and a chill ran down my back. Only one thought went through my mind...

I couldn't let her leave.

"You can't go," I blurted it out as she grabbed the doorknob, not knowing what else to say. She turned, her eyebrows raised as she stared at me. My mind started going through possible excuses I could get her to stay home.

"Excuse me?" She didn't have the patience for my bullshit, standing by the door with her arms crossed.

"You can't go to that bar," I repeated myself. She stayed silent, waiting for me to say something else. I couldn't tell her the truth, but lying to her didn't feel right. "Jason told me about something that happened there last night. I don't think it's safe."

Was it likely this dumbass would be at the same place twice? No, it didn't seem like his motive. But that didn't stop me from wanting to make sure Gwendalyn was as far away as possible from this case.

"I think I'll be fine," she chuckled, her hand turning the knob.

Images of her beaten, in a hospital bed, flashed in my mind.

The darkness took over.

"What the hell is wrong with you?" Gwendalyn hissed at me.

I blinked down at her, and found my hand around her wrist. I crossed my hand over, pulling hers from the doorknob. She ripped it from my grasp before looking up at me, fury filling her eyes.

"Call your friend and tell her you'll meet her at her place or she can come here." As I towered over her, she flinched slightly, pulling away enough so that there was space between us.

I was crossing a line, breaking her trust.

But I couldn't back down.

I had to keep her safe.

"Anthony, this is ridiculous," she huffed, her voice raising. "I'm leaving and meeting my friend. You don't get to tell me what to do."

"I do if you refuse to put your safety first, Gwendalyn," I growled. It took everything inside of me not to blurt out the real reason I wanted her to stay home, but putting that unbearable weight on her would be unfair of me.

"Is that so?" She kept her voice low. A fire lit in her eyes. She shoved her finger into my chest, emphasizing her next point as she found her confidence. "You kissed me, and then left me. Any time I've tried to have a conversation with you, you've ignored me. So no, Anthony, you don't get a say. Now, move."

Her words hit me in the gut.

She was right, of course. I was too scared, too in my own head, to simply talk to her. She pulled her hand away from my chest, taking several steps backwards and crossing her arms across her chest while she waited for me to move.

I was proud of her, but that wasn't going to stop me.

My vision darkened on the edges as I stalked toward her. My hands pressed against the wall behind her, pinning her against it. Our eyes never left each other.

"Daddy, I'm hungry!" The words registered, but the voice didn't, my mind still fogged by the infuriating woman in front of me.

"Oliver is calling for you," Gwendalyn whispered.

Her words lifted the haze. I turned my head, ready to call out to Oliver, when Gwendalyn slipped under my arm. Bolting for the front door, she wretched it open and left without looking back. The slam that followed echoed through the house, making my stomach drop.

I had just royally fucked up.

# Chapter Eighteen

## Gwen

The place was way more packed than I expected it to be. Silently, I wondered if Anthony's warning was actually true, but quickly dismissed the thought. Bars get busy. What's the worse that can happen?

Making my way toward the small crowd, I spotted Carol on a stool with a pint glass already in her hand. As I reached her, she jumped off her chair and threw herself at me to give me possibly the biggest hug I had ever received.

"Gwen! I'm so glad you could make it!" She pulled away and sat down, gesturing with her hand to the empty stool next to her as she flagged down a bartender. "We're doing a round of shots. It's been a week." Looking over her shoulder toward me, she rolled her eyes, telling me exactly how she felt and I couldn't help my laugh. Carol could never replace Ivy, but she became such a close friend since I moved to Chicago.

The bartender stood in front of us, and Carol ordered three shots of tequila. I was about to ask her why we needed three when she turned to me again. "I've already had one, so you need to catch up."

When the bartender was done pouring, he sat a few lime slices on a plate in front of us. Carol gave him the name for her tab, then slid two of the glasses over to me. We clinked the first ones together before I quickly downed it, opting to do the second one before the first even settled.

I shoved a lime in my mouth, letting the tart liquid chase the tequila. Carol laughed at the sour expression on my face. My own laughter joined hers as I discarded the lime into my shot glass.

When the bartender came back to pick up our shot glasses, I ordered a hard cider after Carol insisted I let her buy me a drink since she invited me out. We fell into an easy conversation about how life was going as we sipped on our drinks and enjoyed each other's company.

Several hours later, the buzz from the tequila had slowly waned as the bar continued to get more crowded. Carol and I were clutching our chests with laughter after eavesdropping on two dudes trying to hit on a couple of women seated a few seats down from us at the bar and getting brutally rejected.

In the middle of our laughing, the sound of a faint ringtone sounded and Carol pulled out her phone. Soon after answering, she stopped laughing as concern warped her expression. After she hung up, she continued to sit frozen, as if unsure what to do next.

"Carol? Is everything okay?" I asked. I placed my hand on hers and she looked up from her phone.

"My next-door neighbor is in the hospital. I'm her emergency contact, so they just called me," she said, pulling away to gather her things.

"Oh no! Do you need me to call someone? I can come with you…"

"No, I'll be okay. I'm going to walk. The hospital isn't too far from here and the fresh air will help. I'm so sorry I have to cut our evening short, love."

"Don't be sorry," I said. Carol practically threw herself from her chair before I could say anything else.

"I'll text you," she called over her shoulder as she rushed out of the bar.

I waved after her, not sure she actually saw it. My half finished drink was staring at me as I debated whether to stay or head home.

Not wanting to deal with Anthony's strange behavior, I decided to stay, even going so far as to flag down the bartender to order one more shot. After I did, I sat waiting with my hands wrapped around my pint glass when a man came up beside me.

Thinking he was just waiting for the bartender, I didn't acknowledge him, but when the bartender came back with my shot, he didn't order anything. Instead, he cleared his throat, grabbing my attention.

"Did it hurt when you fell, angel?" His low voice paired with his heated gaze mesmerized me. Instead of withdrawing from the unwanted attention of this stranger, something inside me pushed to indulge his advance.

Maybe it was last drops of alcohol giving me a boost. Maybe it was the leftover confidence from telling off Anthony. Either way, who was I to deny someone who wanted to show me some attention, the pleasure of doing just that.

"Excuse me?" I couldn't help but chuckle at his cheesy line. He leaned against the bar, his arm now extended in front of me, and I took a second to admire the shape of his muscles that were defined under the stretch of his shirt.

"From heaven, of course." His half smile held a mystery that had me practically melting in his presence. "How about I buy you a drink?"

"I have one." I pointed behind him at the full shot glass. He smirked before twisting to reach for it. Out of his gaze, I tilted my head to admire the muscles in his back, my eyes landing on his ass. Men in jeans would always be a weakness. Too soon, he turned back to me, my shot glass in his hand and I took it from him, quickly downing the liquid. His eyes held a hint of surprise.

"What, never seen a woman drink tequila?" I said, sitting the glass on the bar.

"Not without making a face," he chuckled.

"Well, I'm different." My cheeks warmed as he held my gaze and the liquid worked its way down.

"You definitely are." His eyes darkened as he spoke and my stomach twisted, the confidence I was feeling moments ago wavering as the sounds around me started to muffle.

That was probably one shot too many. My stomach was not happy.

"Excuse me. I need to go to the bathroom." Slipping from the stool, my legs were unsteady as I stood.

The man was blocking my path, and I tried to push past him, placing my hand on his chest. His hand flew up to grab my wrist, tears springing to my eyes as his nails dug into my skin.

Adrenaline spiked through my body as I pushed against his chest, trying to put distance between us and a wicked grin grew on his face. Using his grip on me, the man pulled me against his chest, dipping his head down so his mouth was inches from my ear. My stomach rolled, feeling his hot breath.

"I can see why he's so interested in you." His nose running along my ear sent a single chill down my spine.

"Let go of me!" Pulling my head away from him, I struggled against his hold as I tried to figure out how to get out of this situation. My stomach continued doing flips, the night's drinks threatening to make a reappearance when I acted on instinct. Bringing my knee up as hard as possible, I struck the man in his balls, and his grip on me instantly loosened.

"What the hell is happening over here?" Throwing a quick glance over my shoulder, the bartender was wiping his hands on a rag behind the bar.

*Where had he been he five minutes ago?*

Slipping past the man still doubled over in pain, I pushed past several groups of people, heading toward the front door. I could hear the bartender calling after me, but I needed to leave. As I stepped outside into the fresh air, I gripped the side of the building as tears pooled in the corners of my eyes, a few escaping down my cheeks. The adrenaline that coursed through me only seconds ago was nowhere to be seen.

My chest tightened as I placed a hand on my stomach, willing my turning stomach to settle and forcing air into my lungs. Pulling myself together, I found my way to my car in the back of the lot, cursing every few feet as I stumbled and fought to stay upright.

My head swam as I gripped the handle of my car. Something was wrong. There was no way I was this drunk, at least not that quickly after having a shot.

Dropping my hand from the handle, I reached into my bag to find my phone, nearly dropping it when I pulled it out. My only option was to call an Uber... or maybe Anthony?

Pulling up his contact on my phone, my thumb hovered over the dial button. I hesitated for a moment, thinking back to our conversation before I left. He had been trying to intimidate me, and Gwen from six months ago would have let him. But I had found confidence in myself since then, proud of the fact that I wasn't going to let a man control me or my decisions.

Just as I was about to push the call button, a hard body pushed me up against my car, causing me to drop my phone. A large hand slapped over my mouth. My scream was muffled as I tried to push against my attacker. My hands shoved on their chest while I willed my legs to cooperate so I could run.

My wrists were quickly captured and pinned above my head as a deep chuckle came from under the mask at my weak attempts to escape.

Hoping someone would hear the commotion and run over, I tried to scream again, but quickly realized I couldn't, as if someone had shoved a wad of cotton into my mouth.

My knees collapsed underneath me, my body being held up by my pinned hands. My arms screamed in protest from the weight. As my attacker dropped their hand from my mouth, moving it down my body and stopping at the top of my waistband, I realized that I must have been drugged.

Pure terror filled my body, tears stinging the back of my eyes. Forcing air into my lungs was becoming increasingly difficult, and panic clawed at my throat. Calloused fingers dug into the skin around my hip, roughly kneading my flesh until it felt raw. They leaned closer, the fabric of the mask rubbing against my neck.

"There's no reason we can't have a little fun…" Although muffled slightly by the mask, the deep voice sent a wave of panic through my body, a familiarity to the voice that my drugged brain couldn't place.

He pulled away from my neck, stopping only inches away in front of my face as his dark eyes stared into mine. A single spike of adrenaline had my head flying forward as I tried to make contact with any part of the asshole's face, not caring that I had no idea what I was doing. But my body was easily thrown to the ground. Unable to catch myself, the back of my head made contact with the concrete as my arms and legs laid in various directions, unable to move.

"Fucking bitch…" A rough hand on my face forced rocks to dig uncomfortably into my cheek, and the angle made it even harder to breathe. My head was swimming as another hand yanked at the waistband of my pants before undoing the bottom, while a knee was shoved into the already tender skin around my hip, effectively pinning my legs open. "You want it rough, don't you?"

Fingers shoved into me under my pants while the hand on my face released, making its way down to my thigh where fingertips dug into my skin. "See, baby, you like this. Your pussy wants this." I wanted to scream that it hurt, to beg for him to stop.

And I did, but the words wouldn't come out. They were trapped in my head.

I willed my arms or legs to move, trying to remember to breathe through all of it. Tears ran down my cheeks in hot streams as he continued working his fingers in and out of me, my pants shifting down my hips as a wetness that I don't think was arousal dripped down my exposed sex.

Abruptly, wet fingers gripped my throat and my thigh was released. My pants were crudely yanked further down as my airway was slowly cut off.

I closed my eyes and begged for whatever drug was in my system to finally take hold as the faint sound of a zipper pierced the buzzing in my ears. Struggling to take in a deep breath, Oliver's giggles floated through my mind, blocking out whatever else was happening.

*If something happened to me, what would Oliver think? Would he understand?*

My heart broke at the thought of that sweet boy losing another person from his life as the squeal of tires had my eyes fluttering open, watching as the man on top of me looked over his shoulder and cursed.

The grip on my throat released, and I choked on an intake of air. My vision swam, darkness creeping in at the edges as my attacker ran in the opposite direction of the approaching vehicle.

The headlights illuminated the area as a door opened and footsteps bounded toward me. Someone was kneeling near my head, their shadow covering my exposed body. A voice spoke, sounding gargled, as if I was underwater trying to hear them.

A gentle hand rested on my cheek as my eyelids became too heavy, my body numb to the world around me. Letting them close, a familiar voice broke through the haze just before the darkness finally pulled me under.

"I've got you, *luce mia*."

*Anthony...*

# Chapter Nineteen

## Anthony

I closed the door to Oliver's bedroom and let out a huge sigh of relief. That kid was a master negotiator. Technically, it could be considered my fault, since I found it really hard to tell him no when he asked for one more story. Gwendalyn had been the one putting him to bed recently with this new case, so I never minded a couple extra books. That meant more snuggles.

Looking down at my watch, I noticed the time—nearly ten. I was mentally kicking myself for the fight with Gwendalyn. Maybe trying to tell her what to do was a bad idea, but when she said the name of that bar, something inside me snapped.

My instincts were telling me something bad was about to happen and I had no control of the situation. Hell, I didn't even know when she would be home. The only thing I knew was I needed her to be safe. *Oscurità mia* was screaming at me to go to that bar, and drag her home if need be.

Walking to the kitchen, I pulled a beer out of the fridge, taking a swig of it before pulling out my phone. Drafting an email to the tech guy at work who owed me a favor, I would figure out a way to track her phone and give myself some peace of mind.

*You were still an asshole, though.* Exhaling, I took another drink, debating if I should pull out something stronger. This was going to be a long night of self-hatred, and I might as well do it while drinking the good stuff.

Just then, my phone vibrated in my hand, and Gwendalyn's name flashed on the screen as an incoming call. Maybe the universe was giving me a chance to make things right.

"Gwendalyn?" The line was quiet, and it crossed my mind that this was more than likely a butt dial. My heart sank at the thought that she didn't intentionally call me, but I didn't hang up right away, listening closely for any sign that Gwendalyn was on the other end. I just wanted to hear her voice. Instead, the voice I heard had me running to grab my gun and badge before I sprinted across my lawn to Katie's house.

"There's no reason we can't have a little fun..."

Katie saw the panicked look in my eyes and was putting on her shoes to head to my house before I could get a word out. I broke numerous traffic laws racing across town to get to the bar. Pulling into the parking lot, I spotted her car in the back of the lot and slowed down as I drove back to it, scanning the shadows for her.

All rational thought went out the window when I spotted her unmoving body laying on the concrete next to her car. My truck was barely in park when I threw myself out of it, running to her.

"Gwendalyn!" I kneeled next to her, silently begging for some kind of response. But her head was lulled to the side, blood caked her hair, and her eyes were glazed over. "Gwendalyn, I'm here, okay?"

Pulling out my phone, I called for an ambulance, and I scanned her body. Blind rage coursed through me when I noticed her pants were pulled down. I shrugged off my jacket while I talked to the dispatcher. Not wanting to risk moving her and causing further harm, I draped it over her legs.

My hand rested on her cheek, needing her to know it was me, needing to ground myself.

"I've got you, *luce mia*. You're safe," I whispered. Gwedalyn's eyes drifted shut, and my chest tightened.

My brain was going through worse case scenarios as I sat with her, waiting for the ambulance that I swore I called hours ago. It took every bit of strength I had to keep the darkness locked away. I whispered to her over and over that I was there. It was the only thing I knew to do. My body ached to wrap her in my arms, to protect her when I knew it was my fault she was in this position.

The sound of the ambulance approaching pulled me from my thoughts, and I moved out of the paramedics' way when they rushed over. As they worked on her, I moved my truck to an empty spot, having stopped in the middle of the lot.

Everything that followed happened in slow motion. In the ambulance, I sat at the end of the gurney on the way to the hospital, my hand resting on her ankle while I rubbed it with my thumb. I felt useless, but needed to be touching her, needed her to know I was still there with her.

The steady rise and fall of her chest gave me hope that she was okay.

Until her heart rate spiked. Her body flailed, pushing and shoving at an imaginary force. Her eyes were open, but she wasn't seeing what was right in front of her.

"Let me go!" she screamed. Tears streamed down her face. My lungs stopped working. "Let me go!"

"Mrs. Marino, you're okay. I'm a paramedic." The man next to me did his best to calm her, but she was thrashing. Gwendalyn was going to hurt herself, or one of us.

Flashes of baby Oliver sitting in his crib screaming and crying were at the forefront of my mind. I fixed his pain. I got rid of the person who caused him pain. I made things better. But right now...

I was helpless.

"Do something," I growled. My own voice was foreign to me. The paramedic threw a look over his shoulder, one that told me to let him do his job.

He pulled a vial out of the cabinet, drew the medicine into a syringe, then pushed it into her IV. Her screams quieted almost immediately. Her body stilled, and her eyes fluttered closed.

"Anthony..." My name on a whisper, just loud enough to cause my heart to shatter.

"I'm right here." The reassurance was more for me than her. Silence filled the vehicle after that. No traffic, no horns, just the soft, steady beeping that I forced myself to focus on.

When we arrived at the hospital, a trauma team rushed her back to a room while I was directed to a waiting area. I paced the length of the room so many times I lost count.

Everything was numb.

Those screams, the fear in her eyes, I knew what it all meant. Whoever hurt her would suffer a pain worse than death.

Minutes turn into hours. Nurses and doctors passed the doorway, but no one stopped. I was half a second away from demanding answers when a petite blonde nurse stepped into the room. I stopped in front of her, silently demanding answers.

"Mr. Marino?" She didn't even look me in the eye as she spoke. I resisted the urge to through my arms up into the air, and look around me. This was procedure after all, but seriously... There was no one else in this fucking room, but me.

"Yes," I answered, not bothering to keep my voice pleasant.

"Your wife is settled in a room. I can... um, take you back to her." I nodded in response, and gestured with my arm for her to lead the way. She turned on her heel, tablet flush against her chest, and started walking.

My heart hammered in my ears as I followed. We stopped outside a room with an open door. Muffled voices came from inside. A nurse and doctor were standing at the foot of the bed, looking down at a tablet. They shifted as I stepped into the room, and my stomach sank seeing Gwendalyn lying in the bed.

Her head was wrapped, and bruises painted the side of her face. She looked so small, the white sheet and blanket swallowing her frame. A burning in the back of my throat made it hard to breath. My hands clinched into fists at my sides.

The doctor stepped in front of me, and introduced himself. I looked past him, unable to take my eyes away from the woman I cared about. He spent what felt like an eternity updating me, but my gaze never left Gwendalyn.

While examining her, they found a sizable gash on the back of her head. A CT scan discovered there were no major complications. They stitched up the wound, and were hoping for minimal scarring. There was bruising on her abdomen and along her legs, too.

Because she was currently unconscious, there was no way to tell for sure the full extent of her injuries and they weren't able to collect evidence of assault until she woke up to consent. But the doctor was hopeful for no permanent damage from the head wound. They would give her a few hours to hopefully wake up on her own from the sedative she was given en route. Until then, they would run her blood work. He said as long as everything checked out after that, she could rest at home.

I mumbled out what I thought was a thank you, then stepped around them and stood at Gwendalyn's feet. I waited, the soft click of the door indicating I was finally alone.

The chair scrapped along the floor as I dragged it next to the bed. I collapsed into it, and gathered Gwendalyn's hand in mine.

She looked peaceful in sleep. I wanted her to be able to stay like that. I wanted to protect her from what came next, the questioning and the decisions.

It was all my fault. I hadn't been able to protect her.

The adrenaline drained from my body as I watched over her. A nurse came in at one point and checked her vitals, but I paid her no mind. My only focus was Gwendalyn, waiting for her eyes to open. Time passed slowly, and my arm rested on the mattress.

I squeezed her hand and willed her to wake up, while the steady beep of her heart rate filled the room.

# Chapter Twenty

## Gwen

The warmth of the darkness was yanked from me as I came to, but I refused to open my eyes as I gained some sense of my surroundings.

I was laying in a bed, but I know it wasn't mine. The sheets were scratchy against my skin, and the weight of my favorite blanket was nonexistent. While I would have loved nothing more than to go back to sleep, curiosity got the better of me when I registered a heaviness on my right hand and side. Plus, I had an overwhelming need to pee.

Rousing myself, I blinked away the blurriness that was making it hard to see. I internally groaned when the fluorescent lights shined too brightly above me, letting my eyes close once more to block out the harshness. All my senses slowly woke up as a steady beep echoed through the room and disinfectant assaulted my nose.

*A hospital?* My memories from when I left the bar until now were hazy, like I could feel them in the recesses of my mind, but couldn't grab onto them.

Turning my head to the side, the action caused a dull throbbing. I opened my eyes once more, and hoped I could find someone that could help fill in the missing pieces from last night. Instead, the sight in front of me had my frantic mind stopping.

Anthony was fast asleep in a chair flush against the side of the bed, his arm supporting the weight of his head. He had my right hand captured in one of his, and his face was relaxed in a way I hadn't seen before. There were no wrinkles on his forehead, and his eyebrows weren't pinched together in a constant state of pissed off.

I didn't want to disturb him, my need for answers quickly disappearing as I watched him sleep for a few more minutes. Too soon, though, I remembered why I woke up in the first place. My bladder was going to get angry very fast if I didn't get to the bathroom soon.

Gently lifting my left hand so as to not mess up the IV I just noticed, I placed it on Anthony's shoulder that wasn't covered by his head. Before I could attempt to jostle him awake, his eyes opened and his head snapped up as if sensing something.

"Shit, I didn't mean to–Gwendalyn, you're awake!" His eyes found mine, squeezing my hand. He lifted up his free hand to fix a few stray pieces of my hair and tucked them behind my ear, his hand lingering to gently cup my cheek.

I leaned into his touch, closing my eyes and savoring the familiar roughness, before opening them to look back at him again. Concern clouded his eyes, and guilt squeezed my heart for putting it there. "How are you feeling?"

As if his question triggered my pain receptors, my head began pounding. I tried to speak, but my voice was barely there. Trying to clear my throat, I noticed how dry it was. Anthony moved his hand from my face, the warmth leaving with him as he reached over for a cup with a straw sticking out of it on the bedside table. I went to take it from him with my free hand, but he shook his head.

"No, let me help you. Please," he mumbled, adding a half smile that melted my heart. I had no strength to fight him, nor would I have wanted to. The man had said please after all. He held the cup in front of my lips so I could pull the straw in between them.

"Small sips," he softly instructed, and I did as he said, at first, anyway. As soon as that first sip hit the back of my throat, it was like a desert receiving rain for the first time.

I took a huge gulp, and Anthony immediately pulled the cup away. I tried to follow the straw as it was ripped away from my lips. "I said small sips. You're going to make yourself sick if you start chugging water," he chastised.

"But..." A whine escaped as I stuck out my bottom lip, hoping the pout would help me win my case. I threw some puppy dog eyes in there, too, for good measure.

"There she is," Anthony chuckled, a faint smile threatening the edges of his lips as he placed the cup back on the table. "You scared the shit out of me, Gwen." Sadness returned to his eyes and my stomach flipped, his use of my shortened name not lost on me. He had refused to call me anything but Gwendalyn, going so far as correcting Oliver in the beginning until I insisted he could call me Gwen.

"Oh my gosh, where is Ollie?" I frantically looked around the room, half expecting him to jump out from behind the chair. The beeping that echoed through the room picked up pace.

"Hey, he's okay." Anthony grasped my chin with his thumb and finger, forcing me to look at him. "Breathe."

I did, the panic slowly subsiding. His fingers released my chin, once again cupping my cheek.

"Katie is watching him," he answers when my body is no longer in flight mode. "Let's focus on you right now. Do you remember what happened last night?"

"Everything is still pretty fuzzy after I left the bar..." A knock at the door cut me off, and Anthony's head snapped around. His grasp on my hand somehow became tighter, but I was too distracted by the doctor walking into the room to really care.

"Good morning!" The doctor exclaimed, louder than was necessary in the small room. I flinched as the sound bounced around my head like a pinball. "Oh, good, you're awake. I'm Dr. Edwards. How are we feeling?" There was a smile plastered on his face, but I couldn't tell if it was genuine.

"Um, okay, I think," I said, looking between Anthony and him. "My head is killing me, though. Feels like a bad headache." My bladder took that moment to remind me of the now urgent need for a bathroom. "I need to pee, too."

"Well, let me do a quick check and then we can go from there." He stepped around to the left side of the bed and pulled a penlight out from the pocket of his white coat, shining it in my eyes and having me look in varying directions. He asked questions about my pain and if I had experienced any dizziness or lightheadedness since waking. Satisfactory with my answers, he unwrapped white gauze from around my head, and prodded the back of my head with a gloved finger.

Anthony didn't leave my side, but did loosen his grasp on my hand. I was thankful for both of those things.

By the time the doctor was done with his checks, my mind had drifted. If it weren't for the nagging need to pee and the throbbing in the back of my head, I would have fallen back asleep. I was about to close my eyes when the doctor's chipper voice broke through the mental fog. "In regards to the head trauma, that seems to be on the up and up. No lingering effects that I can tell, but of course, that will need to be monitored over the next couple days. Now, in regards to everything else…" He paused, seeming to search for the right words as he met Anthony's stare. "Mr. Marino, would you be so kind as to give us the room?"

Panic flooded my system. The thought of being alone with a strange man had me shaking, and I didn't bother to try and figure out why. All I knew was that I needed Anthony.

"No!" My voice came out louder than I expected, but it got my point across.

"Mrs. Marino, I need to ask about the events that led up to you visiting us last night, and having your husband in the room could influence the answers. I want to make sure you feel comfortable disclosing everything." *Mrs. Marino? Husband? What the hell is going on?* I looked to Anthony for answers, his jaw set as he forced air through his nose.

"Gwen, he has to make sure I'm not the one who did this to you," Anthony answered my unasked question, his voice soft as he did but his eyes shooting daggers at the doctor. When I finally registered what he meant, I quickly turned my head toward the doctor, causing pain that had me wincing. Anthony's hand on mine tightened slightly, the action grounding me.

"Anthony would never hurt me! I went out last night with a friend and I started feeling dizzy and nauseous, so I left the bar and tried to find my car. Things are still kind of fuzzy after that, but Anthony had nothing to do with it. I swear!" I was speaking way too fast and when the doctor looked between me and Anthony, his eyes narrowing and lips pinching together in a line, I knew he wasn't believing me.

I was about to keep word vomiting when, all of a sudden, Anthony stood up quickly and the motion distracted me. He released my hand for the first time since I woke up, and I took a second to stretch my fingers. My eyes followed Anthony's movements, still very confused by the fact that we were apparently married.

"Dr. Edwards, seeing as you were not her doctor upon her arrival, I would appreciate you approaching this topic with more sensitivity. She has made it clear that she has little memory of last night. I think it would be best if you gave her some time before continuing your questioning."

Looking between the two men having a staring contest, Anthony's jaw twitched and his eyes narrowed. The doctor looked at me, his eyebrows raised. He seemed hesitant to leave.

"Alright," the doctor said, breaking eye contact with me. "Let me send in the nurse to help Mrs. Marino to the bathroom and then we can talk more afterward." We both tracked the doctor as he quickly made his way out the door.

Looking down at me, Anthony met my stare, and he read my thoughts once again. "When the ambulance picked us up, I may have told them we were married. I was worried they wouldn't let me stay with you otherwise. I didn't want you to wake up alone." His hand reached out to grasp mine once again, giving it a gentle squeeze.

"Ambulance?" I asked. "Anthony, what happened?"

"You called me. The line was quiet until I heard a voice that wasn't yours. When I found you, you were..." Anthony's voice trailed off as we were once again interrupted by a soft knock on the door. The door cracked open, and someone slowly peeked into the room.

Seeing us watching the door, a nurse with a lot of pep in her steps bounded into the room. Anthony moved closer to my head, but still kept a loose hold on my hand. The nurse basically skipped her way to the bed, bringing with her what looked to be a robe.

"Hey there! Doc said you needed the bathroom. Let's get you disconnected from everything, then we can get you up and moving!" Anthony set my hand down, stepping away from the bed to presumably let the nurse do what she needed to do. I looked up, hoping to convey to him without using words that I didn't want her help. He met my eyes, a look of understanding flashing across his eyes, followed by a quick nod.

Clearing his throat, he speaks up as the peppy nurse starts making quick work of unhooking me from machines and removing my IV. "I think my wife would be more comfortable using the bathroom without a stranger present." While I have never considered Anthony a scary man, his tone of voice definitely relayed that she shouldn't attempt to argue with him.

"Of course." After finishing up, she offered a small smile. "There's a call button in the bathroom and here by the bed if you need anything." She gestured to the button then threw Anthony a nasty look, before quickly leaving the room. I held in the chuckle that threatened to escape my lips. I was sure Anthony's sudden alpha male energy wasn't going to help our case, but I was amused nonetheless.

Before I could blink, Anthony was in front of me, hands out to offer his assistance. "Let's get you to the bathroom. Need any help standing up?"

"Thanks." Carefully, I guided my legs off the edge of the bed, letting my feet touch the floor. Then I took his outstretched hands and leaned into them, pushing myself up into a standing position. I wasn't the most steady at first, my knees nearly buckling when I went to take a step. Anthony quickly reacted, releasing one of my hands and putting it on my waist until I had stopped swaying.

"Are you dizzy?" he asked, concern lacing his words. "I can ask the nurse to come back."

"No, I'm okay. Just need a minute for my legs to adjust." Tentatively, I stepped away from the bed, much more confident in my own strength. Anthony released me, reaching over to grab the robe at the end of the bed and helping me to put it on. His hands returned to their spots, guiding me to the bathroom as I focused on putting one foot in front of the other. Once we reached the door, he let go of my waist, stepping in front of me and bending slightly so I could see his face without straining to look up.

"Do you want a few minutes to yourself?" he asked, reaching to tuck hair behind my ears. I nodded my head, definitely wanting a little privacy. He straightened himself, placing a kiss on the top of my head before flipping the light on in the bathroom. "I'll be right out here if you need me. Just holler."

I stepped into the bathroom, closing the door behind me and going straight to the toilet to relieve my bladder. After getting cleaned up, I stopped in front of the sink and someone I didn't recognize was staring back at me in the mirror. Bruises painted the side of my face and neck, disappearing under the hospital gown. My hair was a mess, and turning my head revealed a bald spot several inches wide that surrounded several stitches.

All of a sudden, memories from the night flooded my mind.

*"There's no reason we can't have a little fun..."* The words echoed through my mind as I pushed away from the sink, stumbling backwards. My back hit the wall and I slid down it, pulling my knees to my chest. I was stuck under him again, unable to breathe.

*Fingers like sandpaper shoved into me as jagged nails dug into my skin, pain shooting through every nerve of my body. "See baby, you like this..."*

I could feel my body starting to shake, and the darkness threatened the edges of my vision. Anthony was right outside the door. I just needed to call out, but I couldn't move or speak. I was left with only the screaming in my mind that I didn't want his body on mine.

*No... Please... Stop.*

# Chapter Twenty-One

## Anthony

Crossing my arms, I leaned against the doorframe of the bathroom. As much as it pained me, I gave Gwen the privacy she needed right now. I closed my eyes to clear my mind for a few minutes, but I couldn't stop thinking about her.

I had no idea how I slept at all last night. When I woke up to her bright eyes looking at me, it was like I could finally breathe again. The mirage of a professional boundary that I had fooled myself into believing was gone. It was time she knew how badly I needed her. I refused to let anything happen to her ever again.

Despite what the doctor and everyone else in this hospital seemed to think, I would never lay a hand on Gwen, on any woman. But I understood the concern. Opening my eyes and standing straight, I started pacing outside the bathroom door. *Why didn't I find a way to make her stay home last night? I should have been able to protect her.*

Gwen may not remember what happened to her right now, but I knew. Someone touched her, hurt her, and I needed to know who. If it had anything to do with the case I'd been working... *Fuck!*

Hearing the toilet finally flush, I stopped my pacing and faced the bathroom door. I waited for Gwen to come out, but she was taking too long. I grew impatient as the questions started circling around in my head. The detective in me was taking over.

Not bothering to knock, I slowly opened the bathroom door, so I didn't hit her if she was standing at the sink. She wasn't, though, and I quickly scanned the room, catching a quick glimpse of her hair in the mirror. Slipping inside, I closed the door behind me before sitting down on the floor in front of her.

Her legs were pulled up to her chest, with her arms wrapped around them. Her head was tucked down as far as it would go. It was almost as if she was trying to hide from something by making herself as small as possible. Reaching out, I placed my hand on one of hers, trying to offer her any amount of comfort she would take. She flinched slightly but didn't pull away. Her reaction to such a small contact telling me everything I needed to know.

The darkness threatened to crawl out of the recesses of my mind. I pushed it down, knowing I would be no use to Gwen if I let it take control. Not even Detective Marino was right for this job. I almost wish my partner was here. Jason was the comforter, he knew how to make the survivors feel safe.

But I needed to try. For her.

"Gwen," I tried to keep my voice soft just like I heard Jason do a million times. "I'm right here, *luce mia*. I'm right here." She lifted her head, and tears pooled in the corner of her eyes. Her eyes barely met mine. She was remembering, feeling...

*Oscurità mia* was raging in my mind, anger forcing its way through my veins causing the hand not holding onto Gwen to flex. I was going to find the person who touched her, and have his body join the dozens of others who thought they could get away with putting their hands on a woman.

*She was mine, luce mia.* No one would ever hurt her again. Shoving down all the anger, I reached out and urged her into my arms as tears started streaming down her cheeks. She came willingly, and I settled her into my lap with her head resting on my chest as I sat on the floor.

Her walls crumbled. Soft cries shifted into sobs. One of my hands found its place on her back, running up and down her spine. My head rested on top of hers as I softly whispered that she was safe, and I wasn't going anywhere.

Time stood still. It felt as if several minutes had passed.

"Gwen, you need to breathe. Please." I mumbled into her hair as I attempted to keep the panic out of my voice.

She tucked her face into my chest, one of her hands fisting my shirt. "I-I can't. Ev-every-everything h-hurts." Her voice was muffled as her body shook. I wrapped both of my arms around her body, pulling her further into me, wanting to take away all of her pain.

I felt useless, my own anger slowly making its way back to the surface at my inability to be enough for Gwen in the moment. Shifting her in my lap, I pressed my lips against her temple.

"Deep, deep breaths," I whispered. "I've got you. You're safe." Her body shifted as she tried in between sobs. She wasn't getting enough air, her chest rising and falling too quickly. She was hyperventilating.

"I'm—I'm sorry, Anthony," she said, barely above a whisper. If I wasn't listening so intently to her, I would have missed it.

Unwrapping my arms from around her, I placed my hands on her cheeks and gently guided her face up. Her eyes were closed, squeezing shut with enough force that I knew it had to be causing her pain, and her face was splotchy. I wanted to kiss away the tears trailing down her cheeks.

"You have nothing to apologize for, absolutely nothing." I encouraged. She shook her head, fresh tears falling onto my hands.

I needed her to know that this was not her fault, but there was no point in arguing with her. Not right now.

My heart shattered when I removed my hands from her face and pain flooded her features, as if my hands were the only thing keeping her in the moment. I ran my hands down her arms, making circles with my thumbs until I reached her hands. I picked them up and pressed her palms against my chest.

"Gwen, you need to breathe. Stop thinking and just breathe. Please." I begged her, forcing my voice to stay steady and calm while I exaggerated my own breathing. It didn't work. She was too deep into the memories. Her own mind was keeping her captive

*Fuck it.*

"*Luce mia,* look at me." I put a little more authority into my voice, hoping it wouldn't make things worse. "Now." Hesitantly, she opened her eyes and stared into mine.

"That's my girl. Keep looking at me." I barely noticed the slight nod of her head as I persisted in pushing my luck being forceful. If that's what she needed, then that was what I was going to do.

"Breathe with me. Deep inhale." I pulled in a breath and she mirrored me. "Slow exhale. You can do this." I did my best to keep the darkness threatening the edges of my vision away as I pressed her palms in my chest harder, the pain from her nails pressing into the skin calming my mind.

Slowly, she took in more air, the rising and falling of her chest evening out. I kept my eyes on her, the darkness around the edges of mine retreating as her tears dried up.

After several minutes, her body stopped shaking, and her shoulders visibly relaxed. I leaned forward, pressing my forehead to hers and closed my eyes. Gwen was safe. She was here. I would never let anything bad happen to her again.

"Gwen," I started, lowering our hands from my chest to her lap, but keeping her hands folded with mine, "I know this isn't what you want to hear right now, but we need to talk about what happened last night."

I didn't want to push her, but I needed to know. It would be best to have the conversation just between us first.

"I don't know if I can," she muttered sadly, her fingers twitching in my hands.

"Oh, *luce mia,*" I sighed and opened my eyes, pulling away and releasing her hands to cradle her jaw. Her eyes fluttered open, sadness flashing across her features, as her body deflated into me. "You can, I know you can. Because you're the strongest person I have ever met." Her face was inches away from mine, and I wanted to kiss her.

I wanted to kiss away all the darkness and leave behind only the light. I couldn't, though. This was my fault. I had let this happen to her.

"Will you help me?" she asked, her question bringing me back to the moment. My chest tightened with emotion. I was sitting here blaming myself, but she never lost faith in me. She never stopped trusting me. For a split second, I even saw a twinkle of hope in her eyes.

"Of course. Whatever you need, I'm here," I said, pulling her in for a hug. I let her wrap her arms around my waist and rest her head on my shoulder with her nose rubbing against my neck.

We sat in a comfortable silence for what could have easily been ages. My own body relaxed into the embrace and I wanted to live in this moment for the rest of my life. Gwen was in my arms and right now, I could protect her. She would have to relive what she went through, but she wouldn't be doing it alone. I would be beside her every step of the way, if she wanted me to be.

Internally groaning, I knew it was time to leave the comfort of the bathroom when my lower back ached from sitting on the ground. Plus, I did *not* want to have the conversation we needed to have in a hospital bathroom. "Let's get you off this floor, okay?" I offered. I felt her move her head against my shoulder but couldn't tell if it was a yes or no. "Gwen, you're going to have to use your words." I swear I heard a faint chuckle, and it gave me hope for what was about to come.

"Yes, please," she responds. Shifting us both so she was no longer in my lap, I stood up then grasped her hands and helped her to do the same. I caught her eyes and held her gaze, not wanting to let go for fear something would happen. It was irrational, but I didn't care.

I pressed my lips to her forehead, breathing in the hint of citrus still left in her hair.

"Let's go sit," I said. Not waiting for a response, I opened the bathroom door and scooped Gwen into my arms, bridal style.

"Anthony," she started, wiggling in my arms, but I held her firmly against my chest. "Put me down. I can walk."

"You can, but you won't," I said, looking down at her. "Let me do this." She smiled, easily giving in and resting her head on my chest.

When we reached the bed, she shifted, no doubt expecting me to put her down. Instead, I situated myself on the bed and settled her in my lap. Gwen relaxed instantly into my chest. Her head rested on my shoulder while her fingers ran along the fabric of my shirt. I ran my hand along her leg, gently resting my head on hers.

I forced myself to take slow, deep breaths, slipping into detective mode as I made sure my own emotions were under lock and key. She didn't need any of my feelings clouding her own.

This moment was about her.

"*Luce mia*, I need to know what happened last night," I whispered, feeling her stiffen against me. Her hand dropped to her lap, and she turned her face, pressing into my chest. "I don't want to push you or force you to do something that makes you uncomfortable, but the more I know, the more I can help. It's important to me that you know your options." I paused, waiting for a response, but none came.

Her breathing was still even, no signs of crying, so I gave her time to think. She needed to sort things out. The mind was a powerful thing and when it wanted to protect itself. It would fight to keep things buried.

She pulled away from me, and I let the arm wrapped around her back slide to her front, my hand finding one of hers. The pressure that had built up in my chest slowly lessened, making it easier to breathe. I ran my thumb over her knuckles, cherishing the feeling of her skin under mine. It had always been soft compared to mine, calloused and rough.

"I met Carol at the bar," she whispered, "and everything was going great until she got a call and had to leave." She paused, her shoulders tensing. "I should have left, but I was upset at you. I didn't want to go back to the house and have to deal with all of that."

"Gwendalyn, I—" I started to apologize.

"No, let me say this." She cut me off. "If you interrupt, I won't be able to get it all out."

I nodded my head, watching as her attention drifted down to our hands. Whenever she was nervous or anxious, she would pick at her cuticles, usually until they bled. I hated seeing her hurt herself, even something so minor as that. But it was a coping mechanism.

Instead of releasing her, I grasped her other hand. My thumb swiped along her skin until she took a deep breath and continued.

"Some guy started flirting with me at the bar. I thought it was harmless, and I had been pissed about what you said, so I didn't think much of it and decided to have a little fun. He offered to buy me a drink, but I had just ordered a shot from the bartender and he handed it to me. Maybe it was my fault for not paying closer attention to what was happening..." She trailed off and I squeezed her hands.

"I got really nauseous, and I assumed the shot wasn't sitting right. The guy was crowding me, though, and I needed air. So I may have kneed him in his balls so he would back up."

I swallowed my ill timed chuckle, but damn was I proud of her.

"Everything is hazy after that. I made it outside and found my car, but I knew I shouldn't drive so I had my phone out debating on if I should call you when I was shoved up against my car. I struggled to scream, but my voice just wouldn't seem to work." She hesitated, and I tightened my grip, trying to silently communicate my presence. "When I tried to get away, they threw me to the ground. I wanted to fight, to do something, anything, but I couldn't." Tears brimmed her eyes as she forced slow breaths into her lungs, her shoulders tensing.

"He forced his fingers down my pants. It felt like someone was shoving sandpaper into me. He said... He said I liked it. That my body wanted it rough. I didn't. But I couldn't move. I couldn't tell him to stop. I just wanted him to stop..." Tears streaked her face. Her chest was frantically rising, and I quickly began taking deep, steady breaths. Slowly, she mirrored my movements and forced firm breaths into her lungs. Her fingers clawed at my palms. I wasn't even sure if she knew she was doing it, but I made no move to stop her.

"Gwen, you don't have to continue," I reassured her, telling myself it was for her benefit. Selfishly, I wanted her to stop. The thought of another man defiling her, using her for his own pleasure, had *oscurità mia* ripping at every lock and key I had thrown at it, and it was terrifyingly close to breaking out.

I would find him. I would *kill* him.

"Would it help if I called my partner? He can get your statement and then we can talk about what happens after together," I gently offered.

Gwen looked up, catching my eyes. A single tear fell down her cheek as she muttered, "What would happen to Oliver?"

My brows stitched together. "What do you mean?"

"If something happens to me, would Ollie be okay?" she whispered, breaking eye contact and staring at our connected hands.

"*Luce mia...*" I trailed off, realization settling in my veins. Even when going through what could only be described as the worst night of her life, it seemed Oliver and I were the ones on the forefront of her mind.

"He has already been through so much," she continued, oblivious to the wheels turning in my mind. "There's no way he would understand. That little boy means the world to me. If something had happened to me, he wouldn't know how much I loved him. He filled a piece of my heart I didn't know I was missing."

My hands were no longer holding hers. Instead, they were intertwined in her hair, pulling myself up to claim her lips. She relaxed into me, and I couldn't help feeling a sense of pride at how safe she felt with me. Her tears mixed into our kiss, the saltiness giving me a renewed sense of freedom.

*Wait, fuck! I can't be doing this.* I pulled away too fast, her hands flying up to my chest at the same time my hands went to her shoulders to help steady her.

"Gwen, I am so fucking sorry. I shouldn't have done that. That was…" She shut me up by crashing her lips to mine, her fingers weaving through my hair and tugging. Cupping her face, I pulled her against me and groaned into her mouth. Our bodies pressed against each other, a heat rising between us as I felt myself pressing into her leg.

She broke our kiss and leaned back, her eyes shining with unshed tears. A smile threatened her lips, and I swore I saw a halo of light around the woman. We stayed like that until a knock on the door had me scrambling to get off the bed like I was a teenager, about to be caught by my mom.

"Mr. and Mrs. Marino? Everything okay in there?" The peppy nurse popped her head into the door just as I was getting Gwen settled into the bed. Hopefully, it looked like we had just made it back from the bathroom.

Letting the nurse do whatever she needed, I excused myself to the hallway to give Jason a call and check on Oliver.

He got to the hospital faster than I thought he would, which meant he probably sped from his house. Jason pulled me in for a hug when he saw me, something I wasn't expecting but was grateful for, nonetheless.

We interviewed survivors multiple times a day, but it never got easier, let alone when it was someone you know. There was no one else I trusted enough to do this. When he stepped through the door, he became Detective Kreugler, asking all the right questions.

The doctor was present at one point, letting us know they had finally gotten Gwen's blood work back and confirmed my suspicions that she had been drugged. She started sobbing at that point, nearly hyperventilating again.

I sat with her and effortlessly pulled her into my lap, breathing with her until she had calmed down and was ready to continue. Much to his credit, Jason stayed professional throughout the entire thing, not even throwing a knowing glance in my direction. She recounted everything from last night in even greater detail while never leaving my arms. I refused to let her at this point. This was where she belonged.

"Alright, Miss Brookes," Jason said, "so from my understanding there was no penetration by the assailant's genitalia?" Gwen shook her head, stiffening slightly in my arms. She had been completely relaxed against me up to that point, a blanket wrapped around her shoulders. I kissed her hair and rubbed her back, small gestures to help ground her.

I peeked over Gwen's head, Jason's gaze finding mine. He raised his eyebrows, a silent question, and I gave my head a slight nod. This next bit would be hard, but *luce mia* had more strength than she knew. He looked back to her and softened his face. I have seen him do this hundreds of times, and it still surprised me how good he was at it.

"So the next step would be to obtain a sexual assault kit to gather evidence," he started. "It's by no means a requirement as we cannot force you to undergo such an invasive exam, but it could help in the future. It's entirely up to you. Is that something you want to go forward with?"

I looked at Gwen, wishing I could read her mind. She turned to look at me and I saw it in her eyes, the question of what she should do.

"I support you, whatever you want to do," I said, losing the internal battle to keep myself composed when a tear slid down her cheek. "I promise you, no matter what you choose to do, I will find that fucker and he will pay for putting his hands on you." Her eyes went wide, and she turned her head to look at Jason, presumably because she expected him to chastise me for threatening someone's life in front of him.

She didn't know him like I did, though, what he did in his free time. Gone was the calm, concerned expression of Detective Kregler.

Replacing it was the same uncontrollable anger that I had been trying to keep hidden from Gwen since I found her in that parking lot last night.

Jason simply nodded his head.

Gwen's eyes returned to mine, still wide, as if trying to connect the dots. Bringing one of her hands to my lips, I gently pressed them to her knuckles. I watched as her expression softened and she exhaled slowly, shaking her head. "I just want to go home," she whispered.

I pulled her back against my chest, kissing the top of her head while it laid on my shoulder. "Of course, *luce mia*," I muttered into her hair. "Let's go home."

# Chapter Twenty-Two

## Gwen

Looking at the radio clock, it felt like it should be much later than two in the afternoon. I was thankful for the quiet drive home. The streets weren't busy yet with rush hour traffic.

Leaning my head against the window of Anthony's truck, I watched the downtown streets morph into suburban roads as the events of the last 24 hours ran through my mind. After Detective Kreugler shook hands with Anthony, he left and the nurse returned one more time with discharge papers and a set of scrubs. She helped me change while Anthony walked his partner out, even though I could tell he wanted to protest.

Honestly, I didn't want him to see the bruises. I didn't even want to see them. If the one on my face was any indication, I preferred to keep them hidden for now. The nurse was kind, seemingly knowing what I needed, and helped make sure I didn't need to see them

I closed my eyes and took deep breaths, a feeling of uncertainty settling in my stomach and making me nauseous. Anthony's hand laid on top of mine, comforting me with little brushes of his thumb.

*I got away. I'm safe.*

Repeating those words in my head over and over, I focused on the motion of the car and the warmth of Anthony's hand. The combination soothed the nerves in my body, and I could feel myself beginning to relax. Listening to the song softly playing on the radio, everything else drifted away.

Anthony's scent enveloped me as I was pressed against a hard chest. I opened my eyes as he carried me from the truck and into the house.

I opened my mouth to protest, but smiled to myself, remembering his insistence on not letting me walk, both in the hospital and when we left. He wanted to take care of me, and I was too exhausted to fight him. I felt how I imagined being run over by a truck must feel like.

All I wanted to do was go to sleep.

I lifted my head as we ascended the stairs, confused where Anthony was taking me. "Where are you going?" I asked, looking up at his face while trying to read his expression. He kept his eyes forward and avoided my gaze.

"Your bathroom doesn't have a bathtub and you can't take a shower with your stitches," he answered. As much as I wanted to argue for him to just take me to my bed, a bath sounded nice. There was a layer of dirt on my skin that I wanted to wash off.

Reaching the top of the stairs, Anthony stepped into his room and went to his master en suite. My jaw dropped at the sight of his bathroom. Across from the double sinks with a beautiful marble countertop was a massive clawfoot tub. Behind it was a glass shower with a waterfall shower head and black tile. I was speechless, and Anthony chuckled.

He walked over to the edge of the tub, sitting me down so I was perched on the edge. Keeping his hand on my waist, he reached over me to turn on the water.

I wanted to cling to him, and I realized there was nothing stopping me from doing just that. I pressed my cheek against his chest as I wrapped my arms around his neck. The familiar scent of pine and bourbon surrounded me. I breathed it in, letting my body relax as much as it could.

Anthony straightened, and kissed the top of my head. My heart skipped a beat, the small gesture holding so much meaning.

"I'll be right back, okay?" he whispered into my hair. I nodded my head as he stepped away, leaving the bathroom.

Immediately, I missed his warmth and wrapped my arms around myself. Not knowing what else to do, I stood up and looked around the bathroom, admiring the massiveness. Running my fingers along the smooth marble, the cold sent goosebumps up my arm. I pulled away, and caught a glimpse of myself in the mirror.

If I thought I looked bad in the hospital, I was a disaster now.

The nurse had gathered my hair back into a low ponytail, understanding my need for my hair to be out of my face, but also being mindful of the stitches. I pulled the ends in front of my shoulder, my fingers running over the streaks of dirt and dry blood speckled throughout.

The bruising on my face had gotten progressively worse, turning a dark red and purple. Standing up, I took a couple steps back, and carefully pulled the scrub top up slightly to look at my stomach in the mirror. The top of a massive bruise disappeared under my pants. I knew if I looked, there would be similar ones on my thighs as well.

"Gwen…" Anthony's voice came from behind me. Startled, I dropped my shirt and turned on my heel. He stood in the doorway, but when our eyes met, he closed the distance between us before I could blink. His hands moved to brush away tears from my cheeks that I hadn't realized had fallen. "*Luce mia*, you're safe now." I took a deep breath, leaning into his touch.

*I got away. I'm safe.*

"Let's get you out of these scrubs and cleaned up," he whispered, "and then we'll get you into something more comfortable."

Panic rose in my chest, and I frantically shook my head. I didn't want him to see. *I* didn't event want to see.

Hugging myself with my arms, I hang my head, avoiding Anthony's eyes. Everything was happening too fast. I wasn't ready to face what happened to me. Not again.

"Gwen, talk to me, please." He was being so gentle…

"The bruises… I… I… can't," I stammered, unable to even finish the thought. How could I even begin to explain it to him?

"*Luce mia*, look at me," Anthony said. I shook my head, but he didn't accept that answer. Placing his hand on my chin, he gently lifted my head until I was looking at him. "Gwen, those bruises do not define who you are. What defines you are the things you do every day, despite what you've been through. I may not know everything about you, but what I do know is that you are an incredible woman who has opened up her heart to my son, treated him with more love and respect than he has ever received, all because you believe there is good in everyone." A few stray tears fell when I blinked up at him.

"Please, let me help," he whispered, drying the wet trail left on my cheek with a swipe of his thumbs. His hands moved to the hem of my shirt, and I pulled away. Every nerve in my body was screaming to run.

But Anthony wasn't forcing himself on me. He was relaxed, his eyes soft as he waited for my consent.

*I got away. I'm safe.*

Closing my eyes, I stepped into his arms and focused on breathing, too scared to see his reaction to my body.

He lifted the hem of my shirt as my hands rested on his chest. I focused on the rise and fall of it once while Anthony maneuvered the top over my head. My eyes squeezed even tighter closed when his fingers grazed my bruised hip, colors exploding behind my lids. Pressure radiated through my jaw from clenching it shut as he quickly untied the scrub pants. They slid down my legs easily, and pooled on the floor around my ankles.

I was anticipating words of disgust, a gasp, anything. That would be the least I deserved. Instead, warm hands cradled my face.

"Gwen, look at me," Anthony said. I shook my head in his hands.

The shame made it impossible to look at him. I couldn't do it.

"Yes. Look at me." There was an edge to his voice, and it left no room for argument.

I took a fortifying breath, then slowly opened my eyes. Hot tears rolled down my cheeks, and my breath caught in my chest. Meeting Anthony's gaze, I expected him to be looking at me with sympathy or disdain. But he wasn't.

"You are beautiful, *luce mia*," he whispered, brushing his thumbs along my cheeks before pressing his forehead to mine. "Nothing will ever change that."

He wasn't lying. My heart pounded in my chest, something close to relief flooding through me. He dropped his hands, his fingers intertwining with mine.

"Let's get you cleaned up now, okay?"

"Okay," I choked out. He pulled my hands to his lips to kiss my knuckles before he led me toward the bath. Carefully, I stepped into the water, letting my body adjust to the warmth of the water as it lapped at my calves.

Sitting down, I pulled my knees as close to my chest as possible before resting my chin on top of them. My shoulders tensed, and my body trembled slightly as it adjusted to the water.

Anthony grabbed a couple washcloths from under the sink, and sat them on the edge of the tub before kneeling next to me. He gently worked the ponytail holder from my hair, being careful not to tug the stitches. My hair hung in clumps against my shoulders when he finished.

He reached for one of the washcloths, dunking it in the water and wringing it out. Carefully, he wiped away the evidence of last night from my hair, while being mindful of the stitches. The knot in my stomach slowly unfurled as he worked, and my eyes closed as the tension left my shoulders.

A comfortable silence fell over the room, the occasional sloshing of water when he cleaned out the washcloth the only sound. It was rarely this quiet in the house, even when Ollie was taking a nap. There was always something making noise.

*Ollie...*

It hit me that as much as I was enjoying this time with Anthony, it wouldn't last forever. He was a father, and I was his nanny. We would have to talk about everything that happened before Ollie came home.

Wondering when that would be, I opened my eyes and lifted my head, turning to Anthony. "When do you have to go get Ollie?" I asked.

"He's having a blast at Katie's. I told him Miss Gwen wasn't feeling good, and *he* told me that I needed to take care of you." Anthony chuckled while my heart nearly exploded in my chest. "I think it's for selfish reasons, of course. He knows you're the fun one and if you can't play, then he's stuck with his boring dad." The edges of my mouth curled up into a smile. That boy had my entire heart. I would do just about anything he asked of me.

"Let's focus on you right now," he muttered, the lightness in his eyes helping to settle the uncertainty I felt moments ago.

Anthony reached for the body wash in the corner of the tub. Putting some on the other washcloth, I was drawn to the bubbles forming as he rubbed the sides of it together. He cleared his throat, and I looked at him again.

"I'll be right back, okay? You wash up and I'll knock when I get back." He handed me the washcloth in his hand, then stood and flashed a small smile over his shoulder as he walked out of the bathroom.

This man... I didn't have to ask, he just knew.

I took a deep breath, then stretched out my legs. These bruises didn't define me. I looked down at my body to take in the full extent of everything.

The one that started on my hip was larger than my hand. The ones on my inner thigh were smaller and spread out.

Gentle at first, I brought the washcloth to my hip to wipe away all the dirt and grim. But as my focus stayed on the physical reminders of what happened last night, a knot formed in my stomach. Tears threatened the edges of my eyes again as I washed harder.

I wanted the bruises gone.

Logically, it didn't make sense, but logic went out the window a long time ago. *This wasn't fair.*

I scrubbed, everything starting to numb as the adrenaline in my body took over. My heart beat faster and faster. The healthy skin around the bruise started to turn pink.

A soft knock barely registered in my mind while I continued scrubbing. The skin was red now, but the bruise was still there.

Another knock followed by Anthony's muffled voice on the other side of the door. "Gwen, can I come in?" I didn't answer. The proof of last night was still on my body. and I wanted it gone.

The water was a light shade of pink now, but it was still there.

The door creaked open and footsteps followed. "Gwen..." Anthony's voice trailed off, my mind not registering what he was saying, even though he was right next to me. I knew what he must have been thinking.

*Disgusting. Useless.*

The tears falling from my cheeks into the water betrayed me. I wasn't sad.

I was angry.

I was angry that I had to look at my body, and have these bruises remind me of what happened. *I just wanted to forget.*

"*Luce mia*, stop!" A voice yelled, grabbing my wrist and yanking it away from my body. The anger in the voice paired with the tightening grasp caused my body to seize.

*No, I wasn't letting this happen again.*

"Let go of me!" I screamed. I was in control. *He* may have taken that away from me before, but not this time. I whipped my head around, but it was Anthony crouched in front of me, not the masked attacker.

He released my wrist and sat back on his heels, putting a few inches between us. It was enough for my body to realize I wasn't in danger. I hastily wiped away the stray tears from my cheeks, then met Anthony's gaze.

Regret washed over me at the sight of his furrowed brows and wide eyes. He had seen me through today and didn't deserve my anger. My face relaxed, an apology forming on my lips.

"It's okay," Anthony said, not letting me get out the words. "I shouldn't have touched you without your permission. I promise I won't do it again." I simply nodded my head to acknowledge his words, unsure what else to say.

"Can I help you get out?" Anthony offered, gesturing to the towel that was draped across his lap. I glanced at my hip, emotions tight in my chest as I saw what I had done. Angry red skin starred back at me. Defeat

"Gwen?" The concern in Anthony's voice pulled me away from the edge of a mental spiral. I looked back up to meet his soft eyes, and nodded my head. I left the washcloth on the tub spout, not bothering to wring it out.

Anthony had the towel open in his arms with his forearm close to my body. I grabbed on, using it to steady myself as I stood. Stepping out of the tub, I turned away from him and wrapped the towel around myself, the warmth enveloping me, surprising but welcoming. It felt like it had been just taken out of the dryer, and I silently wondered if it had.

I turned to thank him, but the words were stuck in my throat, the ones that let him know how much I appreciated him and everything he had done today. If it weren't for him...

Tears burned the back of my eyes. Everything that I had been shoving down was rising to the surface. All the anger, disgust, fear, grief, shame; I no longer had the energy to keep it down.

"*Luce mia...*" Anthony hesitated, keeping his promise not to touch me without my permission. A sob escaped my throat as I threw myself at him, clinging to his shirt. Anthony wrapped his arms around me, while tears streamed down my face.

"I've got you... I'm right here..." he whispered into my hair. Sob after sob shook my body until it wasn't enough. There was too much, and I was going to explode if I didn't let it out.

A scream filled the bathroom. My scream.

But I didn't stop. I screamed again. And again.

I screamed until my throat was raw and my body went completely numb. I screamed until Anthony's hold on me was the only thing keeping me from crumpling to the floor. I screamed until my vision started to darken at the edges, and I could no longer breathe.

"Gwen, sweetheart." Anthony's hushed voice broke through the haze that had settled over my mind. "I need you to take big, deep breaths with me." He exaggerated his inhales and exhales, his chest rising and falling steadily under me, and rubbed my back in long strokes.

I took in several shaky breaths and slowly, the pins and needles in my face from the lack of oxygen disappeared. We continued like that for several minutes, Anthony showing no indication of wanting to let go. When I did finally lift my head off his chest, he looked down at me, a glazed over look in his eyes as if he had been trying to hold back his own tears.

"You are so strong, *luce mia,*" he whispered. "Stronger than you know. When you forget that, I will always be here to remind you." He kissed the top of my head, sealing his unspoken promise. His body shifted and the next moment, he was carrying me from the bathroom to the bed.

Sitting me on the edge, he grabbed a shirt from beside me. He maneuvered it over my head and gently urged my arms through the sleeves before pulling it down over the towel that was still wrapped around my body. I was grateful for the coverage, feeling all too vulnerable. Grabbing the sweatpants next, my heart jumped when he knelt on one knee to lift my feet and legs into the holes. He shimmied them up to my knees before standing up and offering me his hands to help me up. Letting the towel fall to the floor, he pulled up the pants and tied them just below the bruise that was now surrounded by abrasions.

"I'll be right back," Anthony said, before retreating to the bathroom and returning with a clean washcloth and a small tube. He pointed to my hip when he spoke, "I want to dry it off and put on some antibiotic ointment, if that's okay."

"Yeah," I whispered, lifting my shirt. Anthony kneeled in front of me, and the air caught in my lungs. A strangled gasp leaving my lips when his calloused fingers gently spread the ointment along my skin.

My heart nearly stopped beating at the sight of this man on his knees taking care of me. It was all too much.

I would never be able to repay him.

When he was done, he stood to his full height, and left everything in a pile with the towel. He looked down at me with an unasked question in his eyes, one I answered with a pleading look of my own. I swore he could hear my heart hammering in my chest when he rested his hands on either side of my face. Warmth returned to my body, the kind that I knew couldn't last forever.

"Thank you for letting me take care of you," he whispered. My bones felt like lead as I leaned into his embrace. The need for sleep called me even though I knew it was barely evening.

Anthony must have felt the shift because he took my hands, guiding me into bed and I let him. Exhaustion was quickly pulling me under, and I was barely able to keep my eyes open. Anthony pulled the comforter up to my chin, just how I liked it, then brushed my hair behind my ear. "Sleep well, *luce mia*."

He bent down, gathering the pile of discarded things, and turned to leave. Before he could step too far away, I reached out a hand to grab him. "Stay with me, please."

"Of course," he whispered. A smile threatened the corner of his lips as if he was waiting for me to ask. He discarded the things in the bathroom, then crossed the room, turning off the light and closing the bedroom door before making his way onto the bed. He laid on top of the comforter that I was underneath, pulling up a blanket from the end of the bed to drape over his legs.

I knew this was his way of giving me back some of the control that I had lost, and I was grateful to him. My eyes drifted closed as I rested a hand on his chest. His hand came up to rest on top of mine. Blowing out a breath, finally feeling safe.

# Chapter Twenty-Three

## Anthony

A t some point, I must have fallen asleep because the next thing I remember, I opened my eyes to a pitch dark room. I was on my back with Gwen curled up next to me, her head tucked into my side, with my other arm wrapped protectively around her shoulders.

I watched her sleep peacefully, the rise and fall of her chest a steady reminder that she was safe. *Oliver could have lost her. I could have lost her.* All because I had been too stupid to admit how much she meant to us—to me.

Holding her up in the bathroom earlier, listening to her scream until her voice was nearly gone, shattered any remaining resolve I may have had. My heart broke, the same heart that was caged off for years. But when Gwen walked into our lives, the bars started to disappear.

Gwen shifted beside me, pulling me away from my thoughts. One of her hands flopped gently onto my chest and she clenched my shirt in her fist. Beneath my arm, her body trembled, and I tightened my hold on her, hoping it would comfort her. It had the opposite effect, though, and she fought against me, her breathing increasing.

"*Luce mia,* you're safe," I whispered into her hair, kissing the top of her head. The familiarity of the action was becoming an addiction that I wanted to do for the rest of my life.

Instantly, her body relaxed into mine, and she took a deep breath. Her fist released my shirt, her hand lying lazily on my chest as a soft groan escaped her lips. Lying my head back on the pillow, I knew I should check in with Jason, but I didn't want to leave Gwen.

He planned on doing some recon when he left the hospital earlier, and I needed to see if he found out anything about who hurt Gwen. That meant getting my phone.

Carefully, I freed myself from around Gwen's body, kissing the knuckles on her hand as I laid them gently onto the bed. I tucked the comforter around her, draping the blanket that had been across my legs over her for an extra layer of comfort. I went into the bathroom and found our phones that I had discarded next to the sink at some point yesterday. A missed text from Jason waited for me.

> Warehouse. ASAP.

*There was definitely no staying now.*

> On my way.

Noting the time, nearly three in the morning, I slipped my phone into my back pocket. While walking back into the bedroom, I made sure I silenced her phone so it wouldn't go off then plugged it into the charger next to my bed, silently grateful we had the same type.

I pulled a notepad from my nightstand, scribbling out a note in case Gwen woke up while I was gone.

*Running an errand. Be back soon. - A*

The last thing she needed was to think I abandoned her. Checking she was still sound asleep, I tucked the note under her phone then quietly slipped out of the room, heading toward my truck.

Fifteen minutes after backing out of the garage, I pulled up outside the warehouse. I had no idea what to expect when I got inside, but if Jason had texted me when he knew I was taking care of Gwen, it meant he found something. Or *someone*.

I wanted it to be someone.

My blood boiled at the thought of what she went through last night, some piece of trash thinking he could touch her, *luce mia*. I had shoved down the anger for too long. Now it was time to let it out.

Climbing out of my truck, I grabbed my knife from the glove compartment, then made my way into the warehouse. As soon as I opened the door, blood mixed with sweat and fear hit my nostrils and it relaxed me.

*I may not have been able to protect Gwen last night, but right now, I could do something—something I was good at.*

Following the only light, I walked down the hallway to an open door, turning inside to find Jason sitting crossed legged on the floor in front of a man tied to a chair with his head hanging to his chest. My eyes darted to the small cut on the side of his face. A line of blood trickled down his cheek. I smiled at the sight of the blood, and the thought of how much more was yet to come.

"This him?" I asked, stopping behind Jason, who stood from his position before answering.

"Nope," he said. "But this fucker knows who he is. The bartender corroborated Gwen's side of the story. She was arguing with a guy who looked to be getting too handsy. She kneed him in the balls before basically stumbling out of the bar." He paused, gesturing to the man in the chair. "He was icing his balls at the bar for a good hour after that, so he wasn't the one who assaulted Gwen. But I'd say whoever did paid this fucker to spike her drink. This dumbass left his credit card, and the bartender gave me his information. I found him a few hours ago at a different bar, scoring drugs, so I knocked his ass out and dragged him here. He woke up and decided he was going to act tough, so I may have put him in his place a little."

I gave Jason a short nod and pulled my knife from my pocket, twirling it around in my fingers before turning to the man in the chair. Jason moved to take up a place against the door frame. Walking over to the unconscious fucker, I stabbed his hand, embedding my knife into the wooden chair below it. His eyes snapped open, and I ripped out his gag, stuffing it into my front pocket as the scream that escaped from his throat turned to music in my ears.

"What the fuck is wrong with you?" he screamed as I pulled my knife back out of his hand, and I laughed at his question. *Where do I even begin?* I swung my empty fist, connected it with his jaw, then gripped his shirt to pull his face toward me.

"Tell me who hired you," I said, putting as much venom into my voice as possible. He answered by spitting in my face, liquid hitting my eyelids before it ran down my face. My body reacted without direction, my knife finding its way into his other hand.

To his credit, the fucker didn't scream that time. Not until I twisted the knife, anyway.

"Fuck you," he sneered. In a flash, the knife was lengthwise against his throat, just below his Adam's apple, while my other hand gripped his jaw. I put enough pressure on the hilt to cause the blade to nick the skin, a bead of blood to slip onto the metal. His eyes grew.

He was scared. *Good.*

"He-hey man, take it easy," he whimpered. "I don't know what you're talking about."

"Here's the thing," I growled while squeezing his throat. "You do know what I'm talking about. There is a woman at my home right now, a woman I care about very much, covered in bruises because someone thought they could touch what doesn't belong to them. We both know that *someone* paid you to spike her drink. So forgive me, if I don't take it easy."

"Tony." I whipped my head around to face Jason. He hadn't moved from the door frame, but he had a look in his eyes. The one that reminded me I need to get answers *before* I kill him.

Turning back to the fucker in front of me, I released my grip on his throat and pulled back the knife. The fucker started gasping for air and I mentally kicked myself. This asshole seemed to only have a single brain cell, and I deprived it of oxygen.

I needed *his* fucking name.

I wanted blood, though. *Oscurità mia* was scratching to come out, demanding I do more. Maybe he wasn't the one to force himself on Gwen, but he had drugged her.

Plenty of men just like him have sat in this chair. All of them have said the women were asking for it. I don't have the patience to hear his excuses tonight. Not after everything. No, this time I was going to get straight to the point.

"Tell me, how intimidated do you think women will be of you if you're missing a finger or two?" I said, examining the edge of my knife and hoping it would be sharp enough.

"What—?" he muttered, the crunch of bone as my knife crudely severed a piece of his finger cutting him off. His howl filled the room as I worked the knife out of the chair, watching as the piece fell from the chair into his lap.

"I'm done playing games," I said. "Last chance, then the whole hand comes off. Give me his name."

"Fuck, I don't know his name, okay?" he sputtered, his arms trying to free themselves from the restraints as blood oozed from his amputated finger. "I met him in the bathroom and he pointed the bitch out to me. He handed me a pill and a roll of cash. I swear, I don't know his name." It wasn't the answer I wanted, but for some reason, I believed the dumbass.

That didn't stop what came next.

My hand wrapped around the hilt of my knife and slammed it in between the fucker's legs before he could blink. The wail that echoed off the walls brought a smile to my face. Even though he wouldn't be around to see the light of day, there was something about seeing these assholes think they'd have to live without their penis that brought me joy.

I turned my back to the now sobbing piece of trash, knowing he'd pass out soon from the blood loss, and met Jason's gaze.

"Thought I'd have to jump in and actually play good cop," he chuckled.

"You got him from here?" I questioned, pulling the handkerchief out of my pocket and wiped off my face. Fuck, I hoped Gwen was still asleep cause I had no idea how I'd explain this to her. Looking at my watch, I wiped off the glass before reading the time, 4am.

"Yeah, I'll tie up the loose end. How's Gwen doing?" he asked as we walked toward the exit.

"I'm not sure. I left her asleep in my bed," I sighed. "I had every intention of giving her space, but she asked me to stay. I don't blame her. And to be honest, it was the best sleep I've had in a while." We made it to the door, and we both stopped. Jason put his hand on my shoulder.

"I promise we'll catch the guy. You go take care of Gwen. You and Ollie would be a wreck without her."

"Don't I know it," I muttered.

"I'll call if I need you. Go," he said. I shook his hand, then opened the door, heading to my truck and home to my Gwen.

When I pulled up to the house, all the lights were still off. Not wanting to push my luck any further by opening the garage door, I parked in the driveway. It wasn't even 4:30 yet, so the chances of Gwen being awake were slim. Just in case, I decided it best to dispose of my shirt now covered in blood before I went inside. Shoving it under my seat, I inspected my black jeans to make sure there were no obvious stains before I opened my truck door to head inside.

Opening the front door, I stepped into the entryway, pausing for a minute and listening for any sounds. Thankfully, everything was still quiet. I locked up before heading upstairs, being careful to avoid the squeaky step near the top. Carefully opening my door, I checked on Gwen, seeing her still curled up in the same relaxed position that I had left her in.

*Oh luce mia, my beautiful light.*

I decided to leave the door cracked in case she woke up, and walked down the hall to the bathroom that Oliver typically used. Turning on the water and letting it warm, I stripped my pants and briefs while cracking my neck in an attempt to relieve some of the stress that had built up.

I stepped into the shower, letting the hot water wash away all the blood and sweat from the last couple hours. It did little to relieve the tension in my shoulders, though.

Anger had a death grip on me, and there was nothing I could do to shake it. It was anger at the world for allowing bad people like the one who hurt Gwen to walk among us. It was anger at myself for what happened to her.

I should have protected her.

My fists pounded on the tile, and the fight drained from my body. I hung my head, watching the water circle down the drain. When it finally ran clear, I turned off the water, resolving to the fact that I had failed.

Before I could step out of the shower, a blood-curdling scream came down the hallway—one that sounded far too familiar. Ripping back the curtain, I dashed out of the bathroom, grabbing a towel from the hook as I went and wrapped it around my waist.

My stomach dropped when I got to the bedroom, and my fears were confirmed. Gwen was lying in a fetal position in the middle of the bed with the blanket and comforter in a pile by her feet. Rushing up next to her, I reached out to touch her when I remembered my promise.

"Gwen, *luce mia*... Wake up." My voice didn't sound like my own.

"No! Please, let me go! Please!" she screamed, her voice laced with pain.

"*Luce mia*, please," I begged her to wake up, for her subconscious to hear me and reach out so I could hold her. But she didn't. Her hands pulled at her hair as she curled into herself more. Her nails dug into her scalp, and I couldn't tell if her screams were from the memories, or the pain she was causing.

I didn't want to break my promise, but I couldn't just stand here and watch her hurt herself.

Reaching for her, I put one arm under her neck and the other around her waist, then pulled her into my lap. My chest was still wet and my hair was dripping water onto my shoulders, but I didn't care. The only important thing was the woman in my lap being plagued by an anguish that she did not deserve.

"*Luce mia*, you are safe. I promise," I whispered, emotion clogging my throat.

I held her body close to mine as she shook violently, the nightmare still having a hold on her. I wanted to fix this—fix everything. She deserved so much more than what she has had to endure the last couple days.

I kissed her hair, shifting my hand from her waist to rub circles on her back. She whimpered in her sleep as her body slowly stopped shaking. I continued to hold her, my hand tracing the familiar path of her spine.

Resting my chin on her head, I closed my eyes, giving her time to either wake up or completely fall back asleep.

"Anthony…" she whispered, and my eyes flew open. She squirmed against me, pulling her head away from my chest and looking up at me. Her bright blue eyes were still heavy with sleep and sadness.

"*Luce mia*, I'm so sorry. I know I promised not to touch you, but I was worried," I rushed. Gwen sat back just enough so we were eye to eye.

"It's okay. I'm okay. I'm sorry," she said. She tried to look away, and move away, but I refused to let her. Gently, I held her chin, continuing to hold her gaze.

"You have nothing to apologize for, *luce mia*," I reassured her.

"I hate this feeling, Anthony. I hate feeling so out of control," she whimpered, her eyes wandering down to my lips and back up. She brought a hand to my chest, the warmth sending electrical pulses straight to my heart.

*Was she...*

"No, Gwen." I shook my head as I spoke, trying to hide the evident desire in my voice. Because I wanted nothing more than to claim the woman in front of me, to make her feel comfortable and safe in her own body again. This wasn't the right time, though. She would wake up, and regret all of this.

"No. I..." Whatever I was about to say was forgotten as Gwen shifted in my lap. She pulled away from my chest, straddling me as she ran her hands over my chest. Her soft skin set mine on fire. I wanted her so fucking bad.

"Please," she softly begged. "I want to forget." The sadness in her eyes turned to lust as she pulled on her bottom lip with her teeth.

*Fuck it.*

# Chapter Twenty-Four

*Gwen*

"**P**lease, I want to forget," I begged, my voice threatening to break. His face was undecipherable, his brows pulled together and lips in a thin line.

When I woke up from reliving my worst nightmare and found myself curled up against Anthony's bare chest, something inside me shifted. After everything that had happened between Matt and that stupid masked man, I should not have wanted Anthony's hands on me. But he was different. Only he would be able to erase the horrible memories, filling the pain in with beautiful pleasure.

I ran my hands over his chest. The light speckling of hair was damp, which confused me. I pressed into him in hopes I could convey without words how badly I wanted this. His face twisted in an almost pained expression.

Pulling away, I shifted to get off his lap. This was too much to ask of him. I read the signals wrong. *Great fucking job, Gwen.*

The overwhelming urge to scream at my fucked up emotions had me wanting to punch something. Anthony's hands found my face. My body froze between the bed and his lap, then his lips were on mine. I melted into his hold on me as he pulled me closer to him, our chests touching.

He leaned back, just enough so I could look into his eyes while keeping our bodies pressed together. "Gwendalyn, are you sure?" His voice was hoarse but gentle. I nodded my head, pulling at my bottom lip with my teeth. I wanted this man more than words could ever express. "Words, *luce mia.*"

"Yes, I'm sure," I whispered. "Please, Anthony. Help me forget."

He was on me before I could take my next breath. Taking his time, he kissed me in the most rough and passionate way.

My skin was on fire, begging for his touch. His hands moved; one going behind my head to fist my hair at the base of my neck. The other was on my upper thigh, tugging me toward him until I was once again straddling him with my legs wrapped around his waist.

His kisses became desperate, as if he was running out of air and I had the last of the oxygen.

We stayed like that with our chests pressed together, desperately clinging to each other. When his lips left mine, I groaned at the loss.

Using the hand in my hair, he tilted my head to the side and nipped at my neck with his teeth before kissing the skin and soothing the pain. Over and over, his mouth traveled from the base of my ear to my collarbone, leaving a wet trail in its wake. I barely registered my head resting on the pillow as he leaned over me, his hand moving from under my head.

Anthony hovered above. Water droplets from his hair pooled on his shoulder. I wanted to lean up, and lick it off. His fingers danced across my exposed collarbone. Every inch of my skin demanded more of his touch.

"Anthony, please…" I begged, not recognizing my own voice. "I need you to touch me…"

"Grab the headboard, *luce mia.*" He commanded, the low growl sending electrical pulses through my body. "If it becomes too much, if you let go, I stop. But you're going to be a good girl and use your words if it becomes too much, aren't you?"

"Yes…" My answer was breathy, trying to push my body up into his. It was useless. He smirked down at me as I stuck out my bottom lip.

I stretched my arms above me to grab onto his headboard, and my legs fell from Anthony's waist to rest on his hips. His hand moved down to the hem of my shirt, pushing it up until my breasts were exposed. He quickly palmed them, and I moaned when his thumbs brushed my nipples.

"I love the way you respond to my touch, *luce mia.*" His praise sent a flood of arousal between my legs as his mouth latched on to one of the peaks. Sucking it into his mouth, his fingers trailed down my stomach, his touch sparking a fire in my core.

When he reached my hips, my breath hitched, and I pushed into the mattress away from his touch.

"Anthony…" I whispered, not wanting to let go, but needing him to pause. His hands quickly left my body as my mind started a sharp downward spiral.

*The bruises.* I hadn't seen them since before we went to bed, but I knew they wouldn't have just disappeared. *What if this changes things?* A tear escaped from the corner of my eye as I took a deep breath to re-center myself.

"Talk to me, *luce mia.*" His voice was calm and gentle. My chest tightened at his concern as the emotions flooded my body.

"I'm okay. I just needed a minute. The bruises…" I trail off, not knowing how to explain what I was feeling. As if reading my mind, one of Anthony's hands brushed over my hip. I lifted my head, watching as Anthony leaned back on his heels.

"Gwen, I said it last night and I will say it again. These bruises do not define you." His hands snaked under my ass to the waistband of my pants while he talked, working them down my legs until they were off and on the floor. "You are no less because of what he did to you. When you leave my bed, it will only be when you understand how extraordinary of a woman you are. I will worship your body for however long it takes."

His lips found my exposed hip, and nipped at the skin in the same way as before, my skin once again on fire. As he made his way around the bruise, my body responded to the sensations, warmth pooling in my center.

"Anthony..." My head fell back once again, my eyes closing and a moan escaping my lips. My legs tried to straighten and Anthony's lips left my skin, his hands pressing on my thighs, spreading my legs.

"Do you trust me?" He asked, lust coating his words. I nodded my head, certain he could see me from his position in between my legs. When he didn't immediately restart his assault on my skin, I lifted my head to see him glaring at me in warning.

"Yes, Anthony. Of course, I trust you," I answered, offering a small smile to encourage him even more.

My heart skipped a beat watching Anthony look down at my body. Desire consumed his features. His middle finger ran through my center, gathering the wetness that had dripped down my thighs from his earlier admiration of my body. Slight discomfort pulsed between my legs as he gently slid a finger inside me, slowly moving back and forth. My brows pinched together at the intrusion, and I willed my body to relax.

*This was Anthony. My Anthony. I trusted him.*

"Gwendalyn, look at me," he urged. My gaze found his. "Good girl, *luce mia*." My face relaxed with his praise, my tense muscles following suit.

Anthony leaned down, planting a kiss directly above my exposed clit as he added another finger. I gasped, and tried to push up into him for more, but his hand on my thigh tightened, keeping me against the bed.

His head moved, his beard scratching against my hip. I started to ask what he was doing when I got my answer. Pain radiated through my body as his mouth bit down on my bruised flesh. Hot tears burned the corners of my eyes.

"Fuck. Anthony..." My voice came out strangled, somewhere between a scream and a moan. Anthony pumped his fingers faster as he sucked, and my hips instinctively bucked against his hand as the pain morphed into pleasure. His thumb grazed my clit, an orgasm quickly building.

My nails dug into the wood of the headboard, not wanting to accidentally let go.

"Please, Anthony, don't stop," I groaned, my body begging for more.

"I wouldn't dream of it," he smirked, soothing my skin with a flick of his tongue. His grip on my thigh tightened, digging into the bruises already there and making them his.

I wanted to scream, not from pain but from the torture my emotions were inflicting on me. Every cell in my body wanted him to continue, to chase the release I was so close to catching.

But something in my mind held me back from letting go.

Shame and guilt forced their way into my thoughts. *I should not be enjoying this.*

"Stay out of that pretty head of yours, *luce mia*," Anthony said, reading my mind. "Don't think, just feel."

My chest tightened, not understanding how this man saw me as anything other than broken and damaged. But I needed this, to have my body feel like my own again, and who was I to try to convince Anthony otherwise?

His mouth was on my hip again, biting down harder as his thumb intentionally circled my clit. My orgasm was so close, every muscle in my lower body tensed, my toes curling. I just needed something...

"Come for me, *luce mia*," he growled, and that was all it took for me to go toppling over the edge.

I screamed my release, coming so hard that Anthony's hand on my thigh was the only thing keeping my entire body from arching off the bed. Every single one of my nerves was on fire, demanding all the oxygen in the room as my orgasm reached parts of my body I didn't know existed. My soul floated above me as wave after wave of pleasure hit, nearly drowning me as I tried to hang on.

I wanted to live in this ecstasy forever.

Anthony milked every ounce of my orgasm, letting me enjoy the bliss as long as I wanted, coming down from my high in my own time. Once my body sank back into the bed, he slowly withdrew his fingers from me, and I whimpered from the loss.

I lifted my head, catching Anthony's heated gaze as he stuck his fingers, glistening with my release, into his mouth. My hands fell to my sides, nearly numb from how hard I had been clinging to the headboard. Finished with cleaning his fingers, Anthony pushed himself upright until he was sitting on his heels, his hand falling from my thigh. A shiver ran down my spine from the loss of his body heat so close to mine.

I pushed myself up onto my elbows, my body still buzzing from the mind tingling orgasm it has just received. "Anthony, that was…"

*Amazing? Mind blowing? Fucking awesome?* There were no words to describe what had just happened.

"I don't believe I said I was done with you yet, *luce mia.*" His gravelly voice paired with the dark gleam in his eyes should have had me pulling away and running out of this bedroom, especially after everything that had happened. Maybe that was why I chose to stay.

Anthony had shown me what it felt like to be cared for, and I had never trusted a man more completely before today.

"Please, I don't think I can take anymore," I begged as I attempted to pull my thighs together.

"Oh, but you can, and you will." He growled, his gaze never leaving mine as his hands trailed up from my ankles until they reached my knees, pinning them against the bed and effectively exposing every inch of my wet pussy to him. Positioning himself in between my legs, he trailed gentle kisses from my knees until he reached my clit. His warm breath on the sensitive bundle of nerves had my body squirming under his hold. "Now, be a good girl and let me clean up the mess I made."

His mouth was on me before I could comprehend what had happened. The expert way his tongue swiped up my center had my entire body shaking in pleasure, sending sparks of electricity through my body.

His speed was torture as he slowly lapped up the release that was dripping toward the bed. My legs convulsed when he flicked my clit with the tip of his tongue, his hands traveling up to dig his fingers into the flesh of my thighs.

"Anthony…" I moaned his name, my voice sounding foreign. I couldn't process my indescribable need for this man.

He set my skin on fire with a single look. His touch caused every muscle in my body to go weak. I needed to feel him, to make sure this was real.

My hands found his head, and my fingers weaved through his hair, making him groan. The sound sent a vibration through the most intimate parts of me, causing my hips to buck against his mouth, silently demanding more. An orgasm was threatening to take over.

"Patience, *luce mia*," he chuckled, looking up at my body through hooded eyes. "Stay still, or I will find a way to tie you down until I have finished." My breath hitched. *Why did the thought of Anthony tying me up turn me on?*

Anthony bit down on my clit, effectively pulling me out of my thoughts and eliciting a harsh wail to escape from my throat. He already knew his way around my body, adding another reason to the growing list of reasons I was falling for this man. His tongue pushed inside of me, my hands fisting his hair. I was so close and didn't know how much more I could take.

My hips rocked against his mouth, matching his speed while he dug his fingertips further into my thighs. The painful pinch of breaking skin mixed with the pleasure of Anthony's tongue sent me over the edge.

There was no holding back the release that took over my body.

My heels dug into the bed as Anthony held me down, lapping up every drop of my cum before it could leave my body. Only when he was satisfied that he left nothing behind did he finally lift his head and release my thighs.

My body sated, I let my eyes close while Anthony's gentle hands tugged at my shirt until the hem met my hips. The mattress shifted under his weight as he made his way next to me, bringing the comforter with him before he snaked his arms around my body and pulled me toward him until my back was against his chest.

His hands rubbed lazy circles on my hip and everything fell away as I relaxed into Anthony. He would fight every last one of my demons, if they dared return, without me having to ask. Sleep claimed me while he whispered praises into my hair, making me feel more appreciated and cared for then I had in a long time.

# Chapter Twenty-Five

## Anthony

I had done my best not to make too much noise as I made a pot of coffee and something small for us to snack on.

It was early afternoon by this point and Gwen had to be hungry, seeing as she hadn't eaten since the day before last. My stomach had been too twisted in knots to even think about food until now. The coffee machine beeped loudly, and I silently cursed it for possibly waking Gwen. I poured two mugs then added creamer to one of the mugs until it was the perfect light brown. Balancing the plate of fruit and cheese that I had assembled in one hand, I managed to grab both cups of coffee in the other before heading upstairs.

Standing next to the bed now, I looked down at *luce mia*, laying on her side facing away from me with her hair spread out on the pillow around her like a halo. My heart squeezed with love and admiration for the woman in front of me.

*Wait, did I love her?* There was no denying I had strong feelings for Gwen, but I had no idea when they had morphed into something bigger. My head spun with the revelation, a voice deep inside telling me I needed to run.

*She deserved better than what you could offer her.*

A soft hum broke me from my thoughts, Gwen turning to face me as her eyes fluttered open. My self-deprecating thoughts would have to wait until later. I sat down the plate on the bedside table, then settled on the bed next to her.

"Good morning," I said, holding out one of the coffee cups enough so she knew it was for her. She pulled herself up into a sitting position, letting the comforter pool on her lap, then took one of the mugs from my hand. The cup pressed against her lips as she sipped it cautiously.

"Morning," she offered back, a small smile forming after she lowered her mug. "This is the best cup of coffee I have ever had. Thank you."

"No thanks needed. I brought you some food, too. It isn't much, but it's early afternoon and you need something."

"Now that you mention it, I am starving," she chuckled, eyeing the plate next to her.

"Eat, please." I picked up the plate, offering it to her. She took it, settling it in her lap before she popped a grape into her mouth. The tiny moan that escaped her had my cock hardening again. I needed to put space between us before I took her right then and there.

"I'm going to take a quick shower, then give Katie a call to see how Oliver is doing." I stood up, kissing the top of her head to keep from devouring her lips with mine. "Let me know if you need anything, alright?"

She nodded her head, a dreamy far-off gaze in her eyes as she continued eating, and I chuckled. After grabbing fresh clothes, I headed to the bathroom and took my time getting ready for the day ahead.

I called Katie from the bathroom after I got dressed. Of course, the first thing she asked about was how Gwen was doing. I was grateful for the friendship the two of them formed. Katie said she was happy for Oliver to stay as long as needed, but he was asking about us constantly. I told her I would talk to Gwen, and make sure she was up for Oliver coming home.

Stepping out of the en-suite, I started to ask Gwen how she was feeling when I froze in my tracks. She was no longer on the bed. Fear immediately flooded my veins.

"Gwen," I yelled for her as I rushed from the bedroom. My body stopped upon seeing her. She was coming out of the hallway bathroom and in her own world. Turning around, she nearly jumped out of her skin.

"Cheese and crackers, Anthony," she squealed, her hand going to her chest. "You scared me. What are you doing just standing there?"

I rushed forward, wrapping her in my arms and pressing my face into her hair. My racing heart started to slow when she rested her hands on my back, and pressed her cheek against my chest. I breathed in deeply, emotion catching on the exhale. Of course, Gwen noticed.

"Hey, what's wrong?" she whispered, rubbing my back in long strokes in an attempt to comfort me. I didn't answer right away, not knowing what to say, and she didn't push. We stood there in comfortable silence until I loosened my grip on her. She lifted her head, looking up at me through hooded eyes, and I was gone.

Cupping her cheeks, I kissed her, wanting to convey with actions where words failed me. I wanted her to know how much she meant to me and how scared I was of losing her. Her hands covered mine as I claimed her mouth, our tongues dancing together as she melted into me. I swallowed every moan that threatened to escape from her lips

*I needed to stop before things went too far.* It wasn't that I didn't want a repeat of last night, because I definitely did. It was just that her body needed to rest. Plus, there was still that fact that my son was with my neighbor.

I broke our kiss, pressing my forehead to hers and catching my breath.

"I'm sorry if I worried you. I didn't want to interrupt you and I really needed the bathroom," she said, her fingers gently wrapping around my wrists with her thumbs resting on top of my hands. The touch centered me.

"Don't apologize. I'm just on edge," I admitted, a thousand scenarios having run through my mind of what could have happened to her.

"I'm not going anywhere," she voiced, reading my mind. I continued to hold her, wanting to burn this moment into my memory.

I finally pulled away and my hands dropped to hold hers. "Oliver has been asking about us. What do you think about ordering pizza and having a movie night?"

"I would love that. Is it okay if I shower?" she asked.

"Of course."

"I'm going to go down to my room to get fresh clothes. Give me maybe an hour?"

"Take your time. I'll get the food ordered, then go get Oliver."

I leaned down once more, kissing her gently this time. When I was done, I stepped back and released her hands. I reluctantly watched as Gwen went downstairs.

Pulling out my phone, I texted Katie that I would be over to get Oliver in thirty minutes. I walked back into my room, ordering dinner and getting set up for a night with my two favorite people.

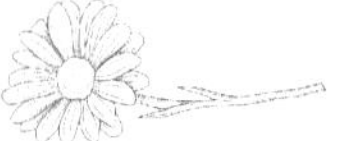

"Here you go, man," Jason offered, stepping up behind me and setting a mug on my desk in front of me. "Also, Steve from I.T. wanted me to give this to you."

He pulled a small box out of his pocket and held it out to me. I took it from his open hand, opening it to check out the contents. After the attack, not only had I made sure I could track Gwen via her phone, but I asked Steve if he could come up with something that I could give her that would be inconspicuous enough that no one would know it was a tracker.

He designed a bracelet that could double as a panic button and would alert me directly. The plan was for her to never need it, but just in case...

Letting out an exasperated sigh, I leaned back in my chair, slipped the box into my pocket, then covered my face with my hands.

Hopefully, Gwen would accept the gift. There was no doubt in my mind she was getting fed up with my inability to make up my damn mind. Whenever I found myself getting pulled in, I would force myself to stop. I didn't want to push her.

It had been a few weeks since that night together, and I didn't know where we stood. We never talked about it. Honestly, I never brought it up in fear she would express a level of regret. It was a childish thought–I knew this–but it didn't change the fact that I knew I would never be good enough for Gwen.

So, I did my best to give her space and threw myself into this case.

Jason and I were certain the person who attacked Gwen was the same asshole who had assaulted all the other women. It had been days of me pouring over the most current files, to the point that words started blurring together.

There was no new information or leads. All the interviews we re-conducted were dead ends. By all accounts, the asshole went into hiding after that night. While I was glad no other woman had been attacked, what didn't sit right with me was that he stopped all of a sudden.

Jason was still talking, going on about updating things at the warehouse because of security concerns, but I couldn't bring myself to care about any of that right now. I needed to figure out what the hell was going on, and why we couldn't find this fucker.

And why it seemed Gwen was the catalyst to him disappearing.

"Earth to Tony," Jason broke through the mental haze, his eyebrows raised in a quizzical look.

"It's been weeks, and we have nothing." The anger was building, my fists clenching on top of my desk. "We need to find him. Now."

"Anthony, we will." Jason put a hand on my shoulder, and the action caused me to jump. My arm swung wide, bumping into the full cup of coffee and spilling the liquid over the files scattered on my desk.

"Shit!" I exclaimed as I tried to keep some of the papers from being soaked.

The coffee started dripping over the edge of the desk, a small puddle forming on the floor. I stared at the liquid as the anger bubbled over. I picked up the offending mug and threw it on the ground, the shattering pieces adding to the storm that was brewing inside me.

We had been too preoccupied with the case to put time and energy into teaching lessons to any other dirtbags. I wanted to feel bones crunching under my fists, and their blood on my knuckles.

Rage clouded my mind. I needed a release.

Blindly swinging, my fist made contact with the first thing it could.

"Fucking damn it!" Jason exclaimed, having been caught severely off guard when my fist found his jaw.

Pain radiated through my hand and wrist. *Apparently, punching Jason was becoming a thing.* Closing my eyes and focusing on the pain, I hung my head and tried to center myself. I took deep breaths, imagining Gwen's warm skin under my hands and her soft lips against mine. She would always be my guiding light.

"Tony…" Jason started, but was quickly cut off by a booming voice that echoed throughout the station.

"Marino, Kreugler, my office. NOW!" Captain was standing at the top of the walkway outside his office, his face pinched in anger as he turned and walked away.

*Shit.*

# Chapter Twenty-Six

## *Gwen*

"**M**y flight is booked and I'm coming out to see you! Just two more weeks, sweet pea!" Ivy squealed into the phone, nearly causing me to drop it into the sink full of water.

"How long are you staying?" I asked, scrubbing away at a pot that looked like Anthony used to make scrambled eggs. There was no way I was letting him near the stove any time soon unless he learned how to properly use non-stick cooking spray and correct cookware.

"Just a week. But I'm thinking of doing a little apartment hunting while I'm out there. My contract is almost up and I've started putting out some feelers at different event centers in the area." Ivy seemed excited, and I was happy thinking about Ivy being in the same state as me.

"I know you'll find something amazing! Anybody would be lucky to have you." I gave her a smile, then returned my focus to the stubborn burnt on eggs in front of me.

"How have you been doing?" Ivy asked. I sighed, really tired of answering that question. But I wasn't going to tell Ivy that. She hadn't been too happy with me when I told her about the attack two days after it happened. She even threatened to hop on a plane right then if Anthony wasn't going to keep me safe. So if she wanted to ask my how I was doing every day, than I would let her.

"I'm okay." And I was, for the most part. It had been weeks since the incident. For the most part, things were back to normal, and I was feeling more like myself. There were still times when I was skittish, especially with loud noises, and would wake up suddenly from night-mares.

But Anthony... His hot-and-cold routine was getting old. It was like he was afraid he was going to hurt me.

"Any news about that dumbass ex of yours?" Ivy asked.

"No. The police in Pittsburgh haven't been able to serve him with the restraining order because they don't know where he's at, if he's even in Pennsylvania. Honestly, I don't care." I shrugged, scrubbing harder at the burnt eggs. "I haven't had an unknown call or text from him in so long. Maybe he finally got the memo."

"Well, I hope for your sake, something bad happened to him and he's gone for good," Ivy said. I would never say it out loud, but I agreed with her. "I'll text you the flight details. Call me soon, okay?"

"Of course," I laughed. "I love your face."

"Love yours more." Ivy blew me a kiss, and I returned it.

Just as she ended the call, the sound of the garage door let me know Anthony was home. The door leading into the house slammed closed, a line of expletives following quickly after as heavy footsteps echoed through the kitchen.

I jumped, causing water to splash from the kitchen sink onto the floor. I dropped the dish towel from my shoulder onto the floor to soak up the water.

The hair on the back of my neck stood up as Anthony walked behind me to the fridge, the smell of pine and bourbon lingering in the air around me as I followed him out of the corner of my eye. Anthony pulled out a beer, opening it and drinking half of it before he closed the door.

"Is everything okay?" I asked softly. All signs pointed to Anthony having had a rough day, and I didn't want to make it worse.

"Just great," he paused, then gestured to the sink. "You didn't have to get those. I would have done them in the morning."

"That's what you said yesterday, and the day before that," I muttered, not sure if he'd hear me, while I put the now clean pan in the drying rack. The chuckle coming from him told me he did. "It's not funny Anthony!" I whipped around to see he had snuck up beside me. A smile stretched across his face as he placed the bottle down on the counter next to me. He knew just how much it annoyed me that he constantly left dirty dishes in the sink for days at a time.

I turned back around to drain the water from the sink and he closed the distance between us. Warmth radiating from him, setting my skin on fire. His arms around my waist teasing the waistband of my pants with his fingers as he kissed my shoulder. I sighed, leaning into his touches and laying my head back.

A shiver ran down my spine when his fingertips brushed over my hips, and his lips found the crook of my neck. I pushed against him with my hands gripping the edge of the sink, feeling his hard cock pressing against my lower back.

"Anthony..." I moaned, wanting more and ready to beg if needed. His body froze against mine before he slowly pulled away.

I spun on my heels, pissed that this was happening once again. This time, though, I wasn't going to just let him walk away. Our gazes locked, and it became a stare down, each of us waiting for the other to break.

It was me.

I shoved at his chest, wanting some kind of reaction from him. When he didn't, I tried again, and this time one of his hands wrapped around both of my wrists, pulling me close to him and pinning them against his chest. He dipped his head close to my ear, the rough stubble on his jaw rubbing against mine and sending electricity down my spine.

"You do not want to do this right now," he growled. His tongue flicked at my earlobe as if he couldn't help himself and I was once again putty in his hands. As quickly as he started, he stopped. Anthony pressed his forehead against mine, our breathing the only sound in the kitchen.

"What if I do?" I whispered.

"I can't—," he started, pulling away to look down at me, but I cut him off.

"Let go of me," I demanded, my voice surprisingly steady with the amount of emotions flowing through me. He immediately dropped my wrists, taking several steps back with his head down, refusing to look at me.

Anger was rising in my chest, the constant rejection from someone who weeks ago worshiped my body finally causing me to snap.

"What the hell, Anthony? Why are we doing this back-and-forth dance after everything that has happened? Did you finally realize I wasn't worth the trouble?" His head snapped up and his eyes found mine once again. They darkened, a warning to stop, but I needed to say this.

"The last three weeks have been nothing short of torture. You have been treating me like I'm going to break at any second. I'm not some fragile flower, Anthony. Do you regret what we did? Cause I sure as hell don't. But if you don't want to do this, if you don't want me, then say it cause I can't do this anymore." I was yelling by this point, my chest rising and falling angrily as I let out all the emotions I had bottled up for the last three weeks.

Anthony didn't move the entire time, his gaze fixed on me. Irritation replaced the anger that had been coursing through my veins.

"Message received. If you don't need anything else, I'm going downstairs before I start throwing dishes." I rolled my eyes as I turned to leave the kitchen. Anthony stopped my retreat by stepping in front of me. "Move, Anthony."

"Did you just roll your eyes, *luce mia*?" His voice was intense as his stare.

"And if I did?" *Don't do it Gwen. Don't poke the bear.* "Nothing you can do about it." *I poked the bear.*

There was a glint in his eye, and every instinct screamed at me to run. But I was frozen in place by all the thoughts of what I wanted him to do.

He stalked toward me, and before I knew what was happening, he had me pinned against the pantry cabinets, my ass pressed against the door with his arms on either side of me. "Maybe I need to fuck that attitude out of you."

"Anthony, I—" I whimpered, his hands on my hips distracting me.

"Is that what you want, Gwen?" One hand was traveling up my stomach, the other was still planted solidly on my hip. "You want to be my good girl?"

"Please." I reached my arms up to wrap around his neck. In a flash, one of his hands pinned of mine above my head against the cabinet.

"Fuck," he pressed his nose against my throat as he spoke, "I shouldn't want to do this so much. I've tried to stay away, to give you space after the assault. But the things you make me want to do to you."

"I don't want space. You make me feel things I never knew I could. Please Anthony," my voice a desperate plea at this point, "Touch me."

"Because you asked so nicely." He pushed my legs apart with his knee while his tongue warmed up on my neck. I was so far gone I barely registered his hand on my hip, moving as his fingers teased into the waistband of my leggings. My breath hitched when they slipped lower, past my upper thigh until they found my center. "You're so wet, *luce mia*. Is all of this for me?"

All I could do was nod my head as his expert fingers moved my own wetness to my clit and began circling the little bundle of nerves. *He expected me to talk right now?* It only took a few seconds of his expert touch before I was practically melting into him. As my head fell back against the door, Anthony took the opportunity to nip at my exposed neck.

That's all it took for an orgasm to overcome me. I closed my eyes and my attempt at staying quiet so Oliver didn't wake up was quickly forgotten as a moan escaped from my throat. Anthony quickly claimed it by covering my mouth with his as his fingers continued their assault on my clit, drawing out my orgasm. Between his fingers and mouth, I barely registered the fact that his body was pressed against mine, until his hard length was pressed against my stomach.

"You feel that? You do that to me." He pushed harder into me as he withdrew his hand from my leggings. I whimpered at the loss, wanting him to continue fucking me with his fingers, not stop.

"Anthony, don't—" My protest was quickly silenced as he released my hands from above my head and lifted me up against his body by grabbing onto the back of my thighs. I gasped as he turned us around and placed me roughly on the kitchen island.

His eyes were now level with my unconstrained breasts, a fact he seemed all too aware of as one of his hands slipped under my shirt until he found my pebbled nipple and began rolling it between his fingers. Just as I began to moan my approval, his mouth was on me again, his tongue not hesitating to explore every inch of my mouth.

His free hand was on the back of my neck, sliding up into the base of my hair, before fisting it. All the sensations put my nerves into overdrive. I was getting closer to the edge, but something was holding me back.

"Anthony, please. Touch me again."

"I'll do one better. I want to taste you again." He pulled his mouth away, taking my bottom lip with him as he gave it a gentle bite, moving his hand to free my other breast and giving it the same attention. "Lift that perfect ass of yours up or I'm going to have to buy you a new pair of pants. I'm too desperate of a man right now."

I groaned as I positioned my hands on the island to push myself up. Then I froze.

Sensing my hesitation, Anthony stopped and withdrew his hand from my shirt. "Are you okay?" His eyes were laced with concern. "Fuck, I went too far."

"No, NO!" I quickly fisted his shirt and pulled him closer to me. "It's just, I'm not wearing cute panties or anything. Not to mention I've been chasing around Ollie all day. This isn't sexy. I'm not sexy. This is—"

As if offended by my words, Anthony scoffed. In a blink of an eye, his hand was holding on to my throat, just below my jaw. The pressure from beneath pushed my head up so I could no longer see what he was doing.

"Now I'm only going to say this once, so listen very closely. I will not tolerate anyone talking bad about what's mine. That includes you." Shifting my head to the side, he marked a path from my collarbone to my ear with his tongue. "I don't care if you're wearing lace underwear or granny panties, it doesn't matter. Because it's all going to look the same, in a pile on my floor."

Goosebumps began to form on my neck as he moved my head so I could look him in the eye. "Lift up so I can claim what's mine, *luce mia.*"

As I shifted my hands back down to the island to lift myself up, he let go of my throat, moving to slide both of his hands under my ass and into the waistband of my leggings, swiftly pulling both them and my underwear off in one motion. I gasped at the feeling of the butcher block on my ass.

I didn't have much time to process it before Anthony had a hold of my knees. He pulled me toward the edge until my ass was barely on the island, the spread my legs as wide as they would go. Positioning himself in the middle, he lowered himself down to one knee with hunger in his eyes.

I grabbed the edge of the counter to keep myself from falling as Anthony moved his head to get his first taste. Swiping his tongue up between my folds, I gasped when he barely brushed my clit with the tip.

"Fuck Gwen, you taste even better than I remembered." Plunging his tongue back toward my pussy, he began his assault on my body. His hands made their way up to my thighs, giving him the leverage to spread me even more. My back arched in an attempt to press myself into him.

"This pussy is mine." He moved his tongue slick with my wetness back up to my clit. As he flattened his tongue to press against it, he moved his hand to position a finger at my entrance.

"Oh God, yes," I sputtered, attempting to push my body onto his finger.

"No God here, *luce mia*, only me. Now tell me, do you want my fingers inside of you again, or should I keep teasing you with my tongue?" He lazily flicked his tongue over my clit several times, making me squirm with need.

*What kind of question was that?* I continued my sad attempts to force his fingers inside me. His hand on my thigh tightened its grip, and I gasped as a light slap landed between my legs.

"Words, Gwendalyn. I need words," he growled.

"Your fingers! Your fingers, please!"

"Good girl." He roughly shoved a finger inside of me as he sucked my clit in between his teeth. Immediately, he pulled out, plunging two fingers all the way in, curling them to hit that spot deep within. All it took was one, two, three strokes and I was spiraling.

My head hung back as I drew my bottom lip in between and bit down to stifle the scream threatening to escape. The force of my orgasm caused me to see stars. Anthony continued pumping in and out of my pussy, not stopping until he had licked up every drop of arousal.

Blinking away the stars, I looked down at him just as he withdrew his fingers and slipped them into his mouth.

"I'll never get tired of this taste," he grinned up at me.

My heart was hammering so hard in my chest I was certain he could see it. Standing, he grabbed a clean dish towel from a drawer, then wet it at the kitchen sink and returned to his spot between my legs.

Kneeling once more, he cleaned me up as I sat happily sedated, watching him work. *I* would never get tired of seeing this man on his knees for me. Anthony stood, and gently grasped my chin between his thumb and finger, pulling me toward him. He kissed me tenderly and once again, I couldn't help closing my eyes and melting into him.

I didn't want this moment to end. I wanted him to take me up to his room and have his way with me.

Gently, he pulled away. His hands found my waist and he lifted me off the counter and placed me on my feet. Bending down, he grabs my discarded leggings and underwear, handing them to me. I stared at the clothes in his hands, dumbfounded.

"Gwendalyn, I can't be gentle anymore," he shook his head, "and you deserve that. You deserve better than me."

"Stop, I thought we already established that I am not some breakable thing. I want you, all of you. So give it to me."

His eyes darkened once more, and I could have sworn I saw him smile. Before my next breath, Anthony threw me over his shoulder and left the kitchen, quickly walking through the house to the steps. I wiggled in his grasp, ready to protest being manhandled, but was quickly silenced by a smack on my ass.

"Anthony!" I gasped, sincerely hoping I hadn't woken up Ollie.

"I'm in charge, *luce mia*. If I want to throw you over my shoulder and smack this ass, then I will. Plus," he paused, slipping his hand in the space where my lower body rested on his chest and between my legs, "it would seem that you enjoy this." His fingers found the pool of wetness caused by the slap from his hand, and I cursed my body for betraying me.

I closed my eyes as he slipped a finger into my center, biting the inside of my cheek to keep from moaning out loud as my sensitive core shuttered from the contact.

My eyes opened when my ass made contact with the mattress. Anthony discarded my clothes by his feet and looked down at me with a darkness in his eyes.

"Last chance, Gwen," he said. "We do this, and I am never letting you go. You're mine, to cherish and protect until my last breath." His declaration depleted the air from my lungs as he continued. "I want you, more than words can explain right now, but I will always put your safety above all else. So if anything gets to be too much, you say stop and I will. No questions asked. Do you understand?"

"Yes."

A fierce hunger joined the heat in his eyes. I squeezed my thighs together as he stalked toward me and grabbed my chin. Tilting my head up, I resisted the urge to squirm under his heated gaze.

"Good girl. Now, *luce mia*, take off your shirt. I want to see those perfect tits."

# Chapter Twenty-Seven

## Anthony

It took every ounce of restraint to not force Gwen down on my bed and use her body however I wanted.

The corner of her lips raised in a cocky smile as she lifted the shirt over her head at a tortuously slow pace. I dropped my hand to my belt and began unbuckling it, needing to free my hardening cock.

Gwen added her shirt to the pile, then worked to undo the button of my pants. They dropped with a heavy thump and I cursed under my breath, remembering my gun that I needed to lock away.

"Don't fucking move," I said to Gwen, picking it up and hurrying to my closet to put it in my safe. I put in the code, opening the door and my eyes caught the shine of a pair of handcuffs that I had forgotten about.

*Perfect.* Grabbing them and the key, I shut the door, strolling back into the bedroom and stopping in front of Gwen. Her eyes went wide when they landed on the handcuffs dangling from my finger.

"Are you going to use them on me?" she said quietly, lust coating her words.

"If you'll let me," I said. Her mouth parted, and she pulled her bottom lip between her teeth. "But I don't have to."

She stood, our chest mere inches from each other. Her fingertips traced the path of hair from my chest to my abs, my cock throbbing from the contact. Her gaze found mine, and I saw my own desire being reflected.

Threading my fingers through her hair, I yanked her to me and our bodies collided together. Her nails dug into the skin near my hips as I claimed her mouth, our tongues dancing together. Panting, I broke our kiss, looking down at her.

"Yes," she breathed, gripping my cock through the fabric of my briefs. "Use the cuffs."

"Fuck, Gwen," I hissed. Feral thoughts flashed through my mind. I wanted to take her, hard and fast, until she was screaming my name, but I wanted to savor the first time I sunk my cock into her pussy. Plus, Oliver was down the hall. I reached over, placing the key on the nightstand, then returned my attention to Gwen. "Turn around, *luce mia.*"

She did as she was told, slowly spinning on her heel while peeking over her shoulder to watch my movements. Grabbing one of her hands, the soft clink of the metal sent a wave of anticipation through my body as I closed it around her wrist.

I watched for any kind of change in her body language, tension in her shoulders or uneven breathing. She stayed relaxed as I moved onto her other wrist, binding them together behind her back. When I was done, I tucked her hair over her shoulder and ran my fingers over the skin of her neck. She closed her eyes, a soft moan leaving her lips as I ran my nose up the path my fingers had just taken.

"You are breathtaking, Gwen," I whispered. My hands slide over her soft skin to the front of her body, cupping her breasts. She sighed and leaned into my touch, the action causing my heart to pick up.

I focused my attention on her nipples, pebbled between my fingers as I pinched them, causing a moan to escape her throat.

"Shhh, *luce mia,*" I muttered, nipping at her ear. "I'd hate for our fun to be cut short."

"Maybe you should do something about that, then," she muttered, gasping when I gave her nipple a tug.

"You want me to gag you?" She relaxed into me further, seemingly granting me permission to do whatever I wanted.

Excitement grew in the pit of my stomach, picturing Gwen with her panties stuffed in her mouth, her words garbled as I laid my claim on her body. Roughly, I grabbed her throat and forced her head back until her hooded eyes were staring at me. "Not today, *luce mia*. I want to hear my name on your lips when you come on my cock for the first time."

My hand traveled from her neck down her body until my fingers slipped between her legs. I brushed past her clit, eliciting a whimper from Gwen when I didn't give it attention, and discovered a pool of wetness waiting for me. Gathering it, I circled the bundle of nerves that she had so desperately wanted me to touch. "Fuck, you are so wet for me."

"Anthony," she whimpered. Withdrawing my hand, I pushed Gwen forward until her chest was resting on the bed, her feet still planted firmly on the floor. I marveled at the way she looked in this position. She was completely vulnerable, her body on full display for me.

I ran my hand down the dip in her back and tugged off my briefs with the other. My cock sprang free, a bead of precum gathered on the tip.

"I don't know how long I will last once I'm inside you, Gwen." I reached into my nightstand as I spoke, and found the silver packet stashed in the back of the drawer.

Rolling the condom over my erection, I stepped between her now spread legs. My nails dug into her ass, marking her perfect skin with tiny crescent shapes.

"Please Anthony," she groaned, pushing back into me as I ran my cock along her slit, coating it in her arousal. I gave her exactly what she wanted, entering her in one motion, only pausing to let her adjust when her muscles tensed under me.

Once her body relaxed, I pulled out until just the tip remained inside, then slowly pushed back in. I kept up the torturously slow pace, relishing in the moans that Gwen was trying to keep muffled by pressing her face into the mattress.

Leaning forward, I twisted her hair in my fist and yanked her head backward, causing her to arch her back. "Fuck, Gwen," I murmured. "You take me so well, like your pussy was fucking made for me."

She hummed in approval as I picked up my speed, arousal dripping down her leg as my balls smacked against the wet skin. Wanting to taste her delicate skin, I hauled Gwen up by her hair.

I continued my fevered thrusts, her cuffed wrists pressing into my abdomen while my tongue ran along the pressure point in her neck. I bit down, causing her to pulse around me and pushing me closer toward my release. Slipping between her legs, I braced my forearm down her body to keep her against me and circled her soaking clit with two fingers until her legs were shaking with the need for release.

"Come with me, *luce mia,*" I grunted, my balls tightening. I drove into her, one, two, three more times.

Gwen let go with a scream, and my hand in her hair moved to cover her mouth and muffle the sound. Her pussy strangled my cock, pulling my own release from me in bursts.

"Fucking hell," I grunted, dropping my hand from her mouth to rest on her collar bone.

Stars danced across my vision as I struggled to stay upright. Resting my chin on the top of her head, I focused on the perfect woman in front of me. Her body fit against mine like a puzzle piece.

Our sweat mixed together as we both tried to catch our breath. When I finally felt like I wasn't going to collapse, I carefully pulled out of Gwen. A small hiss escaped her lips, and I pressed a kiss to the crown of her head.

Reaching for the key on the nightstand, I unlocked the cuffs, rubbing her wrists and checking for any signs of irritation. There was a slight red line on one side, presumably where she was pressed against me and I leaned down to kiss the afflicted skin.

We collapsed onto the bed after that, rolling onto our sides. I tucked Gwen against my chest and drew lazy circles on her hip. Within minutes, her breathing was slow and rhythmic.

As much as I wanted to let my body relax alongside hers, I needed to get both of us cleaned up. I untangled myself, eliciting a groan of protest from the beauty dozing in my head. Chuckling to myself, I headed to the bathroom to dispose of the condom and start a bath.

She was already going to wake up sore in the morning, a thought that had my cock seemingly jumping to life again. There was no reason she needed to wake up feeling dirty.

When the water had warmed up, I searched through the sink cabinet for something I could add to the water. I found a barely used bottle of lavender bubble bath that I must have gotten for Oliver when he was going through sleep regressions, and added a few squirts to the water.

Once the tub was full enough and a nice layer of bubbles formed, I went back to the bedroom and scooped Gwendalyn into my arms. She gasped slightly, her eyes opening when I lifted her off of the bed, peering up at me through hooded eyes. "Where are we going?"

"To take a bath, *luce mia*," I chuckled as she relaxed into my chest. "You'll thank me tomorrow."

Stepping back into the bathroom, I stopped next to the tub, then gently set her down into the water. Her fingertips grazed over top of the bubbles, popping some of the higher formations around the edges of the tub.

"I didn't take you as a bubble bath kind of guy." She grinned up at me, sleep still filling her eyes. Just like the last time she was in here, she sat in the tub with her legs pulled to her chest and her head turned toward me with a cheek resting on her knees.

"Only for you."

"Are you joining me?" Gwendalyn looked up at me through hooded eyes, her wavy hair cascading down her shoulders. If I hadn't already planned on getting in with her, I would have without a second thought.

"Scoot forward."

Water sloshed over the side as I settled behind Gwendalyn and positioned her between my legs. Her hands rested on my knees as I started washing her hair, using a washcloth to squeeze water to get it wet and running my fingers through her waves.

The little moans that filled the bathroom while I massaged her scalp were music to my ears. I would be content to live the rest of my life finding different ways to make her moan like that.

Once I was done with her hair, I moved onto her body, tracing every curve while she leaned back onto my chest. Her head rested just below my shoulder, and I occasionally kissed her forehead while I finished my task. She hummed her approval every time I trailed my fingertips over her skin, leaving behind goosebumps, and I had to keep my thoughts in check.

That was difficult, though. If it were up to me, I would be fully planted inside her again, her warm pussy strangling my cock until she came over and over.

"Already ready for round two?" Gwendalyn asked as she wiggled her backside against my hardening cock. My hands flew to her hips, stilling her body.

"*Luce mia*," I growled in warning. My lips trailed along her shoulder.

"Anthony..." she moaned. "Maybe we should head to bed?"

I stood quickly, Gwendalyn yelping in surprise as she grabbed onto the side of the tub to keep from falling forward. Grabbing a towel from the rack, I dried off, then wrapped the towel around my waist. Gwendalyn had stood up, her body on full display while she wrung the water from her hair. Her skin had turned a soft pink from the heat of the water.

Most of the bruises from that night had healed, no physical reminder of what had happened. Her eyes met mine, one of her eyebrows raised in a quizzical look.

I offered her a smile and a shake of my head to let her know it was nothing. She reached for a towel, and I watched as she dried off the water from each leg before she stepped out of the tub, then wrapped the towel around her frame.

I was lost in a trance when she stepped up to me, standing on her tiptoes to plant a kiss on my lips. My hands wrapped around her body, forcing my tongue between her lips and deepening our kiss.

I needed her like my lungs needed air. Every fiber of my being was consumed with the desire to be inside her. *Fuck it.* I pushed her toward the bedroom, my mouth never leaving hers, until the back of her knees hit the bed. She collapsed onto it, and gasped as her towel fell open, moving quickly to cover herself back up.

"Leave it," I demanded, and her hands fell to her sides to prop herself up. My gaze ran over her body, trying to memorize every freckle, mole, and scar possible. "You are mine, *luce mia.*"

Her moans of pleasure were the last thing I remember before the feral part of me took over.

# Chapter Twenty-Eight

## *Gwen*

Light streamed in through the window over Anthony's bed. My body was blanketed in warmth, the weight of an arm on my side, and I couldn't remember the last time I woke up feeling so relaxed. That was until a small foot kicked me in the back. Unless Anthony shrunk overnight, I was fairly positive a certain someone found his way into the bed in the middle of the night.

Turning over, I found Ollie sandwiched in between Anthony and I. Anthony's arm that had been on me seconds ago was now wrapped protectively around his son. I was glad I had slipped a shirt on before passing out last night.

An ache between my legs reminded me of the numerous orgasms given to me by the god-like man laying near me. Where that man found the stamina to go as many times as we had last night still eluded me.

Slipping out of bed, I pulled on my leggings from last night, then gathered the rest of clothes from the floor and walked them to the hamper. This was my last semi-clean pair of leggings, and as long as I was awake, I might as well do a load of laundry before Ollie woke up. I dragged the basket down the hall to the laundry room, where I started throwing in clothes, checking pockets as I went.

Anthony had a bad habit of leaving pens and important papers stuffed into his, and I found the occasional small train hidden away in Oliver's clothes.

My hand curled around a small box no bigger than the size of my palm from Anthony's pants that he wore yesterday, and I wondered what was in it. I set it aside, telling myself to remember to give it to Anthony, and finished loading up the washer.

Just as I was pushing start, arms wrapped around my waist and pulled me into a hard chest. Anthony's familiar scent flooded my senses, and I instantly relaxed into his embrace, leaning my head back onto his shoulder.

"Good morning, *luce mia.*" His low, still sleepy voice had my pussy pulsing with need as he ran his nose up my exposed neck.

"Mmm, good morning," I softly moaned, not wanting to wake Ollie so I could have a few moments alone with Anthony. He started kissing my neck, and I melted into this touch. "Anthony, as much as I wanted to sneak away for more of this, Ollie is going to be awake any minute. Plus, don't you need to get ready for a shift or something?"

"No. My boss is forcing me to take some time off." He sighed, and I turned in his arms, admiring his shirtless chest and low hung sweatpants for a moment before embracing him. He laid his head on top of mine, relaxing into me. "I may have thrown a coffee mug..." He trailed off as if trying to hide the severity of what had happened. I wanted to push him for details, but decided against it.

"Well, I guess you're stuck with us." I pushed away from him, offering him a genuine smile. Ollie would love having him around for a bit and I wouldn't mind being able to get my hands on him, too.

Anthony bent forward, placing a soft kiss on my lips, then stood up, letting his hands fall from my waist.

"Oh, before I forget," I said, turning to grab the box I had set aside, "I found this in your pants pocket." Taking it from my outstretched hand, he opened it and pulled out a small silver bracelet. It had a round charm no bigger than the size of my thumb, with a chain connected on both sides. My heart pinged with jealousy that Anthony bought jewelry for someone.

Reading my mind, he gestured for my wrist and I held it out for him. "It's for you," he spoke, clasping it on before turning it so the charm was facing up. "I had the IT guy at work make this. It's basically a panic button. If anything ever happened to you again, I wouldn't be able to live with myself."

My heart beat against my chest while my throat clogged with emotion. I threw my arms around Anthony's neck, needing to be as close to him as humanly possible.

Surprised, he stumbled forward, but caught himself with a hand on the washer. I peppered his face with kisses like a high schooler who just got asked to prom by her crush.

Anthony chuckled, lifting me up until I was seated on top of the washer, and nudged my legs apart so he could step in between them. Face to face, I couldn't help but feel proud seeing the smile that spread across his lips.

"Thank you, Anthony. I love it." I pulled him toward me, claiming his lips with mine and deepening the kiss as his hands rested on my hips.

The kiss quickly heated, our tongues dancing together while he expertly massaged my inner thighs. Arousal flooded my center, and I wrapped my legs around his, pulling his body into mine. His hard cock rubbed against my sensitive clit through my leggings, and I remembered I never put on underwear.

One of Anthony's hands made its way up my body until it grazed the bottom of my breast while the other pressed under my ass. Fingers brushed over my nipple, eliciting a breathy moan as I pushed my body harder into his. His lips left mine, nipping at the sensitive spot in the crook of my neck, adding to the pleasure.

"Take what you need. Use me, *luce mia,*" he rasped, his hand kneading my breast.

My hips picked up speed, chasing the orgasm that was building as Anthony's hand under my ass supported me. I was so close, the friction from the fabric on the bundle of nerves pushing me closer to the edge. It wasn't enough, though.

"Anthony, please..." I begged, barely able to get out the words. His hand slipped out from under my ass, sliding into the front of my leggings. Anthony roughly inserted two fingers into me and I grinded against his hand.

"Are you going to come for me, Gwen?" I nodded my head, unable to speak from how hard I was clenching my jaw to keep from screaming out. He rolled my nipple between his thumb and finger, pinching it until a strangled whimper escaped my throat.

Anthony covered my mouth with his, swallowing every sound I made while my orgasm shook through my body. Wave after wave of ecstasy coated my veins until I went limp in Anthony's arms. He slowly withdrew his fingers, sucking them clean, and I shuddered from his heated gaze boring into my soul.

*This man...*

"Daddy!" Ollie's voice traveled down the hall. Immediately, I went into nanny mode, trying to figure out how to look more presentable as I pulled away from Anthony, and attempted to slide off the washer. Instead of letting me go, he pressed a kiss to my forehead.

"Let me get him. You can get ready for the day while I make him some breakfast." He lifted me off the washer, making sure I was steady on my feet before running his hands up and down my arms, warming my skin with his touch.

"No scrambled eggs, please," I teased.

"I'll stick to cereal." He winked, sneaking in one last kiss before leaving me alone in the laundry room. If this was how every morning was going to be with Anthony taking time off, I could get used to it.

Two weeks. Anthony had been glued to my side for two weeks, and I was ready to pull my hair out.

Ollie and I no longer had our routine. Anthony accompanied us everywhere, no matter if we went up the road to a playdate or to the store. While he was nothing short of a doting father and an enthusiastic sex partner, I needed space.

I tried to talk to him about how I was feeling, but it was hard to be upset when Anthony reminded me he had nothing but my safety in mind. Ollie begged to go to a park and when Anthony agreed, I faked an upset stomach and practically shoved the two of them out of the door.

It was nice to just disassociate with a book on the couch with a cup of coffee and my favorite blanket. I was almost halfway through my book when my stomach growled. Making my way to the kitchen, I pulled out everything to make a simple peanut butter and jelly sand-wich when the front door opened.

The sound of Ollie's footsteps carrying through the house as he ran through the house. He threw himself at my legs, and I crouched down to give him a hug.

"Miss Gen, Daddy went down the slide!" Ollie exclaimed as An-thony walked into the kitchen, setting down the water bottles he had taken with them to the park.

"Did you wait at the bottom and catch him?" I asked Ollie, trying not to laugh at the mental image of Anthony trying to fit down a children's slide.

"Yes. Daddy was brave. He did it all by himself." Ollie offered his dad a thumbs up, while I caught his gaze, my eyebrows raised in curiosity as to what went down at the park. Anthony simply shook his head, a smile dancing across his lips. His dimples were hidden by the facial hair that had begun growing wild, no longer restricted to the confines of a professional appearance, but I knew they were there.

Ollie placed two tiny hands on my cheeks, forcing me to look at him. "Miss Gen, do your tummy feel better now?"

"It does, sweet boy." I squeezed him, eliciting a giggle that turned into laughter as I tickled his sides. A ringing cell phone sounded over us and I watched Anthony pull out his phone, turning to leave the kitchen while he answered it. I redirected my attention back to Ollie. "How about some lunch?"

He was set up with a peanut butter sandwich at the dining room table when Anthony came back into the kitchen. His face was void of emotion.

Walking up to me, he wrapped his arms around me, and urged our bodies together. There were often moments like these, tiny bits of peace where everything in the world felt right. We hadn't had an official talk about what our future together looked like, but it didn't matter. As long as Anthony held me like I was his anchor in this world, I would stay by his side forever.

"Jason got kicked off the case," he muttered. "I told him he should have kept his temper in check."

"I'm sorry, Anthony," I said, resting my arms around his neck. "I know not having any control must be frustrating."

"He made copies of the files before he left and wants to meet. He thinks since I've been away for a few weeks, I may be able to look at them with a fresh eye."

"You should go. Besides, Ivy's flight is today and she's coming over for dinner. I want to go to the store and get something special."

"No. If something happened to you or Oliver while I was gone…" His words trailed off, his brows furrowed.

"Anthony, you can't be with us 24/7 for forever. We're going to have to find a new normal. Plus, you made sure you would always be able to find us." I held up my wrist, the silver bracelet hanging loosely. Besides showering, it never came off. "Everything will be okay."

"Alright, *luce mia*. I'm only going to meet him for a few hours, though, and you need to promise me you'll keep me updated."

"Promise," I whispered, standing on my tiptoes to give him a quick kiss. Three little words threatened to slip off my tongue, but I caught myself.

*Was I ready to tell Anthony that I loved him?* He obviously cared for me, in more than one way. But was that enough?

Anthony kissed the top of my head, then walked over to Ollie, who was covered in peanut butter, his sandwich nearly gone. He leaned down, planting a kiss on his head before walking back through the kitchen and to the garage door. His hands hesitated on the doorknob, turning to me. "Call me if you need anything."

I nodded, shooing him out the door. My emotions were all over the place and if he saw me crying, I knew he'd never leave. The clambering of the garage door closing signaled his departure, and I released a shaky breath.

Time to find a new normal.

# Chapter Twenty-Nine

*Gwen*

An hour later, Ollie and I were cruising the aisles of the grocery store. I intended on making the trip a quick one since I knew he would be ready for a nap soon, but I couldn't help myself. Our weekly grocery trips were my favorite activity before everything happened.

There was a simple joy that came from walking through the bakery with the fresh baked bread aroma wafting through the air to finding new things stocked in the freezer section. I understood Anthony's need to keep us safe, but I still craved these little things.

Ollie was talking away when I crouched down to look at something on a lower shelf. I kept my hand on the bar of the cart, making sure it didn't roll away while I was looking. When I went to reach for something, my arm was tugged roughly as if someone was trying to take the cart. Jumping up, my heart dropped into my stomach when I saw the familiar face.

Kimberly had her hands wrapped around the end of the cart. She looked rough, her eyes bloodshot and her clothes disheveled. I was almost certain the smell of rotten food that assaulted my nose was from her.

"Give me my son," she spat, staring at me with rage. "You think you can just move in and play house with my husband?"

"Kimberly, you're scaring Oliver. Let's take some deep breaths and we can talk about this." I whispered to her as if talking to a spooked animal while keeping a firm grip on the cart.

Oliver was as far forward in the seat as possible and had his little hands wrapped around mine. My heart hammered in my chest, trying to figure out a way to get out of here without putting him in danger.

"No!" Kimberly screamed. "I want my son now."

Without taking my eyes off her, I tried to find someone to signal to for help. But we were alone in the systeaisle and no one walked by. *Why was no one around when I needed help?* Making a split second decision, I pushed the cart toward her and caught her off guard. She tumbled backwards, her body flailing until she hit the floor.

Quickly, I scooped up Oliver and ran through the store as fast as possible, making my way to the parking lot. When we got here earlier, the small lot was busy, and I parked in the back. As I sprinted through the now nearly empty lot, my only focus was getting Ollie into the car.

I glanced behind me, not seeing Kimberly. But the hair on the back of my neck stood up. I could feel eyes watching me.

Pulling the keys from my pocket, I unlocked the doors as I came up to the car. Adrenaline coursed me, and my hands shook as I buckled a crying Ollie into his car seat.

I needed to call Anthony.

The hand not comforting Oliver went in search of my phone. My fingers wrapped around it just as a large hand covered my mouth, pulling me backwards until my body was flush against whoever held me.

My head was tipped backwards, and bile rose up my throat when I saw the eyes that haunted my nightmares for weeks. *Why hadn't I recognized those eyes?*

The metallic shine of something shoved into the inside pocket of the jacket flashed in my vision as an arm rushed forward, yanking my phone out of my grasp and onto the ground. The crunching of the glass diminished any hope that had been left.

"Scream and I'll shoot the kid while I make you watch," Matt said through gritted teeth, his hand now resting on what I was certain was a gun.

There was no way for me to get away from him and keep Ollie safe. I *had* to keep him safe.

I nodded my head, what little I could, anyway, with his grip on me. Slowly, he lowered his hand from my mouth, gripping my upper arm tightly enough to make the back of my eyes burn with tears. "Now, close the door and walk to the other side. Slowly."

I went through the motions, closing Ollie's door then rounding the back of the car, while Matt followed closely behind. He opened the rear passenger door, and yanked the car keys from my pocket before shoving me away from him. I turned to face him, scanning the parking lot as I did to try to find someone who could help.

*Where* was *everyone?*

"Matt, please. You don't have to do this," I whispered, deciding to make one last effort to get through to him. "Let Ollie go and I'll come with you. We'll go back to Pennsylvania and we can forget any of this ever happened."

Cold metal struck the side of my face. My vision blurred, and pain radiated through my skull. I slumped backwards, crashing hard against the backseat of my car as my legs were harshly shoved in. The door slammed close behind me causing the whole car to shake.

"Miss Gwen," Ollie cried. A little hand reached out and brushed over the top of my head.

"I'm right here, buddy," I whispered.

The car started moving. I grabbed onto the side of the car seat, and pulled myself up to a sitting position. Ollie's cries turned into sobs, only adding to the pounding in my head. He was scared. So was I.

I put my hand in his lap, softly shushing him as I silently begged my head to quit spinning. The car bumped along, not going too fast. Ollie's cries softened into whimpers. I wanted to tell him everything would be okay, but I couldn't even convince myself of that right now.

We slowed to a stop, the world still out of focus as I tried to blink away some of the fuzziness when someone got into the passenger seat. The car jerked forward, and I held onto the seat for balance.

We drove for a bit, the only sounds being the traffic outside the car. My vision slowly came back, and I could just make out Matt alongside the mystery person in the front seat.

"You had one job. ONE!" Matt's screams suddenly echoed through the car, silencing Ollie entirely. My entire body shook as I forced deep breaths into my panicked body. "How the hell did you fuck it up?"

"Fuck off." The familiar voice sent shivers down my back and everything became clear.

Kimberly was supposed to take Ollie, so I would be distracted. Neither of them planned on me protecting this little boy with every fiber of my being.

Silence filled the car as we drove for what felt like an eternity, my head still throbbing as I tried to focus on the moving scenery outside the car. Something cold and sticky ran down the side of my face, and I knew if I pressed a hand against it, my fingers would be covered in blood.

My stomach flipped at the thought. I breathed through my nose, trying not to vomit or pass out.

*Focus on Ollie. Keep him safe.*

Finally, we turned off the main road, heading down a street that looked like it was ripped out of a post apocalyptic novel. Houses were boarded up and a basketball hoop was on its side halfway into the road. Matt parked behind a beat up black Toyota.

Kimberly cleared her throat. "What's the plan now?"

"I'm switching cars. You can take your whiny ass son and do whatever. I don't give a fuck." Matt climbed out of the driver's seat, quickly making his way around the car.

I looked to Ollie, trying to think of a way to protect him, when the silver bracelet around my wrist caught my attention. *Why was I so stupid?*

Kimberly climbed out of the car, and I acted fast.

Taking off the bracelet, I pushed the charm like Anthony had shown me, and shoved it into the pocket of Ollie's jacket. Anthony may not be happy with my choice, but he needed to be able to find his son.

Ollie was more important. He was all his dad had.

"Daddy will find you, my sweet boy," I whispered to Ollie, kissing his forehead. "You are so brave. I love you so much."

Matt yanked me from the car, Oliver's renewed screams still audible after the door was closed. I forced back the tears threatening to escape. Matt would not get to see me cry.

Kimberly dropped into the driver's seat, a menacing grin on her face as she backed away and drove off. Matt yanked on my arm, causing me to stumble into him.

Matt chuckled into my ear. "Let's go, baby. I have plans for you."

I wasn't going to follow willingly, not now that Ollie was out of the way. Spinning on my heel, I rammed my knee between his legs, making contact with my intended target.

"You stupid fucking bitch," Matt's grip on my arm loosened his hands flew down to cup his dick.

You would think the asshole would have learned his lesson after the first time.

I took a step backward and turned, breaking out into a run with no idea where I was going. Matt screamed something at me, but I forced myself to focus on getting as far away from him as I could.

A shot rang out. Searing pain on my thigh spread through my leg caused my knee to give out, and I fell to the ground. Darkness creeped into the edges of my vision as I laid there. Rocks pressed into my back, and I tried to focus on the pain to keep from passing out.

It was no use. I was fighting a logging battle.

The last thing I saw before my eyes fluttered shut was Matt standing over me with the gun pointed at my head.

"I told you this wasn't over…"

# Chapter Thirty

## Anthony

I had no idea why I let Gwen convince me to meet Jason. The entire time I was gone, the only thing I could think about was her.

Jason understood, but still gave me a raised eyebrow every time I pulled out my phone to check her phone location. We didn't even last an hour before he told me to get lost. I wasn't any use to him, or the case. He was going to keep working leads off the books, and hope he found something. I just wanted to get home to Gwen.

A few weeks constantly in Gwen's gravitational pull, and I was a goner. If this doesn't convince me just how badly I needed her in my life forever, I didn't know what else would.

*I love her, and she deserves to know.*

Leaving the coffee shop, I formulated a plan. There was a wild daisy field not too far from here. We could swing by a store this evening and pick up some things for a picnic dinner. I pulled into the driveway with a smile on my face. There was no doubt Jason would be making fun of me right now if he saw it.

Getting out m of my truck, I thought it was weird that Gwen wasn't back yet. Her phone location was still showing them at the store, but something felt off. It hadn't updated the location in over ten minutes.

As I stared at the screen, trying to get it to refresh, an emergency alert sounded–the one that meant the panic button on Gwen's bracelet had been pressed.

Immediately, I tried calling her, but it went straight to voicemail. Without thinking, I jumped back into my truck and threw it into reverse, pulling up the live location from the bracelet tracker as I backed onto the road. Rage clouded my vision as I drove on autopilot, following the blinking dot as it moved.

*If something happens to her or Oliver...*

No, I wasn't going to think about that. This was probably all a big misunderstanding. Gwen accidentally hit the button while getting things loaded into the car.

She was fine. Oliver was fine.

The dot stopped, and I double checked the street address. The location was showing an apartment building, one known for housing drug dealers and the clientele they sold, too. I pushed on the gas, needing to get there faster.

Whatever was going on, it wasn't good.

I spotted Gwen's car parked in front of a building, the tracker showing they were inside. Jumping out of my truck and grabbing my gun, I ran to the closest door and found myself kicking it down, all reason and common sense thrown out the window.

Nothing mattered more than Gwen and Oliver being safe.

Immediately, smells of marijuana and alcohol burned my nose. I stepped through the doorway, eyes adjusting slowly to the low light.

"Gwendalyn! Oliver!" I called out. Rustling sounds came from a hallway, and I waited for signs of life as I scanned the living area in front of me. It was absolutely trashed, takeout bags and dirty clothes littering the floor. I took a step back out, ready to try a different apartment, when Oliver's voice froze me in my tracks

"Daddy!" Tiny arms wrapped around my legs and I bent down, slipping my gun into its holster and scooping up Oliver. Tears ran down his cheeks, and his little body shook against mine as I squeezed him tightly against me. "Miss Gwen said you find me and you did."

"Always, *figlio mio.*" I kissed the top of his head, not loosening my grip even a fraction. He wrapped his arms around my neck, burying his face into my neck.

"Oliver, where is Miss Gwen? Who's here with you?"

He shook his head and as I started to ask again, a figure stumbled out of a door toward the back of the room and I barely recognized Kimberly. She was holding onto the wall as she walked, her body swaying fully from side to side with each step.

"Who the fuck are you?" she slurred, no doubt drunk. My suspicions were confirmed when the smell of vodka burnt my nose. I had a death grip on Oliver, one hand protectively on his head to keep him from seeing his mother. She reached out as if to grab him, but I turned my body, forcing her to stop. "Give me my son."

"Where is Gwen?" I asked, my voice calmer than I actually was. Her eyes lit up with recognition, the corner of her lips curling up into a smile that had me seeing red.

"Anthony. You came. Now we can be a family again." She was out of her mind.

"Where is she, Kimberly?"

"You don't need her, baby." She tried to touch me, but I shrugged her off. Her smile disappeared as her eyes narrowed and she wavered on her feet, grabbing onto the wall for support to keep from falling. "What do I need to do to make you forget about that little fucking whore? That bitch shouldn't be sleeping with other people's husbands."

"We are no longer married and haven't been for years. I'm only asking one more time, where is Gwen?" I growled as images of my knife sticking out of the side of her neck, and the life draining from her eyes flashed through my mind.

My arms shook as I gripped onto Oliver tighter, focusing on my son to keep from losing whatever small amount of light that Gwen planted in my heart.

"He took her. Good riddance," she spat out, her back now against the wall as the grin returned to her face. "Hopefully he'll finish what he started at the bar."

Kimberly slid down the wall, crumpling onto the floor. I couldn't bring myself to care whether she was okay or not. Her words were like daggers in my chest.

He had her. The man who was raping and disposing of women for months, who had already attacked the woman I loved. He had her.

I stormed out of the apartment, Oliver clutching onto me. Buckling him into the car, I draped a blanket over him while reassuring him that everything would be okay. I barely believed it myself, but Oliver didn't need to know that. He calmed down, relaxing into his seat with his eyes drifting shut as I closed the door. Pulling out my phone, I called in for an ambulance, then shot Jason a text telling him to meet me at the house.

My mind spun and I couldn't think straight as I drove. *How was I going to find Gwen?*

The darkness inside me screamed to burn down this town to find her and bring her home safely.

If that fucker touched her again, I would happily cut off each of his fingers and lay them in his lap. He would receive the slowest of deaths.

Parking in the driveway, I realized I had been running on autopilot. It wasn't until I had stepped out of my truck did I realize there was a woman I didn't know sitting on one of the porch chairs. Making sure Oliver was asleep, I made my way around the truck, a hand hovering on my gun that was still attached to my hip.

"Can I help you?" I called out, grabbing the attention of the mystery lady. She stood up quickly, seemingly startled by my approach. As I got closer, I noticed a suitcase sitting at her feet that I hadn't before.

"Oh, thank goodness. I've been trying to get a hold of Gwen for hours. I wanted to surprise her and took an earlier flight, but apparently my plan backfired a bit." The woman in front of me talked faster than I could process, but the voice was familiar.

"You're Ivy." It came out as a statement, but she replied, anyway, with a quick nod of her head. Her phone pinged in her hand and my heart skipped a beat as she looked at it, furiously typing away at it. Maybe Gwen had found a phone and was reaching out. It would make sense that she had her best friend's phone number memorized.

"It's not her," Ivy said, not looking up from her phone. The last bit of hope I had disappeared with her words. Anger boiled over. I buckled, my hands on my knees as every muscle in my body tightened at once.

A guttural scream pierced my ears, and it took me too long to realize it was coming from me. I needed to punch something, to release this anger so I could focus on what was important, but it was eating me alive.

*Oscurità mia* was taking control, and I was going to let it.

"Tony," Jason's voice sounded from somewhere far away. I looked up, seeing him step off his Harley and jog toward me, my mind spiraling. He put his hands on my shoulders and the motion grounded me.

"Someone has her…" It was all I could get out. His eyes had darkened. Jason cared for Gwen, not in the same way I did, but as a friend.

"Matt took her?" Ivy asked, interrupting our silent conversation. His name had me standing up straight, looking past Jason to Ivy. She was standing with her arms wrapped around her body as if trying to offer herself some comfort. Her eyes were burning a hole in the back of Jason's head.

"Matt?" Why would she assume I was talking about Gwen's ex?

"Yeah," Ivy whispered, finally looking away from Jason. "He's sent her some really threatening texts ever since the day he showed up here. Gwen tried serving him with a restraining order, but they hadn't been able to find him. He's a fucking narcissist bastard and I wouldn't put it past him to do something stupid."

"What?" *Fuck, how had I not known about this?*

"I tried to convince Gwen to tell you, but she refused." My chest tightened at her words.

*Why would she have kept it from me?* My fists clenched at my sides as the storm raged inside me, the desire to punch something growing every second.

Was it possible for that dumbass fucker to be the one assaulting women? Was his plan all along to work up the courage to go after Gwen?

"Tony," Jason interrupted.

"What, Jason?" I yelled, my focus going to his phone in his hand.

"Look at this." He held it out for me, a black and white security video playing on the screen. It was the live feed from the warehouse.

Jason mentioned updating the security around the building after some weird things happened.

I watched as a man stepped out of his car, opening the trunk and rustling around inside of it. Before long, he flung a body over his shoulder, their hands bound behind their back as they hung upside down. As he turned around, anger burned through my veins when I saw her face.

My eyes shot up to Jason's.

There were too many questions that didn't have answers, but they didn't matter. We found her. Now, I just needed to get to her.

*Oliver.*

I turned on my heel, nearly running directly into Ivy, who, it seemed, had been standing behind me. "My son, Oliver, he's asleep in my truck."

"I've got him," she nodded. "Go get our girl back."

I turned back to Jason, who was digging the key to his motorcycle out of his pocket. He tossed it to me as I ran past him. His phone was still in his hand, his thumb hovering over the buttons, but he ignored it.

His attention was on Ivy.

I couldn't worry about where my partnership focus was at that moment. I needed to get to my woman.

The bike roared to life under me. Jason yelled out over the rumble, "I'll call for backup and meet you out there." I sped away, not caring about stop signs or red lights if I could help it. The only thing going through my mind was getting to Gwen before that asshole had the chance to put his hands on her.

*I'm coming, luce mia. Hold on.*

# Chapter Thirty-One

*Gwen*

Every muscle in my body screamed at me as if I had just run a marathon. I was on my back with my hands cruelly tied underneath me, the rope painfully digging into my wrists.

The ground I was lying on was hard, probably concrete, and it made everything hurt even more. The faint smell of bleach burned my nose, which confused me.

*Why did a place that had a concrete floor smell like bleach?*

It wasn't making sense, but neither was anything else. Matt was the one to attack me that night. If Anthony hadn't shown up when he did, there was no doubt in my mind I would be back in Pennsylvania being forced to play the doting housewife to this psychopath.

Fingers brushed my cheek, and a chill traveled down my spine. "I know you're awake, baby." Matt's hot breath near my face made my skin sticky.

Slowly, I opened my eyes, letting them adjust to the dim light in the room. He was squatting over me, looking down at me with lust. The gun was palmed loosely in his hand at his side.

Standing up, he grabbed me by my hair, pulling me up until I was on my feet. The room started spinning, my head throbbing as my lunch made a reappearance. Vomit burned my nose, and made it hard to breath.

"What the hell?" Matt yelled, releasing my hair and stepping back. "Fucking disgusting." He turned and walked away as I fought to stay upright, knowing that I would have a hell of a time catching myself if I fell.

Steadying myself, I realized I must have hit my head when I fell earlier, resulting in a concussion. Then I remembered why it had happened.

The memory of the gunshot rang in my ears. My gaze fell onto a ripped patch of my jeans. I wasn't gushing blood, but there was now a burning pain radiating through my leg.

Wincing, I did my best to stand up straight, and shifted my weight to my other leg as much as possible. Matt was standing in the doorway, looking down what appeared to be a hallway, as if waiting for someone. He turned back toward me and I met his gaze.

"Matt, what are we doing here?" I asked. "Why didn't you take me back to Pennsylvania?"

"I may have done some questionable things." He stalked toward me, his eyes roaming up and down my body. My stomach convulsed, not from the potential concussion but from the way he looked at me. "I tried to fuck you out of my mind, baby. Woman after woman, but they weren't you. That's why I came for you that night."

I tried to take a step back, but my legs refused to move. Matt reached out, his disgusting fingers trying to touch me, and I recoiled from his attempt. He roughly grabbed my chin, jerking my face toward him.

"You would be home where you belong if it weren't for that little detective of yours," he snarled. "So I have to take care of him first."

Fear consumed me and my racing heart made it hard to think straight. I pulled away from Matt, shaking my head.

"Matt, please," I begged. "Don't hurt Anthony. Let's just go home." He grabbed my upper arm, yanking me toward him. Stumbling, he kept me upright with my back pressed against his chest while I struggled against him.

My thigh was on fire, the smallest of movements causing pain to shoot through my leg. I squeezed my eyes shut to keep the tears from free falling down my cheeks

"No," he spat. "I'm going to teach him what happens when someone tries to take something that belongs to me."

"She doesn't belong to you." *Anthony?*

My eyes flew open, immediately meeting his gaze. Anthony stood in the doorway, his gun outstretched as he pointed it at Matt.

"She's my fiancé. She wore my ring on her finger for over a year," Matt exclaimed, pressing the gun into my side and my body harder into his. I winced from the pressure, a hiccup escaping my throat.

"Let her go, Matt," Anthony commanded, his jaw set.

This must be what he was like at work. His body projected confidence as he inched into the room, his muscles flexing as he gripped his gun tighter. There was determination in his eyes.

I wanted him to look at me, to reassure me that everything would be okay.

"No. I'm not the villain in this story. You are!" Matt yelled. The gun moved from my side to point at Anthony, who was inching across the room. "You think no one knows, but I do. You interrupted my fun that night, so when your partner showed up asking questions, I followed him and watched." Anthony stopped his advances, but his eyes never left Matt.

"I may have fucked all those women trying to get Gwen out of my system, but that's nothing compared to what you do. Tell her. Tell her about what happens in this room, or I'll shoot her," Matt hissed. The gun returned to my side, and a quiet sob escaping from my chest.

Anthony's gaze flickered toward me, and worry flashed across his eyes. Was it for me or whatever secret he was hiding?

"Anthony, what is he talking about?" I softly asked. Matt laughed in my ear.

"Gwen, I'm sorry," Anthony muttered. "I never wanted you to have to find out like this." Defeat warped his features, the grip on his gun loosening.

"Anthony…" I whispered, terrified about what he had to say.

"Enough!" Matt yelled, and I flinched, the gun pressing harder into my side. Anthony went stoic once more, his hand tightening around his gun. "It doesn't matter, anyway. Put your gun on the ground and kick it over. Otherwise, you'll be cleaning *her* blood off this ground."

Anthony hesitated for a moment, his shoulders stiffening as he stood there. I wanted to scream at him to leave me, that I wasn't worth it.

Oliver needed him.

But, Anthony lowered his gun, clicking the safety before setting it on the ground. He gave it a nudge with his foot and it slid, stopping a few inches from my feet.

Matt lifted the gun away from my side, aiming it at Anthony once again.

"You better not miss," Anthony challenged, "because if you do, it will be my turn. Any goodness inside me is because of Gwendalyn. You tried to take her from me, from my son. You won't be walking out of this warehouse alive if I'm still breathing."

Every emotion I was holding back broke free.

Warm tears silently ran down my cheeks. Anthony met my gaze, and I wanted nothing more than for his lips to be on mine, comforting me and kissing away every tear that fell.

Matt's arm across my body tightened, and something inside me snapped. I was no longer going to be the damsel in distress.

Everything happened so quickly.

I threw my weight forward as Matt pulled the trigger, causing him to stumble. The gun went off, and my ears began ringing. Anthony rushed us, knocking Matt to the ground as I fell forward.

The gun clattered to the floor as Anthony gripped Matt's shirt and punched him, the unmistakable sound of crunching bone filling the room. I was frozen in place, my feet like lead.

Blood dripped from Matt's nose, but Anthony didn't stop. His fist connected with Matt's eye, once, twice, more blood splattering into the air.

"Anthony," I called out. Matt deserved this and worse, but I didn't want to watch. I needed him to stop. He raised his fist, inches away from landing another hit.

"Anthony!" I yelled, my body shaking. My voice echoed through the room, bouncing off the walls like a bomb going in a million directions.

Anthony froze, his fist now hanging in the air. He looked over his shoulder, and the anger written all over his face should have had me running. Instead, I inched forward, as if approaching a wild animal. Anthony blinked, his glazed over eyes returning to normal as he released Matt, who crumbled to the ground with a groan.

Anthony rushed to me, untying my wrists before pulling me to his chest. "I thought I was going to lose you," he whispered into my hair. A hiss escaped from his throat when he tried to tighten his hold on me. I pulled away, the blood surrounding a hole in his shirt on his left shoulder catching my eye.

"You're bleeding!" I gasped, stepping away and frantically looking around the room for something to hold pressure.

"Shit," he sharply inhaled. His brows pinched together while he examined the hole in his shirt. He tried to walk toward me, but his legs buckled.

I rushed forward, catching his upper half as we both fell to our knees. My thigh screamed in protest as I maneuvered Anthony onto his back. My heart pounded in my ears.

"Fuck. Okay. Shit." I pressed my hands down onto his shoulder as hard as I could to try to stop the bleeding. There was too much, though.

*Did the bullet hit his heart?* The red liquid seeped out from around my fingers, mixing with the tears falling from my eyes. This couldn't be happening. This wasn't real.

He lifted his right arm, his hand resting on my cheek while his thumb tried to wipe away the tears. "Hey," he whispered, causing me to look at him, "it's going to be okay."

I shook my head, causing more tears to fall. His eyes fluttered as his arm fell to his side. I pushed harder onto his shoulder, and Anthony cursed.

A gun pressed into the back of my head. "Get up," Matt spat.

*Fucking damn it.*

Rage snapped through me like a bolt of lightning. I scanned for something, anything, that I could use to fight. Spotting Anthony's disposed gun only a few feet away, the metal nearly unnoticeable in the dim lighting, I knew if I could just get to it...

I made to stand up, but lunged to the side instead. Matt stumbled, unable to recover fast enough. Scooping up the gun, I switched off the safety just like Anthony showed me months ago and aimed it at Matt.

The little color left in his face drained as he stared down the barrel of the gun. The side of his face was covered in red liquid, and one of his eyes was already swelling shut. He should have just stayed down.

His mouth moved, but I didn't care what he had to say.

I pulled the trigger.

Matt hit the floor, the thump of his head bouncing off the concrete reassurance enough that he wouldn't be getting back up that time.

I stared at the spot where Matt had been standing, my mind unable to comprehend what I just did. There was no guilt, no sadness. Just indifference. I did what I needed to do.

Anthony coughed beside me, a wet sound that sent tremors through my body. I dropped to my knees, leaving the gun on the ground as I scrambled back to Anthony's side. His eyes were shut and his breathing was shallow. I cradled his face in my hands, smearing his face with red streaks.

"Anthony! Anthony, open your eyes. Open your eyes, Anthony!" My voice was shaky. I couldn't lose him. He was the only man who had made me feel truly safe. I needed him. Oliver needed him.

"Anthony, please. Don't leave me. I love you."

# Chapter Thirty-Two

## Anthony

*D**on't leave me... I love you...*

Gwen's voice rang in my ears. I wanted to reassure her everything would be okay, but my eyes refused to open. It felt like a hot branding rod was being pressed against my shoulder as she kept her weight on it.

Her quiet sobs wrecked me. She needed to know how I felt. I would never willingly leave her.

The last thing I saw before my eyes closed against my will will forever be burned in my mind. My gun in Gwen's hands, pointed at the asshole who caused her so much pain. Pure fury crossed her face while blood dripped onto the floor where she was standing. Her wrists were red and raw from the rope, but *luce mia* wasn't backing down.

I was so fucking proud of her, and I needed to tell her.

Suddenly, Gwen's body left mine, followed by several hands working to take off my shirt. Jason's voice filled my ears next.

"Shh, Gwen. He'll be okay. You need to let them check on you, too." I had forgotten she was hurt.

The slow beeping of my heart filled the room as I was lifted, presumably onto a gurney. The darkness was beckoning me, but I didn't want to go. I needed to stay awake. I needed to make sure Gwen was safe. I needed to hold her, and tell her I loved her, too.

It was a losing fight, though.

Just before the darkness took me under, Jason's harsh voice pierced through the fog. "Gwen. Gwen, are you okay? Shit. Medics!"

*No, no, no...*

Fingertips brushed against my cheek, rousing my subconscious. "I need you to wake up, Anthony. This wasn't supposed to happen," Gwen whispered.

Her fingers weaved through mine, lifting my hand and resting it against her face. The wet skin against mine told me she had been crying. Maybe still was.

"Oliver needs his dad. That little boy can't lose you. I don't know what to tell him if you don't come home."

Tears fell onto my hand as she continued, her voice breaking. "I need you, too. Please, Anthony. I tried so hard not to fall for you, but no one has ever made me feel the way you do. I thought you were going to be this distant asshole of a man, but you welcomed me into your home with open arms. You always made sure to stop and listen. You bought me daisies. No one has ever bought me daisies. You took care of me during a time that any other man would have run. If it weren't for you, I don't know where I would be." She paused, more tears falling onto my hand.

"If you wake up right now, I promise to never complain about another dirty dish you leave in the sink. Please, Anthony. My heart can't take losing you." I willed my fingers to move, to let her know I was here.

They listened. My hand flexed against her hair. The soft strands threaded through my fingers. I forced my eyes to open, blinking as the bright fluorescent lights blinded me. When everything finally came into focus, her ocean blue eyes were the first thing I saw.

I would happily drown in them every day if she let me.

"Anthony?" she gasped.

"That seems like a very roundabout way of saying you love me, *luce mia*." My voice was harsh, my throat raw.

"Oh my gosh, Anthony!" Gwen lunged for me, her body shaking from the sobs. I pushed through the heaviness holding my limbs hostage to embrace her, slowly wrapping my good arm around her.

"I'm holding you to that dirty dishes promise," I whispered, lifting my head to kiss the top of her hair. She chuckled, and it was music to my ears. I pulled her in closer, not wanting to be separated a second more, but winced as pain shot through my shoulder.

Gwen pulled away, hovering her hands over my chest. I noticed the bandages wrapped around her wrists. "Shit, I forgot. How bad is the pain?"

"Not too bad." I took in a deep breath through my nose, trying to hide just how badly it hurt. The lightning pain dulled slightly, turning into a more localized throbbing that I could handle. I took one of Gwen's hands in mine and flipped it over to examine the bandage on her wrist. "How are you?"

"Anthony, I'm fine," she said softly, taking my hand in hers and kissing my knuckles. The motion relaxed me, sending a signal to my brain to chill the fuck out. "There were a few abrasions on my wrists from the rope. I had a graze on my thigh from when I tried to run from Matt. I fell and hit my head, so I had a minor concussion. Then, when they started wheeling you out of the warehouse, all the adrenaline left my body and I passed out. Jason caught me, though, and I woke up before we got to the hospital." She ran her thumb over my knuckles, and I made a mental note that I owed my partner a case of beer.

"I was more worried about you," she continued. "You were in surgery for way too long. The bullet hit an artery, and you lost a lot of blood. I mean, the doctor said you would be fine, but what if you weren't? I was serious, Anthony. I can't lose you."

"I don't plan on going anywhere. But we need to talk about what Matt meant." Gwen tried to say something, but I cut her off. "Please, let me get this out." Her lips pressed into a thin line as she forced herself to stay quiet, just like how I did for her.

"I'm not a good guy, Gwen. There's a part of me that enjoys hurting people, the part that was forced to watch my parents die." Gwen stifled a gasp behind her hand and I paused, debating if this was too much. No, she deserved to know the whole truth. "My father was involved with organized crime in Italy. He wanted out, though, to give me a better life. So they moved here and started over. But the syndicate found us. They forced me to watch while they assaulted my mother and tortured my father."

Gwen sat up a bit, squaring her shoulders as she listened. But her hand never left mine. That was all the reassurance I needed.

"Because of that night, I do bad things to bad people who deserve to no longer walk among the living." I forced myself to keep going, to get everything out into the open. Gwen showed no sign that she needed me to stop. "I don't hurt just anyone. For the most part, they're the husbands and significant others of the individuals we have interviewed who are too scared to press charges or their abusers who have too much power and won't end up facing their punishment." Gwen was motionless, simply sitting beside me, still holding my hand.

"That fucker who drugged you at the bar? I chopped off one of his fingers for touching you, then shoved my knife through his dick. And, tonight, if you hadn't stopped me, I would have beat Matt until he was dead. He doesn't deserve to breathe the same air as you, let alone walk on the same ground. I warned him what would happen if he missed."

Gwen lunged forward, wrapping her arms around my neck and claiming my lips with hers. I soaked it in, if only for a moment.

Placing my hand on her cheek, I urged her backwards. "I need to know you're okay with this. This is who I am. I can't change that."

"Okay is a strong word, Anthony, but you've never given me a reason not to trust you. I may need a little time to process everything, though." Gwen ran her fingers through my hair as she spoke. "But I know I love you. None of this changes that."

"I love you too, *amore mio,*" I confessed.

I threaded my fingers through her hair and pulled her to me. The kiss was desperate, and I urged her lips apart with my tongue. I needed her more than I needed air, and I was going to show her.

Gwen shifted on the bed, nearly climbing on top of me when a knock sounded at the door and in walked the peppy nurse from the last time we were here. Gwen pulled away so fast, she hit one of the machines on her way off the bed.

"Oh, so sorry," the nurse blushed, looking at Gwen knowingly. "Um, I've just come to check on Mr. Marino. I can page the doctor for you, Mrs. Marino. I'll be right back." She disappeared as quickly as she had appeared.

Gwen looked at me, and I raised my eyebrows. "Mrs. Marino, hmm?"

"Shut up," she giggled. "I couldn't very well correct them."

She wasn't wrong. But one day soon, she would never have to think about correcting people. She would have my last name for real.

Jason and Gwen coordinated getting my truck to the hospital lot. After I was forced to be pushed outside in a wheelchair, I was denied access to the driver's seat.

Gwen insisted on driving home, and honestly, I would do anything to make her happy. Plus, seeing her behind the wheel of my truck was doing it for me.

"Ready?" She smiled over at me.

"Let's go, *luce mia*." I responded, reaching across to place my hand on her thigh and giving it a gentle squeeze.

We drove in comfortable silence, occasionally humming along to the radio that was set to a local country station. A short while later, Gwen pulled into the driveway. She turned off the truck, but didn't move.

"Can I ask you something?" She faced me, her fingers picking at the cuticles. It was a bad habit of hers that I was determined to help her stop.

"Of course." I rested my hand on top of hers, and her fingers relaxed under mine,

"Why do you call me *luce mia*?" she whispered. I didn't respond right away, letting the silence hand between us while I tried to find the right words.

"It means *my light*," I answered. "My dad called my mom his guiding light, and that's what you are to me. You were this ray of sunshine that found its way through my darkness when I needed it the most."

A single tear fell down Gwen's cheek, and I brushed it away with my thumb. She leaned across the center console and I met her halfway, our lips connecting in a kiss filled with more love than I thought possible. My heart hammered in my chest enough that I swore she could hear it.

Gwen whispered against my lips, "Thank you for finding me."

"Always," I sealed the promise with a final kiss. She slowly pulled away, a smile spreading across her face as she looked over my shoulder. I turned my head and watched as Oliver barreled out of the front door. He just made it to the truck as I jumped out and scooped him up with my good arm.

"I missed you, *figlio mio*." I kissed the top of his head. He clung to me, wrapping his tiny arms around my neck and holding on tight.

"Daddy, Miss Ivy is even more fun than Miss Gwen," Oliver said.

"Hey now," Gwen said, coming around the front of the truck. She stopped next to us and Oliver laughed as he let go of me and went to her. Tugging Gwen to me by her elbow, her small giggle caused a smile to form on my lips.

I embraced them both, my two favorite people. *How did I get so lucky?*

I had convinced myself I was unworthy, caging off my heart and focusing on making sure Oliver would never know the kind of pain I had gone through. Then Gwen fell into our lives, and she loved him in a way I would never be able to understand.

Gwen looked up at me from my arms, Oliver seated on her hip, and the dream I had months ago came barreling to the front of my mind. My heart was once again filled with hope and love.

As long as I had Gwen and Oliver in my life, everything else would work itself out.

# Epilogue

*Gwen*

## Eight Months Later

"Ollie, Anthony, I'm home!" I called out, slipping off my shoes by the door. They joined the more than a dozen pairs that occupied the entryway.

After he came home from the hospital, the only place Anthony let me sleep was in his bed. It hadn't taken long for all of my stuff to migrate up from the basement and the space once again became a functional guest room.

Ivy stayed in it for some time, mainly to help with Ollie while I tried to force Anthony to take it easy. He had to take a medical leave of absence for a month after being shot and, while he complained every day about not being at work, we both knew he secretly enjoyed being home.

After Matt kidnapped me, I horrible nightmares of Anthony being shot. My mind was finally trying to process everything that had happened to me, and it wasn't going well. Anthony was patient with me, letting me handle it how I wanted, but when he started back to work, the traumatic dreams only got worse.

He called in a few favors, helping to set me up with a department therapist who specialized in PTSD. I had been seeing her for over six months now and I felt like a better version of myself.

It had taken some time, but slowly, I was able to sleep peacefully at night and trust that Anthony would do his best to stay safe. Now, it was just nice to have someone to talk to about everything.

Everything except what Anthony confessed to me in the hospital. *That* I kept between me and him, and Jason. It somehow made it feel less horrific in my mind that Anthony wasn't doing those things on his own. They kept each other in check. At the end of the day, they were keeping women from having to experience everything I went through.

Strong arms wrapped around my torso, tugging me against a hard chest, and reorienting me to the present. I giggled, relaxing into Anthony's hold, and tipped my head to the side. He nuzzled his nose into my neck and planted kisses along my skin, a trail of goosebumps following as he went.

"I missed you, *amore mio*," he whispered into my ear, my stomach heating from the gentle caresses of his hand.

My heart fluttered like it always did when he called me that. Something about the Italian paired with his lust filled husky voice had me immediately weak in the knees. I turned in Anthony's arms, his rich brown eyes peering down at me, and I pressed up onto my toes to plant a kiss on his lips.

It felt natural, me in his arms, like it was where I was meant to be all along.

Tiny hands embraced my leg, and I chuckled as Ollie squirmed his way between our two bodies. *Nothing like a moment ruined by a toddler.* I looked down at him, his dimples well defined as a huge smile spread across his face.

"Daddy, did you tell her we have a surprise?" Ollie tugged at Anthony's arms as he asked.

"No, *figlio mio,*" Anthony said. "Why don't you go show her?"

"Okay!" Ollie squealed, grabbing my hand and yanking me through the house.

I flashed a questioning look over my shoulder at Anthony, who was following behind us at a leisurely pace. He simply shrugged his shoulders and smiled. I shook my head, returning my focus to Ollie and making sure I wasn't pulled into any walls.

We rounded the doorway into the kitchen, and I stopped in my tracks when my eyes fell upon dozens of bouquets of daisies. Some were in vases while others were just laid onto the countertops. I looked down at Ollie, who was beaming up at me with a sparkle in his eye.

"I helped Daddy pick them out, Mommy," he stated proudly, his hands making fists on his hips as he looked around. My heart skipped, just like every time when Ollie slipped and accidentally called me *mommy.*

It made me happy knowing he saw me as someone he could trust. I truly did love this boy with every part of my heart. Maybe one day I would be able to be his mommy, but I wasn't going to pressure Anthony.

Scooping him up, I pulled Ollie against me for a tight hug, his little giggles filling the kitchen. "Thank you so much, buddy. I love them," I said. "But remember, I'm not your mommy. You can just call me Gwen."

"No," he muttered, jerking his body away from mine and crossing his arms across his chest. Ollie's eyebrows crinkled just like Anthony's did when he wasn't getting his way.

"What's wrong, buddy?"

"Daddy said I can call you Mommy," he huffed. "I want to call you Mommy."

Would Anthony have really said that? I spun on my heel to ask him, and nearly lost my balance when I saw Anthony.

He was down on one knee, a ring box open in his outstretched hands.

I stopped breathing as Ollie slid down from my arms. My hands flew up to cover my mouth, silencing the gasp that escaped.

"*Luce mia*, the first time I laid my eyes on you in my living room, I knew you were going to turn our world upside down. You have brought so much happiness and love into my life—our lives. I never want to think about a future without you. Gwendalyn Brookes, will you marry me?"

I lunged toward him and he caught me, hauling me against his chest as our lips collided. Tears ran down my cheeks as I kissed him. He deepened it, and I was immersed in an overwhelming sense of bliss.

Time slowed as we sat in the moment, our bodies pressed so tightly against one another it was difficult to tell where one of us ended and the other began. Finally, I pulled away and Anthony smiled down at me, his dimples that I had gotten so used to seeing forming near the corner of his lips.

"Is that a yes?" he whispered, his eyes darting between me and the ring.

"Yes, a million times, yes," I squealed. Anthony slipped the ring on my finger just as Ollie wiggled his way between us once again. We fell into a pile on the kitchen floor, all of our laughs mixing as we embraced.

It was a perfect moment, and it was then I realized something.

I found myself.

# Note from Author

Dear Reader,

Finding Gwen was first published in June of 2024 as a huge part of an emotional healing journey that I was going through. I poured my heart and soul into the pages of this story, all for the chance to come out the other side a little more healed than I was before. So many readers expressed to me how much they loved this book and thanked me for writing it.

But deep down, I knew something was missing.

In the past few years, I have grown so much as a writer. I found myself in the middle of an amazing author community. I have meet so many readers who have been excited to read my book for the first time.

Support. It was the thing I was missing.

If you're reading this book for the first time, I promise nothing of mass importance changed. Finding Gwen just needed a little face lift. I hope you enjoyed your time with Anthony, Gwen, and Ollie as much as I enjoyed revisiting their story. If you feel so inclined, please consider leaving a review. It helps indie author more than you think.

xoxo,

Delaine

Keep reading for a sneak peek

at Ivy and Jason's story,

Protecting Ivy

# Prologue

## *Ivy*

The man standing in front of me was a ghost. That was the only possible explanation for what I was seeing.

*Austin…*

Six years. It had been nearly six years since the last time I saw him, the man I had fallen for after less than twenty-four hours together.

His beard was longer now and his exposed forearms displayed several new tattoos that weren't there all those years ago, but it was definitely him. My lungs refused to expand, my chest tightening as Austin reached out to grip Anthony's shoulder.

I wrapped my arms around myself, trying to focus on breathing instead of the two men in front of me who were now locked in on a silent conversation between themselves.

My best friend was missing, a fact I just learned after I had caught an earlier flight to surprise her. She had moved to Chicago to get away from her abusive ex and Anthony hired her as a live-in nanny. Things got heated between her and the single dad recently and the last I heard, things were going great.

I was happy for her. After everything that happened with her ex, she deserved this.

"Someone had her…" I barely made out the words that Anthony whispered to Austin.

*Wait…*

"Matt took her?" I wasn't sure if they heard me, but Anthony rose from where he was crouched on the ground. Austin didn't move, standing sideways only a few feet from me. He reached into his pocket, pulling out his phone.

I couldn't tear my eyes away from him.

*How was he here right now?*

"Matt?" Anthony's voice pulled my attention away from Austin.

"Yeah," Ivy whispered. "He's sent her some really threatening texts ever since the day he showed up here. Gwen tried serving him with a restraining order, but they hadn't been able to find him. He's a fucking narcissist bastard and I wouldn't put it past him to do something stupid."

"What?" If looks could kill, I would be dead on the spot.

"I tried to convince Gwen to tell you but she refused," I muttered. Anthony's eyebrows narrowed, his eyes darkening as his fists clenched at his side.

Glancing at Austin, his head remained down, staring at his phone. It felt like a dream. No, a nightmare. He probably didn't remember me. Just a woman he fucked and left.. It had clearly meant so much more to me than it did to him.

I wasn't a crier but the back of my throat burned with the anger and sadness that was building.

Austin raised his head, meeting my gaze momentarily, and nothing in his expression told me he knew who I was.

"Tony," Austin said, looking away from me.

"What, Jason?" Anthony yelled.

*Jason? Who the hell is Jason?*

"Look at this." Jason held up his phone toward Anthony and I could just make out some grainy video that resembled a security feed. Stepping forward until I was basically on top of the two of them, the subjects of the video became clearer. My stomach dropped. Gwen was hanging upside down, having been haphazardly thrown over a shoulder, with her wrists tied behind her back.

Another silent conversation happened between the two men as their eyes remained locked. Time stood still. My brain was trying to process everything.

Then, Anthony whipped around, nearly knocking into me.

"My son, Oliver, he's asleep in my truck." Even though his demeanor was calm, I saw the panic in Anthony's eyes.

"I've got him," I nodded, letting him know I understood. "Go get our girl back."

Jason, or Austin, or whoever the hell he was, fished a key ring from his pockets, tossing them to Anthony who caught them easily. My eyes tracked Anthony as he turned and sprinted across the yard. The motorcycle roared to life. Burning rubber filled the air as he sped away, off to rescue my best friend.

Out of the corner of my eye, Jason put his phone to his ear. I didn't pay attention to what he was saying, refusing to even look at the man who was now a complete stranger to me.

Walking over to Anthony's truck, I peered inside to check on Ollie. His little head lulled against the side of his carseat, his eyes still shut. I walked around to the driver's door and checked it was still unlocked. Anthony had left it running thankfully.

"Ivy?" Austin's voice warmed a part of me that I forgot existed. It almost made me forget the pain he had put me through.

Almost.

Because his name wasn't Austin. He lied and left me. I went through one of the worst things a woman could go through and by myself because he disappeared without a trace.

His hand on my shoulder caused me to jump and I spun on my heel. I was ready to give him a piece of my mind, but he was standing too close. The heat radiating from his body consumed me. He was standing close enough that his exhale warmed my skin. I looked everywhere but at him. If I did, I knew the hatred I had built toward him would disappear as soon as I gazed into his eyes.

"Ivy." My name was a whisper on his lips.

His hand came up and calloused skin brushed my cheek. I ignored the tightening in my chest, pressing myself against the side of the truck and away from him. "Ivy, please."

I heard the pain in his voice but it only served to fuel the rage that had settled in my heart long ago. My eyes met his.

"Do not touch me," I seethed. My hands balled into fists, my nails digging in the tender skin as hurt flashed across my face. His palm fell to his side and he stepped back.

"Kitten..." he started but I cut him off, not wanting to hear whatever excuse he had come up with.

"I called you. I looked for you," I said, trying to keep my voice even. He would not see me break. "It makes sense though. Apparently, I didn't even know who you really were."

His words were lost among the sirens that seemingly came out of nowhere. The phone call he had made just a few minutes ago. *Or had it been longer?*

His head turned to watch the approaching police car until it stopped at the end of the driveway. An officer inside waved to him and Jason held up a finger to him, silently communicating something. When he looked back, his brows were drawn together, the corners of his lips turned downward.

I didn't give him a chance to speak. Turning my back to him, I walked to the other side of the truck and opened the door to a stirring Ollie.

When I looked over my shoulder, Jason was stepping into the car. I turned my attention back to Ollie, unbuckled him from his seat, and settled him on my hip. We watched as the man I once thought I cared about left and my lungs were finally able to work again.

# Acknowledgements

A new edition means new acknowledgments, but I do want to take a minute to thank the people who made that first addition possible. Kaitlyn, Vanessa, Kelly—You all made Finding Gwen possible that first go and I'm forever grateful for everything you did.

To my bestie, Lindsey—thank you. Honestly, if you hadn't pushed me to start a bookstagram, I don't think this book would exist. You supported this idea from conception. From countless video chats hashing out plot holes and characters to just listening to me vent when I needed to complain about this entire process. Your validation of my feelings means the world to me. These characters and this story are what it is because of you. I could not have asked for a better book bestie!

To the best alpha reader and author friend I could ask for, Ri-anna—thank you. You read Finding Gwen when it was a trash first draft. Just a bunch of jumbled words in a document. Now look at it! You helped me make it the best version possible and I can't imagine doing this without you. This is the best way I know how to tell you how much I appreciate you. Also, I publicly apologize for my lack of dialogue tags during those early stages. And making you skim spice.

To one of my biggest cheerleaders, Jessica—thank you. My journey to publish Finding Gwen that first time was rocky, but you helped me through everything I had to endure. You were a shoulder, a listening ear, and one of my biggest supporter. You helped me see that every story should have their chance to be told. I am forever grateful for your friendship.

To Carla aka the best event PA I could ever ask for—thank you. I cannot believe that this all started because we chatted in a line at a book event. We didn't get a picture that day, but we've gotten in a handful since then. There are no words to express my appreciation and gratitude for all you've done for me. I hope you'll stick around forever cause you know my chaos goblin ass needs the help.

To two of the best readers, Amilia and Alessandra—thank you. You both are always willing to jump in and help whenever I need it. You read my first draft chaos, send me inspirational thirst traps, and never hesitate to offer up your opinions when I need them. I cannot say thank you enough for everything you have done.

To Papa—thank you. You're getting your own spot for this one, if only to tell you that I promise the amusement park stalker romance is coming. But also to express my gratitude for all you have done. And thank you for making my mom happy. We both know she deserves it.

To my mom—Thank you isn't enough. The unconditional support at every turn is everything I could ever dream about. I love you so much.

Lastly, to my readers—thank you. If this is your first time reading one of my books, I hope you stick around. There is so much more to come and I cannot wait. If this isn't your first, thank you for coming back. Your continued support is everything to me.

# Also by Delaine Walsh

<u>**Morally Grey Detectives**</u>

Finding Gwen

Protecting Ivy (Coming Soon)

<u>**Shifters of Maplewood Hollow**</u>

My Neighbor is a Wolf

My Fake Boyfriend is a Bear

My New Bosses are Rats (Coming September 2026)

# About the Author

Delaine Walsh is a spicy romance author who write stories with heat, heart, and a hint of darkness. Each book she writes heals a little part of her soul. Reading has always been an escape for her, and she hopes her stories provide that for others.

She currently lives in Northern Kentucky with her husband and three fur babies. When she's not home writing, she's scouring local bookstores for her next impulsive book purchase.